PENGU

NEW PENGUIN
SHORT STORIES IN JAPANESE

日本語の短篇小説

MICHAEL EMMERICH is an assistant professor in the
Department of East Asian Languages and Cultural
Studies at the University of California, Santa Barbara.
He has translated from Japanese more than a dozen
books of both fiction and nonfiction, including
Kawakami Hiromi's *Manazuru;* Matsuura Rieko's *The
Apprenticeship of Big Toe P;* Takahashi Gen'ichirō's
Sayonara, Gangsters; Yoshimoto Banana's *Hardboiled &
Hard Luck, There Is No Lid on the Sea, Moonlight
Shadow, Goodbye Tsugumi,* and *Asleep;* and Kawabata
Yasunari's *First Snow on Fuji.*

New Penguin Parallel Text

Short Stories in Japanese
日本語の短篇小説

Edited by Michael Emmerich

PENGUIN BOOKS

PENGUIN BOOKS

Published by the Penguin Group

Penguin Group (USA) Inc., 375 Hudson Street, New York, New York 10014, U.S.A.
Penguin Group (Canada), 90 Eglinton Avenue East, Suite 700, Toronto, Ontario, Canada M4P 2Y3
(a division of Pearson Penguin Canada Inc.)
Penguin Books Ltd, 80 Strand, London WC2R 0RL, England
Penguin Ireland, 25 St Stephen's Green, Dublin 2, Ireland (a division of Penguin Books Ltd)
Penguin Group (Australia), 250 Camberwell Road, Camberwell, Victoria 3124, Australia
(a division of Pearson Australia Group Pty Ltd)
Penguin Books India Pvt Ltd, 11 Community Centre, Panchsheel Park, New Delhi—110 017, India
Penguin Group (NZ), 67 Apollo Drive, Rosedale, North Shore 0632, New Zealand
(a division of Pearson New Zealand Ltd)
Penguin Books (South Africa) (Pty) Ltd, 24 Sturdee Avenue, Rosebank,
Johannesburg 2196, South Africa

Penguin Books Ltd, Registered Offices:
80 Strand, London WC2R 0RL, England

First published in Penguin Books 2011

18th Printing

PUBLISHER'S NOTE
The selections in this book are works of fiction. Names, characters, places, and incidents either are
the product of the authors' imagination or are used fictitiously, and any resemblance to actual
persons, living or dead, business establishments, events, or locales is entirely coincidental.

LIBRARY OF CONGRESS CATALOGING-IN-PUBLICATION DATA
Short stories in Japanese / edited by Michael Emmerich.
p. cm.—(New Penguin parallel texts)
ISBN 978-0-14-311833-6
1. Short stories, Japanese—Translations into English. 2. Japan—Social life and customs—Fiction.
I. Emmerich, Michael.
PL782.E8S53 2011
895.6'3010805—dc22
2010054525

Printed in the United States of America
Set in Minion Pro

Contents

INTRODUCTION

So here we are. Something amazing is happening. We are standing right on the verge of it. We are, in fact, already part of it, in its sway—and so is this floppy little book you hold in your hands: the incredible thrill of starting to read, for pleasure, in a language that seemed for so long as if it had been designed expressly to exasperate and discourage. There is a community of people, growing steadily larger, who share the excitement of knowing two very different, very rich languages, and we are joining it. The languages are Japanese and English.

The *Penguin Parallel Text* series got its start in the 1960s with the publication of five volumes of stories in six languages: *Soviet Short Stories/Sovetskie Rasskazy* appeared first, in 1963, and was followed over the next three years by collections in German and English, Italian and English, French and English, and Spanish and English. Each volume was later followed by a second; then, beginning in the 1990s, the whole series was supplanted by the *New Penguin Parallel Texts*, whose more global perspective was marked by a subtle revision of the titles: the old *French Short Stories/Nouvelles Françaises* was jettisoned in favor of *Short Stories in French/Nouvelles en Français*; *Spanish Short Stories/Cuentos Hispanicos* reemerged as *Short Stories in Spanish/Cuentos en Español*; and so on. All well and good, of course, except that the Eurocentrism of the old series lingered on in the selection of languages, and none of the books was any help whatsoever to English speakers studying Japanese, or Japanese speakers studying English. For almost half a century, Penguin left people like us out in the cold.

Now all that has changed. And what a change it is! Just imagine: for the first time in the history of this venerable *Parallel Text* series, we've got a collection whose texts are not at all parallel.

On one page, the Japanese text streams down in vertical columns like the rain, progressing one line at a time from right to left, just as in a Japanese book; on the other, horizontal English text gushes across the paper to meet the Japanese in the gutter. For the first time in the history of these volumes, two languages have overcome the stand-offish, never-the-twain-shall-meet dictates of parallelism, and have discovered a means of coming together. It's stunning. It's exhilarating! And it is a *very* welcome addition. English-speaking students of Japanese, and Japanese-speaking students of English, need more books like this. Different types of books, put together in different formats, for students at different levels who learn in different ways.

And of course it's not a simple matter for an American publisher to put out a collection of this sort. Penguin has had to throw the whole idea of the "parallel text" out the window, and switch the right- and left-hand pages—in previous volumes the original text was on the left and the translation was on the right, but here it's just the opposite—and even learn how to typeset Japanese, and how to print kana readings alongside kanji. Penguin went all out, practically turning the notion of the *Parallel Text* series inside out to create this collection. And so . . . here we are! *Short Stories in Japanese*/日本語の短篇小説. A title we've been waiting for. A book we've been wanting, and needing. A book that will be useful and, I hope you will agree, thoroughly enjoyable.

Unfortunately, that still doesn't mean it's going to be easy. It's probably going to be hard. It's going to take a lot of time and energy. This book has more notes than any of the others in the series, I believe, but in a book like this the notes aren't the point. The stories are the point, and the process of figuring out on your own how each sentence means what it does, whether you decide to go for the Japanese first and then read the English, or vice versa—whether you are good with English and want to improve your reading of Japanese, or good at Japanese and trying to work on your English. And that, by the way, is one of the things that makes a book like this so unique and wonderful: it reminds those of us who grew up with English, within English, or maybe learning it somewhere along the way, that if it sometimes seems as though we will never manage to learn everything we need to know to feel at home reading Japanese, there are people who are approaching the gutter from the other side, and that it's every bit as difficult for them as it is for us. By the same token, it reminds those of us who are Japanese speakers struggling with English how much trouble English speakers have learning Japanese. The texts in this collection may not be parallel, but there are, in fact, parallels between the processes of learning Japanese and learning English. Ultimately we're all in the same boat. Or we're all trying to get into the same boat. We are learning to share these languages.

So while it may not be easy, and though it will almost certainly be a bit bewildering at times, there are people doing it all around the world, right at this very moment, and as long as you're willing to put in the work, you can do it, too. Every two-page spread in this book points you in the right direction.

Or who knows, maybe you've never studied Japanese and just bought this book for the translations, because you've noticed that the contemporary Japanese fiction you've read has been pretty amazing and want to read some more, or because you're a big fan of one of the writers whose work is included here. If so . . . well, it's never too late to start! I know a few people who started studying Japanese in their sixties and have made such speedy progress that by the time this book comes out, they probably won't need it anymore—at least not as a study tool. I hope even very advanced students of Japanese will get a lot out of this book, if only because of the extraordinary variety of fiction it contains.

Whatever sort of reader you are, I think you'll find not only that the stories in this collection are powerful and engaging but also that they do a nice job of suggesting—though certainly not representing—the incredible range of fiction that has been written in Japanese over the past few decades. You'll encounter writers of different ages who come from different backgrounds and have vastly different notions of what literature is or should be—or, at the very least, of the sort of fiction they want to create. You'll find stories that are driven by plot, and stories that seem to shy away from it, verging toward the poetic or the essayistic; stories that feel intensely real and are set in actual places, and stories with a charmingly surreal air that are set in a world that obviously isn't our own; straightforward stories that hit hard precisely because they are so straightforward, and stories that leave you reeling because they are downright bizarre, perhaps even incomprehensible—but incomprehensible in a thrilling, edgy, provocative way. You'll find some works relatively easy to read and some rather difficult; some are short enough to get through in one sitting, even if you like to make flashcards as you go, while others are longer and could take a few days to read carefully. Some stories are by internationally renowned authors, while others were written by people whose names you may never have heard before.

Perhaps you could think of this collection as the language learner's equivalent of a fitness enthusiast's well-balanced workout at a fully equipped gym: you've got cardio and weight training, a lap pool, a sauna, and even one or two machines that you aren't entirely sure you're using correctly but like to fool around on anyway. You go through the whole routine, you sweat buckets, and you come away feeling somewhat sore but also energized and light on your feet, having done all kinds of healthy, good things to muscles that ordinarily you don't even know exist. I'm afraid I can't tell you which story in this collection is the lap pool and which is the elliptical trainer, though if I had to go out on a limb and suggest a candidate for the not-sure-what-this-is-or-how-to-use-it machine, the chances are that Abe Kazushige's magnificently quirky and oddly titled 「馬小屋の乙女」(which I have translated here as "The Maiden in the Manger") is probably it.

The important thing, of course, is that you will be encountering all kinds of different prose styles in these pages, different ways of constructing sentences, different ways of representing dialogue and thought, all kinds of grammatical patterns, and lots of vocabulary. Variety and balance. This is how this book will help you exercise particular linguistic muscles, and build up the basic strength you need to become a proficient reader, whether of Japanese or of English. You will quickly discover that the kana reading (*furigana* or *rubi*) for a particular kanji or combination of kanji is given only the first time it appears in each story, so those of you who are studying Japanese will have to exercise your memories, too, making a concerted effort to remember the readings, if you want to be able to hear the Japanese in your inner ear as you read. Japanese-speaking students of English aren't so lucky: you'll have to look up any pronunciations you aren't already familiar with in a dictionary that includes phonetic spellings. (Sorry about that.) I suppose that means your fingers will get a workout, too.

A trip to the gym affects more than just particular muscles, of course: it makes you feel good all over. It makes your whole body work. And that's what this book tries to do as well.

In fact, I would go so far as to say that the *main point* of this volume is to help you build up your overall health, strength, and endurance as an English-speaking student of Japanese or a Japanese-speaking student of English. By the time you arrive at the end of this collection, you will undoubtedly have picked up lots of new words and grammar, but more important, you will have had the opportunity to practice getting along *on your own* as a reader, without relying on detailed notes, simply using the translations to figure out *why* the original means what it does, and *how* it means it, or vice versa. You might suspect that reading a translation alongside the original would make the process almost ridiculously easy, like one of these "lose weight while you watch TV and eat ice cream!" diets that you hear about from time to time. Well, it's not. If you want to get the most out of this collection—the most improvement, but also the most pleasure—you'll have to put some effort into it. Reading a book like this—seeing how the original and its translation converge, and where they depart from each other—is a lot of fun, but it's also hard work. It's precisely the sort of enjoyable effort that helps us get our bilingual brains, the whole brain, in shape.

If you should happen to have friends who might want to read this book along with you, or if you are using it in a class, you'll find that it offers a wealth of material for discussion. In fact, while I did my best to arrange the stories roughly in order of increasing difficulty—though at this level, the different varieties of difficulty one encounters cease to be so easily ranked—I paid even more attention to the content of the stories themselves: to the themes, images, situations, and ideas that emerge from them. I chose works that resonate with one another in some way, or in any number of ways, and tried to arrange them so as to make those resonances as apparent as possible, and as interesting as possible. This collection is meant to get you involved, to give you a chance not only to read and understand the sentences in these stories but also to be moved, and think thoughts, and make connections, in the language you are learning. And then, if you're lucky enough to have people around you with whom you can share those thoughts and emotions, to give you an opportunity to connect with those friends or classmates in conversation in the language you are learning. Exercise together. Join the group of people hanging out by the rack of dumbbells, chatting. That's part of the workout, too. Indeed, that may be what it's all about.

Finally, a few words about the landscape of Japanese literature over the past few decades and the writers included in this collection.

In 1979 a young jazz bar owner named Murakami Haruki published a novel called 『風の歌を聴け』(*Hear the Wind Sing*, in Alfred Birnbaum's translation) to somewhat less than universal acclaim: when the work was nominated for the prestigious

Akutagawa Prize, future Nobel Prize laureate Ōe Kenzaburō, a
member of the prize committee, dismissed it without even
bothering to mention Murakami's name, or the book's title. "One
entry was a clever imitation of an American novel," he
commented, "but since the author made no attempt to develop his
own creative abilities through this imitation, I thought it was a
complete waste of both his own time and his readers'."

A lot has changed in the last thirty years. Murakami Haruki
has become an international phenomenon and a *New York Times*
bestselling author, and there are persistent rumors that he is in the
running for a Nobel Prize of his own. And in retrospect,
Murakami's appearance on the Japanese literary stage seems to
have presaged a new trend, the coming of a new style: the writers
of Ōe's generation, who specialized in brilliant, intense, often
disturbing fiction that conveyed a sense of density and weight,
were about to be joined by a crop of equally brilliant writers with a
taste not for gravity but for levity, or, at the very least, with a
certain easygoing, approachable lightness of touch. Except that
when I say "Ōe's generation," I'm not referring to his age—it's a
matter of *literary* generations. Tsushima Yūko and Yoshida Sueko
were both born in 1947, for instance, just two years before
Murakami Haruki, and yet they seem to share more with Ōe than
with Murakami. If anything, Murakami seems to belong with
Yoshimoto Banana, who was born in 1964 and published her first
collection of stories,『キッチン』(translated by Megan Backus as
Kitchen), in 1988. And indeed, Yoshimoto has become almost as
much of an international phenomenon as Murakami: in 2002,
when the Italian translation of a collection of Yoshimoto's stories
sold 100,000 copies in less than six months and continued finding
new readers at a brisk pace even after that, she became the first
Japanese author to sell more copies of a book abroad, in just a
single country, than she had in Japan.

So as you make your way through this collection, you'll be
encountering fiction that can be described, or could once have

been described, as relatively "orthodox" in style, written by true masters of that style, and works by writers who struck out in a new direction starting, for the most part, in the 1980s, and whose popularity eventually led to the creation of what has now come to seem like an orthodoxy of its own. (This, I think, is part of what makes Japanese literature so thrilling: the sense one often gets that individual writers are engaged in a kind of communal effort, supporting and working off one another, and that the lines between the different groups and styles they create are relatively clear—the sense one gets, in other words, that there are battling orthodoxies.) And then there are stories by a brand-new crop of writers who began publishing fiction in the 1990s, or even, in the case of Koike Masayo, in the first years of this century. As you'll discover, members of this most recent group write in all different styles, and while certain authors do seem to have affinities with each other—Kawakami Hiromi and Ishii Shinji, for example—for the moment, at least, there doesn't seem to be any particular governing style or mood that might hold them together as another "generation." Indeed, if anything links the writers in this last batch, it's the incredible variety of their interests and backgrounds, and the fact that they stepped into literature from outside. Kawakami Hiromi (born on April Fool's Day, 1958) worked as a high school biology teacher for a number of years before she became a writer; Ishii Shinji wanted to be an illustrator; Abe Kazushige started writing novels when he noticed that the descriptive passages in the film scenarios he had been writing as a student at the Japan Academy of Moving Images kept getting longer and longer; and Koike Masayo, recipient of the 2007 Kawabata Yasunari Prize, slid into prose fiction from poetry.

Such are the contents of this volume: two generations and one nongeneration; writers whose ages range from thirtysomething to sixtysomething, and who come from places as mutually distant and different as Jinmachi, way up in the north of Honshū, and Okinawa, all the way down in the south; and fiction written in the

1980s (Tsushima Yūko's「黙市」"The Silent Traders," first
published in 1982, and Yoshida Sueko's「嘉間良心中」"Love
Suicide at Kamaara," first published in 1984), the 1990s (Murakami
Haruki's 1995「夜中の気笛について、あるいは物語の効用について」
"Concerning the Sound of a Train Whistle in the Night *or* On
the Efficacy of Fiction"), and the 2000s (Yoshimoto Banana's
「小さな闇」"A Little Darkness," first published in 2000; Kawakami
Hiromi's 2001「鼹鼠」"*Mogera Wogura*"; Koike Masayo's
「げんじつ荘」"Genjitsu House" and Abe Kazushige's「馬小屋の乙女」
"The Maiden in the Manger," both published in 2004; and
Ishii Shinji's 2005「ボウリングピンの立つ所」"Where the Bowling
Pins Stand").

This collection is packed with all kinds of goodies—eight
stories, five of which are appearing in English for the first time. I
hope you like them.

A number of people provided invaluable assistance as I was
preparing this collection. First, I would like to thank all the
authors for graciously allowing me to include their works here in
both Japanese and English. My deep gratitude, as well, to
Geraldine Harcourt and New Directions for allowing me to
reprint "The Silent Traders," and to Yukie Ohta and the University
of Hawai'i Press for letting me include "Love Suicide at Kamaara."
Kobayashi Satomi of the Kokusho Kankōkai and especially Matsui
Hatsumi of Kaifūsha helped me to track down Yoshida Sueko.
Sakai Tatemi and Sakai Harumi of the Sakai Agency helped me
obtain permission to reprint three of the stories and to print or
reprint their translations in this collection; Amanda Urban and
Liz Farrell of International Creative Management helped out with
others. My thanks also to both the Yoshimoto Banana Office and
the Murakami Haruki Office for their assistance. Takahashi
Gen'ichirō very kindly interceded to try to convince Nakahara
Masaya to let me include one of my favorites among his stories, the
brilliantly whacked-out「あのつとむが死んだ」(which I translated,

perhaps too extravagantly, as "Who'd Have Thought Tsutomu Would Die?") even though Nakahara has declared that he has given up writing and never wants to have anything to do with publishing again. Unfortunately, he wasn't successful. My gratitude, finally, to John Siciliano of Penguin, who managed with grace and good humor to make it possible, despite innumerable obstacles, to produce this beautifully nonparallel, very, very new *New Penguin Parallel Text*.

—Michael Emmerich

Short Stories in Japanese
日本語の短篇小説

Concerning the Sound of a Train Whistle in the Night
or On the Efficacy of Fiction

夜中の汽笛について、あるいは物語の効用について

Murakami Haruki

Translated by Michael Emmerich

The girl has a question for the boy: "How much do you love me?"

He thinks for a moment, then quietly replies, "As much as a train whistle in the night."

She waits in silence for him to go on. Obviously there has to be a story there.

"Sometimes, just like that, in the dead of night, I wake up," he begins. "I don't know what time it is, exactly. Maybe two or three, around then, I'd say. The time doesn't actually matter. The point is that it's the dead of night, and I'm totally alone, not a soul around. I want you to imagine that for me, okay? It's completely dark, you can't see anything. And there's not a sound to be heard. You don't even hear the hands of the clock, ticking out the time—for all I know, the clock could well have stopped. And then all of a sudden, it hits me that I've become isolated, that I'm separated some unbelievable distance from everyone I know, from every familiar place. I realize that no one in this whole wide world loves me anymore, no one will talk to me, that I've become the kind of person no one even wants to remember. I could just disappear and no one would even notice. I feel like I've been pushed into a box with thick iron sides and sunk way down to the very bottom of the ocean. The pressure is so intense it makes my heart ache, I feel like I'm going to explode, to be torn in two—you know that feeling?"

The girl nods. She thinks she knows what he means.

The boy continues. "I think that's one of the most painful experiences a person can have in life. I feel so sad and it hurts so much that I wish I could just go ahead and die, seriously. Actually I take that back, it's not that *I wish I could die:* I can tell that if things go on in this way, the air in the box is going to get so thin that I really *will* die. It's not just a *metaphor*. It's reality. That's what

女の子が男の子に質問する。「あなたはどれくらい私のことを好き?」

少年はしばらく考えてから、静かな声で、「夜中の汽笛くらい」と答える。

少女は黙って話の続きを待つ。そこにはきっと何かお話があるに違いない。

「あるとき、夜中にふと目が覚める」と彼は話し始める。「正確な時刻はわからない。たぶん夜二時か三時か、そんなものだと思う。でも何時かというのはそれほど重要なことじゃない。とにかくそれは真夜中で、僕はまったくのひとりぼっちで、まわりには誰もいない。いいかい、想像してみてほしい。あたりは真っ暗で、なにも見えない。物音ひとつ聞こえない。時計の針が時を刻む音だって聞こえない——時計はとまってしまったのかもしれないな。そして僕は突然、自分が知っている誰からも、自分が知っているどこの場所からも、信じられないくらい遠く隔てられ、引き離されているんだと感じる。自分がこの広い世界の中で誰からも愛されず、誰からも声をかけられず、誰にも思い出してももらえない存在になってしまっていることがわかる。たとえ僕がそのまま消えてしまったとしても誰も気づかないだろう。それはまるで厚い鉄の箱に詰められて、深い海の底に沈められたような気持ちなんだよ。気圧のせいで心臓が痛くて、そのままふたつにびりびりと張り裂けてしまいそうな——そういう気持ってわかるかな?」

少女はうなずく。たぶんわかると思う。

少年は続ける。「それはおそらく人間が生きている中で経験するいちばん辛いことのひとつなんだ。ほんとうにそのまま死んでしまいたいくらい悲しくて辛い気持だ。いや、そうじゃない、死んでしまいたいというような ことじゃなくて、そのまま放っておけば、箱の中の空気が薄くなって実際に死んでしまうはずだ。それはたとえ

it means to wake up all alone in the dead of night. You still following me?"

The girl nods again, saying nothing. The boy lets a moment go by.

"And then, way off in the distance, I hear a train whistle. It's really incredibly far off, this whistle. I don't even know where the train tracks could be. That's how far away the sound is. And it's so faint that it's right on the edge of being inaudible. Only I'm certain it's a train whistle. There's no doubt about that. So I lie perfectly still, in the darkness, listening as hard as I can. And then I hear it again. And my heart stops aching. The hands on the clock start moving. The iron box begins to rise up, nice and slow, toward the surface of the sea. And it's all thanks to that little whistle, you see. A whistle so faint I could barely hear it. And the point is, I love you as deeply as that whistle."

With that, the boy's brief story is over. And the girl begins telling her own.

なんかじゃない。ほんとうのことなんだよ。それが真夜中にひとりぼっちで、目を覚ますことの意味なんだ。それもわかる?」

少女はまた黙ってうなずく。少年は少し間を置く。

「でもそのときずっと遠くで汽笛の音が聞こえる。それはほんとうにほんとうに遠い汽笛なんだ。いったいどこに鉄道の線路なんかがあるのか、僕にもわからない。それくらい遠くなんだ。聞こえたか聞こえないかというくらいの音だ。でもそれが汽車の汽笛であることは僕にはわかる。間違いない。僕は暗闇の中でじっと耳を澄ます。そしてもう一度、その汽笛を耳にする。それから僕の心臓は痛むことをやめる。時計の針は動き始める。鉄の箱は海面へ向けてゆっくり浮かび上がっていく。それはみんなその小さな汽笛のせいなんだね。聞こえるか聞こえないか、それくらい微かな汽笛のせいなんだ。そして僕はその汽笛と同じくらい君のことを愛している」

そこで少年の短い物語は終る。今度は少女が自分の物語を語り始める。

A Little Darkness

小さな闇

Yoshimoto Banana

Translated by Michael Emmerich

I tagged along to Buenos Aires on a business trip with my dad, who runs an import company, only to find myself at a loss, overwhelmed by all I didn't know. It felt strange to be in a city where everyone was white and the buildings looked utterly European, and yet everywhere I looked jacaranda trees stretched their branches into an unmistakably South American sky, clear and deep and almost achingly blue.

The young women I saw walking down the streets all looked curiously old, and though I was twenty-one I imagine I must have looked like a girl in junior high. No one tried to hit on me or rob me, even when I was alone. It may have helped that I was wearing an old pair of jeans white enough to disturb the maître d' at the hotel restaurant, and an even older *Slam Dunk* T-shirt that I had won years ago. With my jean jacket completing the ensemble, it must have been clear from a mile off that I was a low-budget tourist. My dad had said I couldn't be too careful walking alone, so I wasn't even carrying a purse.

My dad was off on his own that day, having gone to buy a guitar. He played classical guitar as a hobby, and was good enough to be a pro. He hadn't come to this country to sightsee, or even, truth be told, on business; his real goal was to buy a guitar. He had finished his business the day before, so he had been in a tizzy all morning, unable even during breakfast to take his mind off the guitar shop. I went with him at first, entering the small shop and gazing at the truly beautiful guitars lined up inside. Musical instruments created by hand, lovingly assembled, carefully polished . . . eventually someone would come along who would play them, giving a new depth to their living, breathing shine. There was something practical in their beauty. My dad's eyes gleamed as he took up one guitar after another, sighing at his indecision. They were all so splendid, he couldn't choose. Realizing he was going to be there all day, I said I'd meet him back at the hotel and left the shop.

———————

輸入業を営む父親の仕事にくっついてブエノスアイレスに来たものの、なんの知識もなかったのでとまどうばかりだった。街が白人ばかりなのも、街並があまりにもヨーロッパに似ているのも、それなのにくっきりと濃い、南米特有の悲しいほど青い空に、ジャカランダの木が枝を伸ばしているのも、新鮮だった。

街を行く女の子たちはみんな妙に老けていて、二十一歳の私なんてまるで中学生に見えるのだろう。ひとりで歩いていてもナンパもされず、スリにもあわなかった。ホテルのレストランがいやがるほどの古いジーンズに、懸賞で当たった古い古いスラムダンクTシャツを着ていたのがよかったのかもしれない。そこにGジャンをはおれば、どこから見ても貧乏な旅行者だった。その上、ひとりで歩くなら用心しすぎてもいいくらいだ、と父が言ったので、私は手ぶらで歩いていた。

その日、父は私と別れてひとりでそそくさとギターを買いに行ってしまった。父はクラシックギターが趣味で、演奏はプロ級だった。父はこの国に、観光に来たのでも、本当を言うと出張で来たのでもなく、ただ単に、ギターを買いに来たのだった。取り引きをまとめる仕事は昨日で終わり、父は朝からうきうきしていて朝食の間もギター屋のことで頭がいっぱいだった。はじめは私もその小さな店に入って、本当に美しいギターが並んでいるのを見ていた。人が手をかけて、心を込めて作り、磨きあげ、やがて演奏することによってまた生命の輝きを深めていく楽器というもの……そこには目的のある美しさがあった。父の目は輝き、次々に手にとって演奏しては、きっと彼は一日中ここにいるだろう、と思い、ホテルで集合することにして、私は店を出た。

I had watched that Madonna movie *Evita* in preparation for our trip, so I decided to pay a visit to Evita's grave. I got on one of the *colectivo* buses and headed for Recoleta, the neighborhood of the city where the cemetery is.

There were so many trees in the graveyard that it looked like a park. Crowds of people were wandering around outside with their dogs. One man was walking more than a dozen. That must be his job, I thought. There was a church with a tall steeple. I went into the cemetery.

With rows of imposing structures lining the paths, it was completely different from the graveyard I had been imagining. Each grave was a building, rising high overhead. This cemetery almost seemed like a residential area. The pseudohouses stood on both sides of the broad paths, stretching into the distance. The chambers inside were large enough to hold several people, not just one. Houses for corpses. Then more houses . . . They were decorated with statues of angels, people, Christ, or Mary. Some had their own small chapels; some even had automatic glass doors that led inside. Magnificent coffins could be seen inside the chambers, arranged in layers. Some graves had stairs leading underground. Evita's was decked out with all sorts of lovely flowers—not a surprise, given the unending stream of visitors—but the grave itself wasn't particularly impressive, in the context of the museumlike splendor of the cemetery as a whole. So many silent houses for the dead, standing in the quiet afternoon sun . . . I remembered going with my parents to see the ruins at Pompeii. The silence of that city, left precisely as it had been long ago, even though the people who once lived there were gone. Streets of stone that hung heavy with an intimation of life, drifting through them like a scent. Silent buildings, eternally dead, set against the background of a blue sky.

Any one of the lavishly decorated buildings in those endless corridors of graves could have held about fifty of my mom's gravestones.

Really. Her grave was so little . . . even among the more modest

来る前にマドンナの映画を観て予習した私は、エビータのお墓でも見てみようか、と思い、コレクティーボに乗って、レコレータ地区にある墓地を目指した。

墓地は公園かと思うくらい緑が多かった。たくさんの人が犬の散歩をしていた。ひとりで何十匹もの犬を散歩させている人もいた。きっとそういう仕事があるのだろう。聖堂があり、高い塔がそびえたっていた。私は墓地に入って行った。

そこは、私の思っていたような墓地とは全然違って異様に立派な建物が並んでいる場所だった。ひとつひとつの墓が一軒の建物になっていて、高くそびえたっていた。これはもはや住宅街だ、と私は思った。広い通路の両脇に、ずらりと家のようなものが並んではるかに続いていく。納骨堂は何人でも入れるくらい大きい。死んだ人たちが入っている家、また家。天使や人物やキリスト様やマリア様の彫像がそれらを彩っている。小さい教会がついてる墓も、ガラス張りで自動ドアの納骨堂がついた墓もあった。中には美しい棺桶が段になって置かれていた。中に階段があって地下に降りて行ける墓もあった。エビータの墓は確かに今も絶えず人々が訪れるだけあって新鮮で美しい花がたくさん飾られていたが、墓地全体の豪華な、まるで美術館のような様子に比べて、それほどのインパクトはなかった。

静かな午後の光、静まり返る死者の家たち……その様子はちょうど、昔両親と行った、ポンペイの遺跡を思い出させた。街はそのままなのに、住んでいる人たちが消え失せたあの静寂。今も当時の活気が匂いのように漂っている石の街。青空を背景に、いつまでも死んだまま静かにしている街。

ずらりと並ぶその墓の街の装飾された建物は、どれもが母のお墓が五十くらい入りそうな墓ばかりだった。

そう、母の墓は本当に小さくて、日本の墓地の中でもさらに見つけることが困難なくらいかわいらしいもの

graves in that cemetery back in Japan, it was hard to find.

These are really cool, I thought. If I were rich, I would build her a grave like this. But almost instantly that feeling vanished.

Because it struck me that she would have hated these little houses.

It felt oddly natural to be remembering her here, where the dead outnumbered the living. No matter how many corners I turned, this town of graves just kept going: the same buildings, decorated with the same lovely carvings, the same flowers. The sun cast such deep shadows that I felt like I was walking in a dream. It struck me that if I kept walking around long enough, the border dividing this world from the land of the dead might disappear, and then I could go there, too.

My mom died of cancer three years ago. I'm an only child, and I was closer to her than to my father, so I grieved for ages. I didn't graduate that year, and stayed in high school longer than usual. Members of the basketball team who had started out a year behind me were now in the same year as me, but they still talked to me as if I were a year ahead, calling me "the senior." That became my nickname. It was really great when I graduated, because everyone, even people in the same year, kept telling me, "Congratulations, senior!" By then, the faint, delicate aura that had lingered in the house after my mom's death had entirely evaporated, and my very undelicate dad and I had settled into our new, sloppy lifestyle. My mom had slipped quietly away from the world. She was gone.

She'd always had a vaguely fragile air about her, and even when I was little I had the feeling she might not live very long. She never let her desires show, hardly ever laughed out loud—she

だった。

かっこいい。私がお金持ちになったら、母にこんなすごいお墓を作ってあげようか、と私は思ったが、すぐにその気持ちは消えた。

そうだ、母はこういう小さい家に入ることがなによりもいやだった、と思い出したからだ。

死んでいる人のほうが多いこの場所では、死者を思い出すことが妙に自然だった。角を曲がっても曲がっても、同じような美しい装飾や花に彩られた「墓の街」が続く。光に照らされて陰影がくっきりとして、夢の中を歩いているようだった。ここをいつまでも歩き回っていたら、自然に、死者の国と境がなくなり、足を踏み入れることができそうだと思った。

母は三年前、癌で死んだ。私はひとりっ子でお母さんっ子だったから、ずいぶん長い間悲しみにくれて、高校を卒業しそこない、人よりも長く高校時代を送ってしまった。バスケットボール部の後輩たちが同学年になり、私はなぜか先輩！　とよばれる同学年になったため、あだ名は先輩、になってしまった。卒業の時は、後輩からも同級生からも、先輩、卒業おめでとうございます！　と言われて愉快だった。その頃には母が残していた薄くて柔らかい気配も家からすっかり消え、がさつな父と私の気ままな生活の型ができていた。母はこの世からひっそりと消えていった。

母はなんとなく影の薄い人で、小さい頃から、もしかしたらお母さんは長生きしないかもしれないなと私は思っていた。母は欲望をむき出しにすることをせず、大声で笑うこともあまりなく、なにかをあきらめているよ

looked, somehow, as if she had given up on something. I always assumed this was the influence of my father, who was subdued and tended not to get too excited about things, but when I met her old friends at the funeral they said she had always been like that. Never had much of a will to do anything, always kind of passive. That, they said, was the sort of person she was.

My mom's mom, my grandmother, was the mistress of a famous painter who lived in Paris. So my mom was an illegitimate child. My grandfather spent three months out of every year in Japan, and basically my grandmother was his local wife. She and he were both dead, and I had never met either of them, but I would always go see my grandfather's paintings when they were brought over for an exhibition, and I'd stand before them, musing. How strange to think I was related to the man who had painted them. I felt that every time I saw those canvases, with their liberal use of bluish green. There was a portrait of my grandmother. I wanted to buy it because her eyes reminded me of my mom's, but the price on it was ridiculous.

In his old age, my grandfather had suddenly gone mad with love, abandoning both his official wife and my grandmother to marry a girl in her twenties. I don't know what happened to his wife, but my grandmother went crazy. She had lost all she'd ever had, and I guess she just fell to pieces.

My mom became weirdly intense when she told that story. Those were the only times I ever saw her like that.

I always worried that she might suddenly vanish, because she seemed so fragile, but somehow whenever she recounted that story, she was strong.

Glancing at my watch, I saw that it was almost three.

うなところがあった。私はそれは父のあまり盛り上がらないおとなしい性格の影響かと思っていたが、母はずっとそんな感じだった、とお葬式に来た昔の友達はみんなそう言った。ああしたい、こうしたい、というのが薄く、いつもなんとなく受け身な感じがする人だったと。

母の母、つまり祖母は、パリに住んでいる有名な画家の愛人だった。母は、私生児だった。祖父は年に三ケ月くらいは日本に住み、祖母はその間の現地妻だったそうだ。どちらももう死んでしまったので私は祖母にも祖父にも会ったことはないが、たまに展覧会が来ると行き、「ほほう」と思う。血がつながっているんだ、と不思議に思う。私の好きな浅葱色を多用しているその絵を見ると、そう思う。祖母の肖像もある。目元が母に似ているから、買いたいと思ったら、法外な値段だった。

祖父は老境にさしかかってから突然恋に狂い、正妻も祖母も投げ出して、二十代の娘と結婚した。正妻がどうなったかは知らないが、祖母は精神に異常をきたした。すべてを失った祖母の、その時の嘆きようはものすごかったらしい。

母は、その話をする時だけは、奇妙に熱を込めた。

私はいつも、影が薄い母がふと消えてしまうのではないか、と不安だったが、その話をしている時の母は、なぜか力強かった。

時計を見ると、午後三時になろうとしていた。

I wandered slowly among the graves, the sun beating down hard on everything. I passed by Evita's grave again, looking at all the different dedications, and at the sparkling flecks in the granite. Then I sat down to rest for a while on the root of an enormous tree. The faint breeze dried my sweat. Why do graveyards always have trees like this, with branches that droop down low to the ground? Are they here to comfort the dead, or do they grow so large by sucking up their energy?

I wondered if my dad was still trying to choose his guitar.

My dad. A good guy who likes classical guitars more than anything.

My parents came here for their honeymoon. My dad bought a guitar then, too. My mom stayed with him the whole time, he said, listening patiently as he played one guitar after another. And then she pointed to one and said, This is your sound. That's the guitar I got, the one I have back at home. She had this mysterious side to her that let her do things like that, and that's what I fell for, he said.

For the most part my mom got along very well with my dad, but he definitely had his oddities—even I could see that. I'm close to my paternal grandparents, and as far as I can tell there's nothing odd about them, so I figure my dad's weirdness is completely his own. He's been like that ever since I was little.

For instance, on my dad's birthday, my mom always prepared his favorite foods, and would start cooking in the morning. My dad would promise to come home early, saying he would call if it looked like he might be late. I would hurry back as soon as I was done with my after-school activities. Eventually, though, when I got slightly older, I learned what to expect. On those occasions, my dad always came back late, and he was always drunk. He never called. He didn't do that on our birthdays, of course. He never missed our parties, even if he had to leave work early or call in sick. But when he got promoted, when he started his own

墓の中は陽ざしもきつく、私はゆっくりと歩いて、またエビータの墓の脇を通り、そこに飾られた様々な献辞や、黒いみかげ石の光るところを見た。そして、少し休むためにとても大きな木の根元に腰を下ろした。かすかに風が渡っていって汗が乾いた。墓場にはどうしていつも、低く枝を伸ばす大きな木があるのだろう？　死者を慰めるためなのか、死者のエネルギーを吸い取って育つのか。

父はまだギターを選んでいるだろうか。

気のいい父、クラシックギターがこの世でいちばん好きな父。

父と母は新婚旅行でやはりここに来たという。その時も父はギターを買った。母は、ひとつひとつの試し弾きに耳を傾け、根気よく、父の買い物につきあった、と父は言った。そして、お母さんは、あるひとつのギターを指差して、あなたの音はこれ、と言ったんだ、それがうちにあるこのギターだよ。お母さんにはそういうミステリアスなところがあって、そこにすっかりやられてしまったんだね。俺は……と父はのろけたものだった。私は父方の祖父母をよく知っているが、特に変わったところはなさそうなので、それは父が独自に持っている癖のようなものなのだと思う。小さい頃からそうだった。

母は父と基本的にとても仲が良かったが、父には私から見ても奇妙なところがあった。

たとえば、父の誕生日、母は父の好きな食べ物を朝から用意している。父は、必ず早く帰るし、遅くなるようだったら連絡をする、と言う。私もそれを心得て、部活が終わるとすばやく帰った。しかし、ある程度の分別がつく年齢になった頃にはもうわかっていた。そういう時、必ず父は酔って遅く帰ってくる。連絡もしない。それが母や私の誕生日だったら別だった。早引けしても病欠してでも、父は家にいた。しかし父の昇進の時

company, even when we fixed a dinner to help him recover from the shock of a close friend's death in an automobile accident— anytime we were waiting to eat with him, for him, he would run away. It was even worse if we had invited relatives or guests. We would end up eating without him, and only after everyone had left would he show up, brought back in a drunken stupor by friends or coworkers.

How many times did my mom and I get angry at him for that? How many times, from when I was a little girl to when my mom died?

"I can't help it," my dad muttered sadly. "When I think of you waiting for me, I get scared. I drag my feet, it gets late. And then it's even harder for me to call. So I drink. The second I start thinking I might not be able to live up to your expectations, it's over. I can't help it."

This was something he had inside him, we realized, and so eventually, little by little, we stopped holding open celebrations for him. Something about these events seemed to touch a wound somewhere deep inside him. I couldn't help marveling that he had been able to launch his own business when he had a problem like that, but I suppose the truth of it was that the harder he pushed himself outside, the more he unraveled inside.

Even so, my mom and I tried to come up with new ways to celebrate.

Once, the night before his birthday, we waited until he was sound asleep, then quietly got everything ready, setting out presents on the table and cooking without making a sound. Then, at two in the morning, we shook him awake and toasted to his birthday in our pajamas. I think our creative celebrations really helped him. The next morning, on his birthday, he went off to work half-asleep, and that night he came back just as always and had an ordinary dinner at home. It never occurred to us that if we had to go to so much trouble, we might as well not celebrate. That was how we showed him our love; that was what human

も、独立の時も、親友が事故で亡くなってがっかりしている父を慰める会の時でさえ、いつもなにか父を中心に、父を待って食事をしようとすると、父は逃げ出した。親戚とかお客さんを呼んだりすると、ますますだめだった。

結局父なしで食事をして、お客さんが帰った後に、つぶれて運ばれてくる父を見るのがおちだった。

幼い時から母が死ぬまで、母も私も何回父を責めただろう。

父は悲しそうに言った。

「どうしても、待たれていると思うと、こわくなってしまうんだ。自分でもどうしようもないんだ。そして、足が重くなって、遅くなってしまう。そうするとますます連絡しづらくなって、飲んでしまうんだ。もしも期待に応えられなかったら、と思うだけで、だめなんだ。」

これは、心の病かもしれない、と思い、私と母はやがてじょじょにだが公にする祝い事をとりやめていった。きっとそれは父の深いところにある傷に触れるなにかなのだろう。それにしてもよくそれで独立して事業をはじめることができるものだ、と私は思ったが、外で無理すればするだけ、できてしまうほころびがそのポイントだったのだろう。

それでも私と母は、創意工夫をして、意地でも祝ったりした。

誕生日の前夜には父が寝静まってからこっそりと支度をして、夜中の二時に父を叩き起こし、みんなでパジャマを着たまま乾杯をしたこともあった。そういう時、その創意工夫に父は本当に救われたと思う。そして誕生日当日は寝ぼけて会社に行き、普通に帰ってきて、普通の夕食を食べていた。そんなにしてまで、とは思わなかった。それが愛情の示し方であったり、人間の弱さという

weakness looked like.

My mother talked to me about it only twice.

I was in elementary school the first time. In those days, my mom and I were still trying to correct that bad habit of my dad's. I don't remember what it was we were celebrating. Maybe it was the time he suggested we go on a trip abroad for summer vacation, and my mom was so happy she decided to make something special.

She had decided to make tempura, of all things. She had gotten everything ready, and we were sitting there waiting, just waiting. I knew my dad wasn't going to be coming back, because he never did, and so when I couldn't wait any longer, I fixed myself a cup of instant ramen. I offered my mom some, too.

She took a mouthful, then said, "Of course, it'd be a lot worse if he were seeing another woman or something, wouldn't it?"

"That's true," I said. "His problem is, he takes things too seriously. He just can't deal with it when we try to do something special at home."

"To tell the truth, though, when I've gotten all these things ready, put the oil in the pot, prepared all the ingredients I'm going to fry, and we're sitting here waiting for a dinner we know we're not going to have, I feel just like I'm in a box."

"In a box?" I said. I didn't see the connection.

"You see, this feeling—I think it's a lot like what you father feels out there, when he doesn't come home. And when I think maybe

ものだと思った。

私が母にその話を聞いたことは二回しかない。

一度は、小学生の時だった。その頃はまだ私も母も、父の悪い癖を矯正しようとしていた。なんの祝い事だっただろう。父が夏休みに海外旅行に行こうと言い出したので、そのお礼にごちそうを作ろうという日だっただろうか。

母はよりによって天ぷらを用意し、じっと待っていた。私は耐えきれず、だいたいどうせいつものように父は帰らないだろうと知っていたので、勝手にカップ麺を作ってとりあえず食べていた。母にもひとくちあげた。

母は麺をすすり、ひとこと言った。

「他に女の人がいるとかいうほうが、よほど深刻よね。」

「そうよ。お父さんはまじめすぎるから、こういうかしこまった場が家にあるのがだめなのよ。」

私は言った。

「でもね、こうして、用意をして、天ぷら鍋にも油を入れて、材料もみんなそろえて、ないはずの夕食の時間を待っているとね、お母さん、箱に入っている感じがするの。」

「はあ。」

私は言った。わけがわからない比喩だと思った。

「この感じは、きっと、今、お父さんが外にいる気持ちと似ていると思うの。そういうところがお互いにひかれ

that's what attracted us to each other, I can't stand it. Because I start thinking it's the awful, painful feelings we carry inside us that resonate. All the bright, happy things we've built up, things in our lives that have their feet on the ground— it all starts to seem like an illusion, and I feel like I've been shut up in a box the whole time. He shuts me up in a box because he loves me, because I'm important to him. Why is he so afraid of being a perfect husband? Or maybe . . . maybe we all have something like that. That's what really scares me."

"Forget it," I said. "I'm here, aren't I? Maybe you two are in a box, but I'm not. There's no point waiting when we know he's not going to come. Can you just fry my tempura for me? We could leave him a heap of cold tempura and go off to bed, just to get back at him. That'd be good. I bet he'd find it easier that way anyway."

My mom smiled, then started frying my tempura.

After that night, my mom no longer insisted on waiting. Of course she did wait some, but she would start cooking things a little at a time, and we would eat them once they were ready. I pictured the two of them before I was born, trapped together. A man and a woman, suffering in the heat of their love.

I understood about the box the second time.

One day when my mom and I went shopping in Aoyama, I suggested we stop by Spiral Building to see an art show. It was an exhibit of miniature buildings by a foreign artist. Visitors could bend down and step inside, and look out through their colorful windows.

Let's go in, I said. But my mom said she would wait outside.

合ったのかもしれない、と思うと、たまらなくつらいところで、向き合っているような気がしてくるのね。お互いのたまらなくつらいところで、向き合っているような気がしてくる。そうすると、ふだん積み上げてきた明るいものや、地面に足の着いたものがみんな幻想に思えてきて、ずっと箱の中にいたような気がする。好きだから、大切だから、箱の中に入れられてしまっているような気がする。完璧なお父さんになるのがこわいっていう心が、お父さんの中になぜあるのか？　いや、誰の中にもあると思う。それがこわいの。」

「いいじゃん、私がいるじゃん。二人で箱に入っていても、私はそこに入ってないもの。無駄だよ、来ないもの待っていても。それより私のために天ぷら揚げてよ。冷えたやつをいやみがましくとっておいて、先に寝てしまえばいいじゃない。お父さんもそのほうがいっそやりやすいと思うよ。」

私は言った。

母はにっこり笑って、私のために天ぷらを揚げはじめてくれた。

その夜以来、母は意地で待とうとはしなくなった。もちろん待ちはしたが、少しずつ、先に作って食べているようになった。私は私で、私が生まれる前の息苦しい二人を想像した。愛の熱に苦しむ男女の姿を見た気がした。

箱については別の時にわかった。

ある時、私と母は青山に買い物に行き、私の希望でスパイラルビルに展覧会を見に寄った。[11]　外国のアーティストが、小さな建物を作って展示していた。見に来た人は、その色とりどりの窓がある小さな建物にかがんで入って、中から外を眺めることができるようになっていた。

入ろう、と私が言うと、母は外で待っていると言った。

I kept pressing her to come, asking her why she didn't want to, pointing out that the interiors were the best part, but she said she would wait. I thought it was odd. She had the same look in her eyes then that my dad had when he talked about why he couldn't come home. It occurred to me that they actually were bound together, very deeply, by the wounds they carried inside.

I stepped into the little buildings, which were about the same size as the graves lined up in the cemetery where I was sitting now, and peered out all the windows, looked at the little furnishings and the pictures on the walls, enjoying myself. And then I went back outside. My mother was waiting for me, a smile on her face, back to her usual self.

"I'm beat," I said. Then, heading toward the expensive café on the ground floor of Spiral Building, I said, "Let's get something to drink."

After finishing a cup of coffee, which she drank happily, as if it were something very special, making it look like it was really good, she began to explain. That's the sort of person she was. She didn't like ambiguities. And she always looked thrilled by whatever food or drink she was putting in her mouth, as if it were the last thing she would ever be eating or drinking. It always hurt me to see her like that.

"You thought I was acting weird before, didn't you?" my mom said.

"Does it scare you to be in boxes like that?" I asked. "Did you have some sort of bad experience once?"

"I've never told you this before, but you know that your grandmother got sick and had to be hospitalized, right? Well, she committed suicide. It was a sanitarium, actually, not a regular hospital, so there were no knives around, but she extracted the

なんで、内装が見どころなんだよ、入ろうよ、と私はしつこく誘ったが、母は待っている、と言った。おかし

い……と私は思った。その時の母は、家に帰れない話をしている時の父と同じ目をしていた。本当にこの人たち

は心の傷をポイントに深く分かちがたく結ばれているのかもしれない、と思った。

私はその小さな建物、ちょうどこの墓地に立ち並ぶお墓くらいの大きさだった……に入り、いろいろな窓から

外を見たり、小さな家具や飾られている絵を見て、楽しんだ。そして、外に出た。母はにこにこして、もとの母

に戻って待っていた。

「疲れたから、お茶でも飲みましょう。」

と私は言って、スパイラルの値段が高いカフェに母を誘った。

一杯のコーヒーを嬉しそうに、おいしそうに貴重なもののように飲み終えた後、やはり母は切り出した。母は

そういう人だった。曖昧にすることを好まなかった。そして、母はなにかを口に入れる時、いつもそんなふうに

この世の最後に飲み食いするもののように楽しそうにした。私はいつもそれを切なく思った。

「さっき、変に思ったでしょう？　お母さんのこと。」

母は言った。

「お母さん、箱に入るのがこわいの？昔なにかあったの？」

私は言った。

「今まで言わなかったけれど、あなたのおばあちゃんは、病気になって、病院に入ったことは知っているわ

ね。おばあちゃんは、自殺したの。精神病院だったから、刃物はなかったのに、えんぴつ削りの刃を取り出して、

blade from a pencil sharpener and slashed her wrist. She was always very good with her hands."

I'd had no idea. I knew she had been overwhelmed by grief, but no one in my family had ever told me the details.

"How old were you then?" I asked.

"Eight," she said calmly. "When your grandmother went crazy, she and I were living alone, just the two of us. Your grandfather never came to the house anymore, and your grandmother was afraid even to let me go to school. One day, when I got back home, she was waiting for me inside with a little house she had built out of cardboard—actually, it wasn't that little. It was about as big as those buildings we were just looking at. She had cut out windows, and put my toys and a table inside, and there was a candle burning on the table. She had even papered over the walls, so the inside was decorated with flowers she had painted. She had an artistic flair, and it was a really adorable cardboard house. She told me she had built it for me, and she asked me, crying, to live inside. So I decided that I would."

"You did!"

"I lived in that house for two weeks. All day, all the time. I never so much as set foot outside. She brought in a potty and kept the place very clean, she took good care of me, and she never forgot to bring me my meals. When the sunlight shone into the

手首を切ったの。すごく器用な人だったから。」

私はそんなこと知らなかった。失意のうちに死んだというのは知っていたが、それは親戚の誰からも聞かされていなかった。

「お母さんがいくつの時?」

私はたずねた。

「八歳の時よ。」

母は淡々と言った。

「お母さんは、おばあちゃんがおかしくなった時、二人で暮らしていたの。もうおじいちゃんがその家に来ることはなくなって、おばあちゃんはお母さんが学校に行くのも恐ろしくなったみたいだった。ある日、学校から帰ると、おばあちゃんは家の中に、段ボールで小さな家を、って言っても、さっきのあの家くらいの大きなものだったんだけど、とにかくそれを作って待っていた。窓がくり抜いてあって、中にはおもちゃのテーブルが置いてあって、ろうそくが灯っていたわ。壁紙もきちんと塗ってあって、中は花柄が描いてあった。絵心があったから、とてもかわいらしい美しい紙のおうちだった。おばあちゃんは、お前のために家を建てたからここに住んでほしい、と泣いて頼んだ。私は、そうしてあげようと決めた。」

「ええ?」

「それから二週間、その家の中で私は暮らしたの。徹底的に、その中だけで。一歩も出なかった。おばあちゃんはおまるまで持ち込んで清潔を保って世話してくれたし、食事もまめに運んでくれた。陽の光は部屋の窓から、

room, it shone into the window of my little house, too."

"You sure could put up with a lot, huh?"

"Because that was all I could do for her. She seemed so happy when she was taking care of me. She smiled. She had a sort of sacred air to her then. She had been crying ever since my grandfather left, and that was the only way I could cheer her up. And of course your grandfather had only come to see us every once in a while, so your grandmother was everything to me."

"Wow . . ."

"My teacher came to check up on me when I didn't show up at school, and I was taken into custody, and your grandmother was hospitalized. After that, as you know, I went to live with my aunt, and she raised me."

"It's too much for words," I said.

My mom nodded.

"Even now, I sometimes dream of waking up inside that house. Curled up, feeling the smooth cardboard against my skin, a thin line of sunlight streaming in through my little window, shining on the purple flowers your grandmother, my mother, had painted. I smell the paint, and miso soup. And I hear the joyful, vibrant noises of your grandmother bustling around outside. It felt like before, waiting for your grandfather to visit. I couldn't leave, even if I wanted to. Because I was so frightened of hearing your grandmother wail. I just stayed inside all day, not doing anything. Curled up, perfectly still . . . I would wake up wondering if I'd be able to leave that day, but somewhere deep inside I knew that when

その小さな家の窓にも射し込んできたわ。」

「お母さん、すごい根性だね。」

「それしかしてあげられることがなかったんだもの。にこにこしていた。神々しかった。おじいちゃんが去ってから、ずっと泣いていたおばあちゃんを、喜ばせるにはそれしかなかったの。だって、お母さんにとっては、あんたのおじいちゃんは、たまにしか来ないよく知らない人だったから、おばあちゃんがすべてだったのね。」

「はあ……。」

「私が学校に行かなかったから、教師が様子を見に来て、私は保護され、おばあちゃんは病院に行った。後はあなたも知っているとおり、お母さんはおばあさんのところに引き取られて育ったのよ。」

「それって、言葉につくせない体験だったんだろうね。」

私は言った。母はうなずいた。

「今も、時々あの家の中で目覚める夢を見ることがある。体を丸めて、かさがさした段ボールの感触を感じて、小さな窓から細く陽が入ってきて、おばあちゃんの、私のお母さんが描いた紫の花柄を照らし、絵の具の匂いがして、それから、お味噌汁の匂い。おばあちゃんの立てる楽しそうな、活気のある物音。おじいちゃんが来るのを待っていた時のようだった。そして、私はそこから、出ようとしても出ることができない。出てしまって、金切り声でおばあちゃんが泣くのがこわかった。私はその中で一日中、じっとしている。体を丸めて、じっと……。今日は出ることができるのかな、と思いながら目覚めて、そして、ここを出る時はおばあちゃんと別れる

I did finally leave, that would be when I had to leave my mother. So I felt like I had nowhere to go. I thought about sneaking out and calling my grandfather in Paris, but I knew that would also mean saying good-bye to your grandmother. I made up my mind to stay with her until the end, even if it meant I was going to die."

"How awful . . ."

I understood the secret of my mom's personality then. And I realized that part of her was probably still there in that house.

"So when your father doesn't come home, I sometimes find myself going back to that world. I feel as if that time, the waiting, will go on forever. I know that I'm being shut up inside on purpose, because I'm loved, but it hurts too much."

"Have you told Dad what happened?" I asked.

"No, I haven't." My mom laughed. "I don't want to."

"Why not?"

"And let him know my weak spot!" she cried. "Just kidding."

My mom was the sort of person who held fast to her decisions. I realized that she must have made up her mind to act as though none of it had happened. She never did tell him about that house, right up until her death.

————————————

時だって、どこかで知っていたわ。行き場がない気持ちだった。そっと出て、パリのおじいちゃんに電話しよう、と思ったこともあった。でもそれは、自分からおばあちゃんと別れることになる、ってお母さんは思ったの。死んでもいい、とことんつきあってやる、と決めたの。」

「そう……。」

母の性格の秘密を私はその時知った。母の一部は今もその家の中にいるんだろうということも。

「だから、お父さんが帰ってこない時、お母さんの世界はあそこに帰って行ってしまうことがある。この時間は永遠に続くという気がしてしまう。愛されているからわざとその時間の中に閉じ込められているというのはわかるけれど、苦しくてたまらなくなる。」

「お父さんにそのこと話した?」

私はたずねた。

「話してないわ。」

母は笑った。

「話したくないのよ。」

「どうして?」

「弱味を知られたくないの、なんてね。」

母は言った。母はこうと決めたらなんとしてでもやる人だった。結婚前に、そのことをなかったことにしたのだろう、と私は思った。死ぬまで、母はそれを父に言わなかった。

The whole time I was occupied with these memories, the afternoon sun was slowly ripening into a golden dusk.

I sat frozen beneath the tree, gazing up at its big leaves. The sun filtering down through the branches played at my feet, forming a beautiful patchwork of light and shadow. Any number of couples passed by, walking arm in arm. A few dogs came over to me, then wandered off.

It was a quiet time. So quiet I almost forgot I was in a foreign country.

The cross on the steeple gleamed in the sun.

In a little while, I'll go back to the hotel and praise the guitar my father bought. I'll ask him to play for me. And then . . .

Should I tell him Mom's story tonight, over dinner?

I thought about it.

No, I shouldn't do it, I decided. It would only make him sad, make him feel bad. He would only look back in sorrow at how the little darkness he carries inside had called to the darkness in her, how they had suffered and loved together.

What darkness do I carry in me? I have no problem going home when I know people are expecting me, and I'm not afraid of boxes. Eventually, though, I thought, it will appear. That's what growing is all about. How will I face it? How will I learn to deal with it? I'm still young, fearless. I can even look forward to it. I want to see for myself what it's like. From the outside, our family was ridiculously sweet, almost too peaceful, and yet we harbored a little, deep darkness with a secret history as pregnant as the silence of this graveyard. It wasn't anything to be ashamed of.

I sat thinking for ages, protected by leaves alive with sunlight.

そんなことを考えている間にも、午後の光は夕暮れの金色に向かって、ゆっくりと熟していった。

私は木の下で、大きな葉をじっと見上げていた。木漏れ日が足元でおどり、美しいまだらを作っていた。何組もの恋人たちが腕を組んで通っていった。何匹かの犬が私のところにやってきては去っていった。

外国にいることを忘れてしまうくらい、静かな時間だった。

塔のてっぺんの十字架が陽を受けて光っていた。

もう少ししたら、ホテルに戻って父の買ったギターをほめてあげよう、演奏も聴いてあげよう。そして……。

私は今夜食事をしている時、母の過去を父に話すだろうか？

と私は考えた。

やめよう、父が悲しんで後悔するだけだ、と私は思った。自分の中の小さな闇が、母の中の闇に呼応して苦しみ合ったことや愛し合ったことを悔いるだけだろう。

私にとってのそれはなんだろう？

私の中からいつかそれは姿を現すだろう？　期待されると帰宅できない性分でもなく、箱がこわいわけでもない。でも、き合うのだろう？　どう対処するのだろう？　私はまだ若く、恐れを知らない。楽しみですらあった。私はそれとどう向いと思った。外から見たら大甘の平和すぎるほど平和だった私の家族の中に小さな深い闇があり、その闇はこの墓地にある静けさと同じくらい、歴史を秘めて豊潤なものだった。それは恥じるべきことではない。

陽にきらきら光る葉に守られて、いつまでも私はそのことを考えていた。

Genjitsu House

げんじつ荘

Koike Masayo

Translated by Michael Emmerich

I got a call from Yoriko. How'd you like to come over for dinner Saturday evening? she asked. I was startled. And pleased. Of course I'll come! So tell me, how've things been?

In the winter of her forty-fourth year, Yoriko gave birth for the first time to a baby girl. They say it's practically a miracle for a woman her age to give birth naturally, though never having had children myself I don't have a good sense of what that means. I remember calling Yoriko one day just about a year ago, soon after she had the baby. Her voice sounded youthful and energetic, as if the adrenaline rush of childbirth hadn't completely worn off. Usually they do what's called a see-zare-ian section, where they cut your abdomen open, you see, Yoriko said, as though not having needed that procedure was something she could be proud of.

Yeah, I've heard about see-zare-ian sections. I guess if I ever had a baby, that's what it'd have to be, don't you think, Yoriko? I'm not as strong as you, I replied, mentally converting the sounds see-zare-ian into the word *Cesarean* and wondering with a touch of suspicion how the procedure came to have such an imposing name.

I heard a baby crying, *wanh wanh,* on the other end of the line. With a note of surprise in her voice, as if she had just noticed something lying on the floor, Yoriko cried, Oh my goodness, you're going to have a baby! I mean, I think it's so wonderful that you're even considering it! And then, more slowly, a scolding tone in her voice: You're such a weakling when it comes to pain that you'd probably be better off having a see-zare-ian. They give you local anesthesia, so you don't feel any pain at all, it seems, even though they're actually cutting your belly open. And of course you're totally conscious, so you hear the baby crying and all.

This *having a baby* thing had always seemed like something that happened to other people; now, all of a sudden, I felt it sliding unobtrusively into the range of my own personal

よりこさんから、電話がかかってきた。土曜日の夕方、食事に来ないかと言う。わたしはびっくりした。そして、うれしかった。

もちろん、行くわ。どう、元気でやってる？

よりこさんは、四十四歳の冬に、初めて女の子供を産んだ。子のないわたしには、ぴんと来ないことだが、その年齢で自然分娩というのは、奇跡に近いことがらなのだそうだ。ちょうど一年前、よりこさんに赤ん坊が産まれてまだ間もない頃のこと。彼女に電話したことがある。電話口から聞こえてきた声は、まだ出産時の興奮が収まらないという感じで、若々しく、華やいでいた。普通はテーオーセッカイといって、おなかを切るのよ。よりこさんはそれだけは自慢していいことだというように、わたしに告げた。

ふうん、テーオーセッカイか、わたしはよりこさんほど丈夫じゃないから、産むとしたら、きっとそれね。頭のなかで、「テーオー」という音を、「帝王」という漢字に変換し、なぜ、こんなりっぱな名前が付いているのかしらといぶかしく思いながら、わたしはよりこさんにそう答えた。

電話のむこうでは、赤ん坊がぎゃあぎゃあ泣いている声がした。よりこさんは、落し物でも見つけたように、あらっ、あなた、産むのね、その気持ちがあるのね、それは素敵じゃない、と言ったあと、ゆっくり諭すように言ったのだ。痛みに弱いあなたに、テーオーセッカイはむしろ向いてるわ。麻酔されるから、おなかを切るっていったって痛みなんか少しも感じないらしいわよ。もちろん、意識ははっきりしてるから、赤ん坊の泣き声だって、聞こえるし。

いままではまるで他人事だった「産む」ということが、わたしの可能性の範囲のなかに、そっと入ってきた

possibilities. It was a warm, puzzling sensation. Maybe I could still give birth, even this late, I murmured to myself, without actually speaking the words. On the other end of the line, the baby's bawling grew ever more frenzied, until it was hard for me, even listening from a distance, to take it anymore. Well, I guess I'll be going now, I just wanted to say congratulations, that's all, I said hurriedly, then tried to hang up. But Yoriko stopped me, her tone startlingly gruff and vehement, and I could tell she wanted to keep talking a little longer. Only there wasn't much left for us to say.

This was the first time I'd heard her voice since that conversation.

I got to know Yoriko at a publishing house where I used to work. She was a colleague in the editing department, and we worked together for about five years. A few years after I quit, she left the company, too, and now she was doing an impressive job supporting herself as a translator, working out of her apartment. Well, you know, it's not a steady income, but I can work from home, and translating really suits me, I think. It's like you stare down really fiercely into the chasm between two languages, and then you build a bridge over it, you know what I mean? That was how Yoriko described it. I'm sure it must have been difficult, working with a baby to care for, even though she could work at home. She was raising the baby all by herself. She wasn't married to the baby's father. He was already married.

I was fully aware of Yoriko's situation, and yet somehow, over the course of an entire year, I had never done a single thing to help her. I was mad at myself for being such a useless friend, though it occurred to me that she had never asked me for help, either, which was kind of sad, and when I tried to imagine how she spent her days, my heart ached even more.

It really has been ages, hasn't it? I'll fix something to bring, of course. I mean, preparing it all yourself would be too much work,

瞬間だった。それはあたたかくて不思議な感触だった。まだ、わたしにも、産めるかもしれないわね、声に出さずに、そう、自分につぶやいた。電話の向こうの赤ん坊の泣き声は、いよいよ激しく、聞いているこちらが、いたたまれなくなってくる。もう切るわね、とにかく、おめでとう、って言いたかったの。急いでそれだけ言って切ろうとすると、よりこさんは、思いがけない、ドスの効いた低い声を出し、わたしをひきとめ、もう少し話したそうにした。しかし話すことはもうあまりなかった。

彼女の声を聞くのはあれ以来だ。

よりこさんとは、昔勤めていた出版社で知り合った。編集部の同僚として、五年間ほどいっしょに働いた。私が辞めた数年後、彼女もまた会社を退職し、今では自分のアパートの一室で翻訳をしながら、りっぱに生計をたてている。収入は不安定だけど、在宅でできるし、翻訳って仕事、すごく性にあってるの。ふたつの言語の谷間をにらみつけて、そこに橋をかけるような仕事じゃない？よりこさんは、そんな言い方をした。いくら在宅の仕事といっても、赤ん坊をかかえての仕事は大変だったろうと思う。なにしろ、彼女は、赤ん坊を一人で育てているのだ。相手がすでに結婚してるからだ。赤ん坊のお父さんとは、結婚していない。そういうよりこさんの現実を知りながら、この一年、わたしは結局、彼女のために、なにひとつとして力になれなかった。そういう自分をふがいなく思い、しかし彼女もまた、わたしに少しも助けを求めなかったことをさびしく思いかえし、いったい、どうやって日々をまわしていたんだろうと、考えれば改めて胸がいたむ。ほんとに久しぶりね。わたし、何か作ってもっていくわよ。だってよりこさん、用意するのもたいへんでしょ。

right? Now, don't go overboard, okay? I said, starting even as I
spoke to think about what I could manage. I could make
salmon-cream croquettes and pot stickers, and I'll pick up some
cream puffs on the way. . . . I would make a whole lot of the
croquettes and pot stickers. She could just freeze whatever was
left and have it some other day.

After I hung up, it struck me that one usually takes
something along for the baby on these occasions, but I had no
idea what to buy or where to buy it. It came as something of a
shock to realize how utterly separate my life was from the world
in which people had babies.

I recalled that my aunt—an extraordinarily greedy woman—
had once mentioned that when someone gives your child a
present, it really doesn't matter how small it is, even a single
pencil makes you happy. Yoriko is undoubtedly the same way, I
thought, but perhaps this time I had better just stick to the food,
and assume she won't mind. First, I would see what it was like
living from day to day with a baby, then I'd help out in whatever
way I could.

Yoriko's apartment was in a place called Chitose Funabashi
on the Odakyū line. I hadn't gotten off at that stop for ages. The
convenience store that had opened in front of the station gave
the area a bland, unremarkable look that it didn't used to have.
But when I stepped into the street behind the station, the
familiar stores were still there, just like always: the flower shop,
the photography studio, the bank (its name had changed), the
vegetable store. I found myself recalling a haiku by a poet
named Nagata Kōi:

the coffee shop
will be here forever
autumn rains

あんまりがんばらないで。そう言いながら、わたしは同時に頭のなかで、鮭のクリームコロッケと、ぎょうざを作り、シュークリームを買ってもらっていこうと、さっそくに算段を始めていた。コロッケやぎょうざはたくさん作ろう。余ったら冷凍にして後日食べてもらえばいい。

電話を切ったあと、そういえばこういうときは、赤ん坊のために何か持っていくものだと思ったが、何を買ったらいいのか、どこで買ったらいいのか、想像力がまったく働かない。赤ん坊のいる世界から、まったく遮断されて暮らしている自分に、そのとき気づいて呆然とした。

わたしの叔母が——彼女は大変強欲なひとなのだが——、子供にもらうものは鉛筆いっぽんでも、どんなつまらないものでも、うれしいものだと、かつて言っていたことを思い出す。よりこさんもきっとそうに違いないが、今回はこれで許してもらおう。赤ん坊のいる生活を、まずこの目で見てから、わたしにできることを助けようと思った。

よりこさんの家は、小田急線の千歳船橋というところにある。この駅に降り立つのは、ずいぶんひさしぶりだ。駅前にできたコンビニエンスストアが、この町をありきたりの顔つきに変えてしまっていた。それでも裏通りに足を踏み入れると、花屋、写真館、銀行（名称は変わっていたけれど）、八百屋など、なつかしい店が変わらずにある。わたしは、ふと、永田耕衣という俳人の句を思い出した。[13]

コーヒー店永遠に在り秋の雨

At first glance, things appear to have changed, but somewhere in this area, too, there is a coffee shop that remains forever unchanged. Inside, perhaps, you will find a man behind the counter who never gets any older, forever grinding beans. To the casual observer, this is just a regular coffee shop. But the second you open the door and step inside, you enter a space in which "time" itself is oddly distorted. A present that streams ceaselessly forth like a fountain, sandwiched between a past and a future that stretch like taffy. A "now" that is linked to the eternal . . .

Walking on, daydreaming, I came to the florist. Suddenly I realized that, of course, flowers were the thing to take! I'd buy the most extravagant bouquet I could find and offer it to Yoriko as a present to celebrate the birth of her child.

There was a man out front who seemed somehow not to belong at a flower shop; he called out in a raspy voice, inviting me inside. He was a solid, big-framed man, getting on in years. I gazed at his strong arms, with the sleeves rolled up, and at his hands, swiftly plucking tulips and roses from the buckets, bundling them up. The care with which he moved his hands, as if he were handling something breakable, had an odd allure. The flowers, wrapped in his rough hands, were somehow obscenely inviting. The man must have noticed how my gaze was fixed upon him, because he said, "The thorns cut you, and you've got to work with water, you know. Soft hands won't get anything done at a florist's." I was slightly taken aback, though I tried not to show it; he offered me a dismayed sort of smile, doing the same sagging thing with his eyebrows that Tsuruta Kōji used to do. In the end, I had him wrap up fifteen yellow tulips.

Yoriko's apartment wasn't far. It was in a plain two-story building with several apartments in it, obviously intended for single residents; most of the people who lived there were, I would guess, students from families without very much money. The sign outside gave the name of the building as GENJITSU HOUSE. Yoriko had been living here since she was thirty.

Genjitsu. Was it *genjitsu* as in "reality"? For some reason the sound of this building's name always took my thoughts in the

変わってしまったように見えて、この町のどこかにも、永遠に変わらないコーヒー店がある。そのなかで、永遠に年をとらないマスターが、永遠に豆をひいているかもしれない。ふと見た者の目には、ありふれたコーヒー店。でも、一歩、ドアを開けて足を踏み入れれば、そこは「時」が、奇妙にゆがんでいる空間である。飴のようにのびていく過去と未来のあいだで、泉のようにあふれてやまない現在。14 その「いま」は永遠に通じている……。

そんなことを夢想しながら歩いてると、花屋の前を通りかかった。とっさに、そうだ、花だと思った。きょうはよりこさんの出産祝いに、思い切り、派手な花を買っていこう。

店頭には、花屋にはどことなく不釣合いな感じのおじさんがいて、いらっしゃい、としぶい声をかけてくれた。がっしりした骨太の初老の男性である。袖をまくりあげたたくましい腕と手がチューリップや薔薇を、バケツからついと抜いたり、束ねたりしている。壊れ物を扱うような丁寧な手つきが、妙になまめかしく目にうつる。おじさんの無骨な手が添えられた花々は、なぜかみだらに、なまめいて見えた。わたしがじっと見ている視線に気がついたのだろうか、おじさんが、とっさに、「とげで傷ついたり、水を扱うからね、ヤワな手にゃあ、花屋はつとまらないよ」と言った。内心少しびっくりしていると、鶴田浩二みたいにまゆげを下げて、困ったような笑顔を向けた。16 結局、黄色のチューリップを、十五本、包んでもらうことにした。

ここからよりこさんのアパートはすぐである。一目で独身者向けとわかる質素な二階建ての集合住宅で、借り手の多くは、おそらく、あまり裕福でない学生たちだろう。入り口のところに、げんじつ荘というプレートがかけてある。ここに、よりこさんは、三十のときから、住み続けているのだった。

げんじつというのは、現実のことなのだろうか。その響きは、かえってわたしに、いつも超現実的なものを感

opposite direction, evoking a sense of something beyond the merely real. Stepping through a gate called reality, you pass into the space of the unreal. Yoriko was charmingly cross-eyed; there was something in her temperament, too, that seemed out of line with reality.

Whatever the case, I found it odd and intriguing that she went on living for so long in that cheerless apartment building surrounded by students.

The building belonged to an old woman, unmarried and going on eighty, who lived directly beneath Yoriko. Yoriko always kept an eye on her elderly landlady, treating her like a relative. Maybe that was why the landlady told her she could stay on even after the baby was born, that in fact she was hoping Yoriko would agree to stay.

It gets dark fast in winter. The sunlight had faded quickly, all around; one of the fluorescent bulbs that lit the hallway in the building kept flickering forlornly on and off. One of the washing machines that had been set up outside the building trembled violently for a while, fell silent, and then, after a pause, emitted a series of shrill mechanical beeps to indicate that the cycle was over. Other than that, the place was silent; there was nothing to indicate that anyone lived there.

Knock knock knock. Yoriko's apartment didn't have a doorbell. Rapping on a door as thin as plywood, I heard her call out, I'm coming! and then the door opened.

Welcome, hi! Please, come on in. Oh my, just look at these tulips, they're gorgeous. Thank you so much!

There were only two rooms, the kitchen and another room, so once you were in the door you could survey the entire household. Stepping up into the six-mat room, I saw the same old work desk and bookshelf I remembered from before, and a small bed, and then, scattered all around, diapers, stuffed animals, and toys— a warm "disorder" had found its way into a room that had

じさせた。げんじつという名の門をくぐり、そこより先は、異空間に入っていくのだ。よりこさんは魅力的な斜視の目の持ち主で、気質もどこか、現実からずれたところのあるひとだった。

それにしても、学生たちにまじって、いつまでも、わびしいこのアパートに住み続けているというのは、実に不思議で興味深いことだ。

大家さんは独身の八十になるおばあさんで、よりこさんの部屋のすぐ真下に住んでいる。高齢の大家さんを、いつも肉親のように気にかけていたことのみかえりなのか、よりこさんに子供が生まれても、そのまま住み続けてよい、むしろ住んでくれと拝まれたそうだ。

冬の夕がたはすぐに暮れる。あたりは急速に日がおちて、アパートの通路を照らす、蛍光灯のひとつが、さびしく点滅を繰り返していた。外に設置された洗濯機の一台が、がたがたとはげしく揺れたのちに静まり、一呼吸おいて、ぴーっ、ぴーっ、ぴーっという、洗濯終了を告げる機械音を響かせた。しーんとしていて、ひとが住んでいる気配がない。

とんとんとん。よりこさんのアパートに、呼び鈴というものはないのである。ベニヤ板のような薄いドアをたたくと、なかから、「はあい」というよりこさんの声がして、ドアがあいた。

いらっしゃい、こんにちは。どうぞ、入って。わあ、すごいチューリップ、豪勢ねえ。ありがとう。

台所ともう一部屋の二間しかないから、玄関を入れば、そこから、よりこさんの家庭はすべてを見渡せる。六畳間のほうに足を踏み入れると、見覚えのある、いつもの小さな仕事机と小さな本棚のほかに、小さなベッドがあり、そのまわりには、おむつだの、ぬいぐるみだの、おもちゃが散乱し、修道女のように簡素だった部屋に、

once been as austere as a nun's.

Here, have a look at the baby. I was carrying her on my back before and she just went right to sleep. Perfect timing. I'm sure she'll wake up in a little, but when she's up, she's just such a hassle, you know? Yoriko said, keeping her voice down. Okay, tea first, come have some tea, she said a moment later, and trotted off to the kitchen.

I peered down at the sleeping baby. Her mouth was open the tiniest bit. Her cheeks were bright red; she looked like a baby monkey. Her chin was her most prominent feature. It curved, jutting out, like a three-day-old moon. She must have gotten that from her father. Her head was long, too, like a peanut. This thing in front of me seemed less like a baby than like some other kind of creature, unusual and unlovely.

The words *How cute!* had been on the tip of my tongue, but I swallowed them, blurting out instead, So what's her name? At which Yoriko said, seeming somewhat embarrassed, Her name is Kunugi—you write the tree radical with the old character for *fun* next to it. I know, it's difficult, she added. I could never write it, even after hearing her explanation.

Kunugi, you know, the trees that acorns grow on? Some kind of oak. She's a girl, of course, but when she came out and I saw that face, it hit me right away that she looked less like a flower than like a tree. *Donguri* was another possibility, at first, for acorn, but I decided that might not be a very pleasant name to have.

So she's a little Kunugi, isn't that cute. Little Donguri isn't bad, either, though, I said with a laugh. Yoriko chuckled along with me. She seemed to have lost weight, her cheeks weren't so chubby; I found myself noticing how pretty she had become.

To think a whole year has gone by already; I suppose you must have been incredibly busy. It's true, these days time zooms by like a giant, with enormous strides. It seems like she was born only yesterday, and now, the next day, she's standing. I've never had a year go by so fast. Yoriko turned, revealing her thin profile.

あたたかい「乱れ」が混入していた。

赤ん坊を見てやって。おんぶしてたら、すぐに、寝てしまったの。ちょうどよかったわ。そのうち起きてくるだろうけど、起きてると、うるさいからね。よりこさんは、小声で、そういうと、まず、お茶よ、お茶を飲んで、と台所に立った。

わたしは、眠っている赤ん坊をのぞきこんだ。口をうっすら開いている。ほっぺたが真っ赤で、まるで小猿のようだ。そして、なによりも、あごに特徴があった。しゃくれあがった、三日月あごなのだ。きっとお父さんから受け継いだものなのだろう。おまけに頭全体が、ピーナツのように細長い。そこにいるのは、赤ん坊というよりも、珍妙で不細工な生き物だった。

わたしはかわいいという言葉をのみこんで、思わずなんていう名前？　と尋ねたのだ。するとよりこさんは、なにやら恥ずかしそうに「くぬぎ」と言って、きへんに楽しいの旧字を書くの、ちょっと難しいわね、と付け加えた。18　言われても、わたしには決して書けない字だ。

ほら、どんぐりの実が生る木。女の子だけど、出てきた顔を見たら、花よりも木かしら、と咄嗟に思ったの。

最初は「どんぐり」も候補にあったんだけど、さすがにちょっとかわいそうかな、と思って。

へえ、くぬぎちゃん、かわいい音ねえ。どんぐりちゃんも悪くはないよ。そう言いながら、わたしは笑った。

よりこさんも笑った。少し痩せたのか、頬のあたりがすっきりとして、綺麗になったなあ、とわたしは思った。

あれから一年だね、大変だったでしょう。うん、いまは、時間が、巨人が大またで歩くようにすぎていく。きのう、この子が生まれたと思ったら、きょうは、この子が立っているの。こんなすばやい一年はなかったわ。よ

Just then, the window started shaking, rattling. There was a
helicopter flying overhead, and the wind from its rotors shook
the window. Just then, the baby woke up and started
whimpering, then a little later she opened her eyes wide and
began watching the ceiling. No matter what angle you saw her
from, she was not a cute baby.

Until she was born—Yoriko said, setting two cups of green tea
on the table—I was happy. When I look back now on my
pregnancy, it's kind of weird. I was the one who was pregnant, and
yet somehow I had this sensation that it was actually someone else
who was pregnant with me. Like I was enveloped in this clear
membrane. But it came to seem like that only after I had her, when
I looked back on it all; at the time, I was just trying to carry the
child inside my womb as carefully as I could, and it was exhausting.
I have this image of myself, a pregnant woman walking down the
path that led to the birth, completely focused, and when I turn and
look at that image of myself now, I can see that I was really happy
then. You don't understand that happiness when you're right in the
middle of everything. But when you look back, finally you realize
that, wow, I was extremely happy then. After all, the goal is to have
the baby, right? What comes after that is actually a much bigger
deal, but you only discover that after you've had the baby; when
you're pregnant it's all about giving birth, that's the goal, the
destination. As if once you get there, that's it, there's nothing more.
In that sense, giving birth is like consciously deciding to die.
Because you can't think about what comes after. Right after you
give birth, and this is true of any woman, you feel so exhilarated it's
as though a hundred hundred-watt bulbs have all been turned on at
once. I kind of think maybe that's because giving birth actually
kills a woman, once, and then brings her back again. I mean, you
actually feel like someone is pregnant with you, even though it's
you who's pregnant, and like you're the one who's been born, even
though you were the one to give birth.

Yoriko kept her slightly crossed eyes lowered as she spoke,
explaining to me with a hint of excitement something that had

りこさんはやせた横顔を見せた。そのとき窓が、がたがたと音をたててゆれた。ヘリコプターが上空を飛んでい

る。その風力で窓がゆれたのだ。すると赤ん坊が目をさまし、ううん、ううんと声をあげ始め、やがて、ぱちり

と目を開けて天井を見た。やはり、どこから見ても、かわいい、とは言えない赤ん坊である。

この子が生まれる前は──とりこさんが言う。緑茶をテーブルに置きながら。──幸せだったわ。身ごも

ている時期って、振り返ると不思議なのよ。身ごもっているのは、自分なのに、まるで、自分自身が誰かに身ご

もられているような感触があって。何か、透明なフィルターのなかに包まれている感じ。でもこれは産んだあと

に、ああ、そういえばって、思い返したことで、あのときは、おなかのなかの子を、ただ大事に運ぼうという、

しんどい思いしかなかったわねえ。赤ん坊が生まれるまでの、途上の路をいっしんに歩いている妊婦のわたし、

そのわたしのイメージは、いまからふりかえると、とても幸せなものなの。その幸せは、その渦中にあるときは

よくわからないのね。でも、あとで振り返って、ああ、あんな幸せのなかにいたんだなって、ようやくわかる。

なにしろ、目的は、産むということでしょ？　それから先のほうが、実は大変なのだけれど、そのことを知るの

は産んだあとで、孕んでいるときは、とにかく、産むことがゴールなの、目的なの。まるでその先なんて、ない

みたいに。その意味では、出産って、意識的な死のようだわ。その先を考えることができないんだから。産んだ

直後は、どの女も、百ワットの電球が百個くらい一度についたような高揚感のなかにいる。あれは、もしかした

ら、出産が、女を一度、死なせて、生まれ変わらせるからかもしれないわね。自分が身ごもっているのに、自分

が身ごもられているように感じたり、自分が産んだのに、自分が生まれたように感じたりするんだもん。

よりこさんは斜視の目をふせながら、自分の身に起きたことが、いまだに、よくわからないことだというよう

happened to her, but which she still didn't quite understand.

And how is it now?

Now I don't even have time to think about whether I'm happy or not. I mean, I've got her here with me, right in front of my eyes, and there's an unending series of things that have to be done, day after day, to keep her going. Only occasionally do I remember the time when I was pregnant—that dreamlike, weirdly swollen period—and realize how irreplaceable it was. In those days, say I got on a bus, for instance. Well, right away, someone would ease out of the way to let me sit down. Men would just say, Here, and stand up, but usually women past a certain age would be very friendly, they'd ask me stuff like, So what month are you? And then they'd start telling me about their own kids and grandkids, and every time the conversation would expand. Simply because my stomach was big, that provided the occasion, you see, for me to come in contact with these lives, lives I knew nothing about, the lives of total strangers. It was like I had this special passport with marvelous powers, and I was a character, day after day, in the story of a birth. I'm sure I've never been shown more kindness in my life than I was during those months.

I remember once I went out to get lunch, and I went into a sushi place. Do you mind if I tell you this story, about when I ordered a sardine rice bowl from the lunch menu? You see, I got this idea in my head that sardines had to have a lot of the nutrients a pregnant woman needs. But when I started eating, there was a tightly packed layer of sardine sashimi on top, and then underneath I found two full slices of red tuna. At first I just thought, Huh, that's funny, they put tuna in the sardine rice bowl, too, but then it dawned on me that it was kind of odd, and I looked around, and then, without even thinking about it, I looked over at the quiet man making sushi behind the counter, right in front of my eyes. He must have secretly slipped the tuna in, because I was pregnant and tuna has a lot of iron, that was the only explanation. What do you think you're supposed to do in cases like that? You can't just say, Thanks for adding the tuna! After all, he's pretending that

に、少し興奮気味に語った。

いまはどう?

いまは、幸せとか不幸とか考える暇もない。ただ、目の前にいる子を、せいいっぱい生かすことで日々が追われてる。ただね、身ごもっていたときの、不思議な膨張した、夢のような時間を、かけがえのないものとして、時々思い出すのよ。あのころは例えばバスに乗るでしょう。すると、誰かが、すっと席をゆずってくれる。男のひとは、ただどうぞ、って立ち上がるだけだけど、ある年齢以上の女のひとなんかは、たいがい、いま、何ヶ月? とか聞いてくるのよ、そこから自分の子や孫の話が出たりして、いつも会話がひろがっていく。おなかが大きいという、ただ、それだけのことで、そのことがきっかけになって、他人の見知らぬ生に、触ってしまう。まるで自分が、特別の不思議なパスポートを持っていて、ひとつの誕生劇に、主役として参加しているような日々が続いたわ。おそらくわたしの生涯で、もっともひとから親切にされた一年だったでしょうね。

いつか、お昼を食べに、すし屋に入ったことがあるの。ランチメニューで、いわし丼というのを注文したとき、いわしっていかにも、妊婦に必要な栄養が入ってるような気がしたのよ。食べ始めたら、いわしのさしみがぎっしり乗った下のほうに、なんと、まぐろの赤身が、ふた切れも入ってるじゃない。最初はあら、いわし丼なのに、まぐろも入っているのね、と思い、その次に、でも変ね、と思いなおし、まわりを見渡し、それから、思わず、目の前で調理している無口なすし屋のおじさんを見ちゃった。こういうとき、どう考えても、わたしが妊婦だから、鉄分の多いまぐろを、こっそり入れてくれたとしか思えない。なにしろ、おじさんは何もないような顔いと思う? まぐろを入れてくださってありがとう、なんていえない。

nothing has happened, calmly making sushi. So I just quietly ate my rice bowl, thinking to myself that I had to remember this. That I wanted to remember that I had been pregnant. To remember this man, this day, this time. And then, without even saying thank you, I just paid the bill and went out. That was such a special moment. All the words were gone, and all that was left in the silence were the invisible feelings passing between us, moving. I know I'll never forget how I ate that sardine rice bowl without saying a word.

Yoriko spoke with the simple directness of a college girl, and then, with a look on her face like she had been suddenly jolted back into reality, she got up and went into the kitchen. Just then, the baby awoke again and started howling, her face even uglier and more hateful than before, and no matter how I tried to soothe her she wouldn't calm down. Yoriko grabbed a cord that she had nearby and with remarkably deft movements hoisted the wailing baby up and tied her onto her back. Instantly the baby stopped crying. Secure on Yoriko's back, she looked as pleased as if she had conquered the world. She looked in my direction, grinned broadly, then pointed at me and said *Aa*.

Lately whenever she discovers something new, no matter what it is, she points at it and says *Aa* like that. She doesn't know what things are called, so the desk, the phone, the lightbulb, everything gets the name *Aa*. You're an *Aa* now, too, Yoriko told me, amused.

There was something wonderfully refreshing and pure, something that made you feel as if your ears had been cleaned out, in the sound of the *Aa* that burst from the baby's mouth. With that one word, ever so cleanly, she cut the world open. And come to think of it, this is the first sound of the Japanese language. It struck me that perhaps, at this very moment, I was witnessing the beginning of language itself.

で、すましてすしを握ってるのよ。わたしはいわし丼を静かに食べながら、わたしはこのことを覚えておこうと思った。わたしは妊婦だったことを覚えておこうと思った。そして、お礼も言わずに、ただ、普通にお金を払ってその店を出てきたの。得がたい時間だった。言葉が消えてしまって、その無言のなかに、見えない気持ちだけが通って動いていた。沈黙のなかで食べたいわし丼のこと、わたし、いつまでも忘れないわ。

よりこさんは、女子学生のように、そんなことをまっすぐに言うと、またふいに現実に戻ったような顔で、台所へ立ち上がった。その瞬間、赤ん坊はぎゃあと泣いて目覚め、その顔は、いよいよ不細工に憎たらしく、わたしがあやしても、どうにもならない。よりこさんは、そばにある紐をさっととると、みごとなてつきで、大泣きしている子供を、ひょいと背中におぶった。子供はぴたりと泣き止んだ。おぶわれた子供は、よりこさんの背中で、天下をとったように晴れ晴れとしている。わたしを見て、にっと笑い、「あっ」と言ってこちらを指差した。

いま、この子、何でも新しく発見したものを、「あっ」といって指差すのよ。物の名を知らないから、机も電話も電球も、すべては「あっ」という名前なの。あなたも「あっ」の一員よ。よりこさんは、おかしそうにそう言った。

赤ん坊の放った「あっ」という音は、確かに耳が洗われるような、まじりけのない、実にすがすがしい音であった。切っ先鋭く、そのひとことで、世界を切開する。そういえばこの音から、日本語は始まる。わたしは、ことばの源泉の風景に、いま、立ち会っているのかもしれなかった。

Evidently something had happened somewhere, because the helicopter had been circling around and around overhead all this time. Each time it drew near, the cheaply installed windows of Genjitsu House shook, violently clattering. Once again the ugly baby pointed, this time up at a sky she couldn't see, and cried out, again and again, *Aa, aa.*

どこかで事件でもあったのだろうか、さきほどから上空を、ヘリコプターが何度も何度も旋回している。そのたびに、げんじつ荘の立て付けの悪い窓ガラスが、がたがたと激しい音をたてて揺れる。不細工な赤ん坊は、今度は、見えない空に向かって、「あっ」「あっ」としきりに指差すのであった。

The Silent Traders

黙　市

Tsushima Yūko

Translated by Geraldine Harcourt

There was a cat in the wood. Not such an odd thing, really: wildcats, pumas, and lions all come from the same family, and even a tabby shouldn't be out of place. But the sight was unsettling. What was the creature doing there? When I say "wood," I'm talking about Rikugien, an Edo-period landscape garden in my neighborhood. Perhaps *wood* isn't quite the right word, but the old park's trees—relics of the past amid the city's modern buildings—are so overgrown that the pathways skirting its walls are dark and forbidding even by day. It does give the impression of a wood; there's no other word for it. And the cat, I should explain, didn't look wild. It was just a kitten, two or three months old, white with black patches. It didn't look at all ferocious—in fact, it was a dear little thing. There was nothing to fear. And yet I was taken aback, and I tensed as the kitten bristled and glared in my direction.

The kitten was hiding in a thicket beside the pond, where my ten-year-old daughter was the first to spot it. By the time I'd made out the elusive shape and exclaimed, "Oh, you're right!" she was off calling at the top of her voice: "There's another! And here's one over here!" My other child, a boy of five, was still hunting for the first kitten, and as his sister went on making one discovery after another he stamped his feet and wailed, "Where? Where is it?" His sister beckoned him to bend down and showed him triumphantly where to find the first cat. Several passersby, hearing my daughter's shouts, had also been drawn into the search. There were many strollers in the park that Sunday evening. The cats were everywhere, each concealed in its own clump of bushes. Their eyes followed people's feet on the graveled walk, and at the slightest move toward a hiding place the cat would scamper away. Looking down from an adult's height, it was hard enough to detect

　森に猫がいる。そのこと自体は、別に妙なことでもない。猫の仲間には、山猫や、ピューマ、ライオンもいる。

　たとえ家猫でも、森は居心地の悪くない場所なのに違いない。しかし、私は森に猫を見つけて、あんな生きものが、と動揺した。森、と言っても、家の近所にある江戸時代の名残りの、六義園という日本庭園のことなのだ。

　森と呼ぶのは少しおかしいのかもしれないが、まわりはビルばかりになってしまっている都会に残った古い庭園の樹木は、あまりにも鬱蒼と茂りすぎていて、塀沿いの道は暗く、昼間でも物騒な感じがする。やはり、森、という印象しか受けない。そして、その森にいた猫も、山猫のような猫だったわけではなく、白い毛に黒いぶちのある、生後二、三ヶ月の仔猫にすぎなかった。こわいどころか、見たところは可愛い生きものだ。こわくはない。

　しかし、私はうろたえ、身構えていた。仔猫がこちらを睨み据え、身構えていたから。

　仔猫は池のそばにある茂みのなかに隠れていた。一緒にいた私の十歳の娘が、気がついて、教えてくれた。あ、本当だ、と私が見つけにくいその姿をようやく確かめた時には、娘は、あっちにもいる、こっちにも、と騒ぎだしていた。もう一人の、五歳の男の子は、はじめの猫もまだ、見つけられず、傍では、自分の姉が次々に猫を見つけていくので、焦って、どこなの、どこにいるの、と泣き声を張り上げ、地団駄を踏んでいた。姉は得意顔で、弟に身をかがめるように言い、はじめの猫の位置を教えてやる。まわりにいた何人かの人たちも、娘の声に釣られて、猫を探している。日曜の夕方で、入園者の数は多かった。

　猫は何匹もいた。一匹ずつ、それぞれの茂みのなかに身を隠し、砂利道に動く人間の足の動きを見つめていた。その足が一歩でも自分の方に近づくと、素早く逃げ去って行く。眼の位置の高い人間のおとなには、猫のいることに気づくのはむずかしい。まして、数え上げることなどはとてもできない。数えられないと、やたらたくさん

them all, let alone keep count, and this gave the impression of great numbers.

I could hear my younger child crying. He had disappeared while my back was turned. As I looked wildly around, my daughter pointed him out with a chuckle: "See where he's got to!" There he was, huddled tearfully in the spot where the first kitten had been. He'd burst in eagerly, but succeeded only in driving away the kitten and trapping himself in the thicket.

"What do you think you're doing? It'll never let *you* catch it." Squatting down, my daughter was calling through the bushes. "Come on out, silly!"

His sister's tone of amusement was no help to the boy at all. He was terrified in his cobwebbed cage of low-hanging branches where no light penetrated.

"That's no use. You go in and fetch him out." I gave her shoulder a push.

"He got himself in," she grumbled, "so why can't he get out?" All the same, she set about searching for an opening. Crouching, I watched the boy through the thick foliage and waited for her to reach him.

"How'd he ever get in there? He's really stuck," she muttered as she circled the bushes uncertainly, but a moment later she'd broken through to him, forcing a way with both hands.

いるように感じてしまう。

下の子どもの泣き声が聞えた。いつの間にか、姿が見えなくなっている。あわてて辺りを見渡した私に、上の娘が、あの子、あんなところにいる、と笑いながら教えてくれた。はじめの仔猫のいた場所に、下の子どもはうずくまって泣いていた。仔猫を見つけて、勢いこんで茂みに飛び込んだのはよいが、仔猫はさっさとどこかに行ってしまい、残された子どもは茂みの外にどうやって出たらよいのか分からなくなって、泣きだしたのだった。

なにしてんだよ。お前につかまえられるわけないのに。

娘はしゃがみ込んで茂みのなかにいる弟に呼びかける。

ばかみたい。早く出ておいでよ。

姉の面白がっているだけの声は、弟の助けには少しもならない。低く垂れた枝の檻に閉じ込められた形になって、そこは光も届かず、蜘蛛も巣を張っていて、男の子は怯えきってしまっている。

だめよ、あれじゃ。あんたが行って、連れ出してやってよ。

私は娘の肩を押して、言った。

自分で入れたのに、どうして出られないんだよ。

娘は不満そうに、それでも早速、茂みのまわりを歩きだし、枝が少しでも透いている箇所を探しはじめた。私は重い葉叢の向こうに見える男の子を、しゃがんで見つめ、娘がそこに辿りつくのを待った。どうやって入ったのかな、大変だよ、これは、などと言いながら、娘はまわりをためらいながら歩いていたが、やがて無理矢理、枝を両手で押し分けて、男の子のもとまで行くことができた。

When they rejoined me, they had dead leaves and twigs snagged all over them.

After an attempt of her own to pick one up, my daughter understood that life in the park had made these tiny kittens quicker than ordinary strays and too wary to let anyone pet them. Explaining this to her brother, she looked to me for agreement. "They were born here, weren't they? They belong here, don't they? Then I wonder if their mother's here, too?"

The children scanned the surrounding trees once again.

"She may be," I said, "but she'd stay out of sight, wouldn't she? Only the kittens wander about in the open. Their mother's got more sense. I'll bet she's up that tree or somewhere like that where nobody can get her. She's probably watching us right now."

I cast an eye at the treetops as I spoke—and the thought of the unseen mother cat gave me an uncomfortable feeling. Whether these were alley cats that had moved into the park or discarded pets that had survived and bred, they could go on multiplying in the wood—which at night was empty of people—and be perfectly at home.

It is exactly twenty-five years since my mother came to live near Rikugien with her three children, of whom I, at ten, was the youngest. She told us the park's history, and not long after our arrival we went inside to see the garden. In spite of its being on our doorstep we quickly lost interest, however, because the grounds were surrounded by a six-foot brick wall with a single gate on the far side from our house. A Japanese garden was not much fun for children anyway, and we never went again as a family. I was reminded that we lived near a

私のもとに戻ってきた二人は、体中に、枯葉や小枝をつけていた。

あんなに小さな猫でも、ここで育っているからには、普通の野良猫よりももっと動きが早くて、抱いて可愛がることなど誰にもできないことなのだ、と娘は、自分も一度追いかけてみて悟ったことを、弟に教えて、私にも同意を求めた。ねえ、ここで生まれたんだよね。この猫なんだよね。でも、そしたら、お母さんもいるのかな。

二人の子どもは、改めて、辺りの木々を見まわした。

いるのかもしれないけど、絶対に見られないところにいるんじゃないの。見えるようなところにうろうろしているのは、子猫だけよ。親猫は、そんなうっかりしたこと、しない。あの木の高いところとか、人間がとても近づけないようなところから、こっちのこと見てるわ、きっと。

私は木の梢の方を見上げながら言い、そして自分で、その見えない親猫が気味悪くなった。街の野良猫が住みつくようになったのか、それとも、ここに捨てられた猫の何匹かが生き延び、子を産み増やしているのか、いずれにしろ、夜は無人の状態になる森は、猫がどれだけ増えようが、居心地の悪い場所になるはずもなかった。

六義園のそばに、私の母が三人の子どもたちを連れて越してきたのは、ちょうど二十五年前、末の子どもである私が十歳の時だった。母から六義園の由来を聞かされ、越した当初は、なかの庭園を見物にも行った。しかし、いくら六義園のそばとは言え、その庭園は三メートルほどもある高いレンガ塀で囲まれていて、門のある場所とは反対の方向に家があったので、子どもには日本庭園など格別、楽しいところでもなく、すぐに興味を失い、家族で行くことなど、それからあと、一度もなくなってしまった。大きな庭園のそばに住んでいることは、その

park, though, because of the many birds—the blue magpies, Eastern turtledoves, and tits—that I would see on the rooftops and in trees. And in summer I'd hear the singing of evening cicadas. To a city child like me, evening cicadas and blue magpies were a novelty.

I visited Rikugien with several classmates when we were about to leave elementary school, and someone hit on the idea of making a kind of time capsule. We'd leave it buried for ten years—or was it twenty? I've also forgotten what we wrote on the piece of paper that we stuffed into a small bottle and buried at the foot of a pine on the highest ground in the garden. I expect it's still there as I haven't heard of it since, and now whenever I'm in Rikugien I keep an eye out for the landmark, but I'm only guessing. We were confident of knowing exactly where to look in years to come, and if I can remember that so clearly, it's puzzling that I can't recognize the tree. I'm not about to dig any holes to check, however—not with my own children watching. The friends who left this sentimental reminder were soon to part, bound for different schools. Since then, of course, we've ceased to think of one another, and I'm not sure now that the bottle episode ever happened.

The following February my brother (who was close to my own age) died quite suddenly of pneumonia. Then in April my sister went to college and, not wanting to be left out, I pursued her new interests myself: I listened to jazz, went to movies, and was friendly toward college and high school students of the opposite sex. An older girl introduced me to a boy from senior high and we made up a foursome for an outing to the park—the only time I got all dressed up for Rikugien. I was no

一帯に鳥の多いことで、納得させられてはいた。オナガやキジバト、シジュウカラなどを、屋根や庭木に見ることができた。夏になれば、ヒグラシの声が聞えた。町なかで育った私には、ヒグラシも、オナガも珍しいものだった。

小学校を卒業した時に、同級生の何人かと六義園に行き、そこで誰かがタイム・カプセルのようなものを思いつき、十年後だったか、二十年後だったか、とにかくその時まで埋めておこう、とこれもどんなことを書きつけたのか忘れてしまったが、紙きれを小さな瓶に入れて、庭園でいちばん高い場所に生えている松の根もとに埋めた。その後、誰からもその瓶のことを聞いていないので、おそらく、今でも埋まったままになっているのだろう、と六義園に行くたびにそれとなく、目印の松を探してみるのだが、さっぱり見当がつかない。当時は、ここなら何年経っても分からなくなる心配がない、と確信していた。その記憶だけははっきり残っているので、どうして分からないのだろう、と不審に思う。しかし自分の子どもたちがいるのに、その眼の前で、今更、土を掘り返して確かめてみよう、という気にもなれない。別々の中学に進むから、実は、瓶のことも、あれは本当だったのか、と感傷的にそんなものを残したのだった。その後、無論、互いのことを思い出すこともなくなり、曖昧な気持になってしまっている。

翌年の二月に、私のすぐ上の兄が呆気なく肺炎で死んだ。その四月に、姉は大学に入った。つまり、ジャズを聞いたり、映画を見たり、そして異性の大学生や高校生とも知り合いになりたがった。年上の女友だちに高校生を紹介され、六義園に四人で遊びに行ったことがあった。六義園に行くのに精いっぱいのおしゃれをしたのは、その時限りのことだ。しかし

beauty, though, nor the popular type, and while the others were having fun I stayed stiff and awkward, and was bored. I would have liked to have been as genuinely impressed as they were, viewing the landscape garden for the first time, but I couldn't work up an interest after seeing the trees over the brick wall every day. By that time we'd been in the district for three years, and the name "Rikugien" brought to mind not the tidy, sunlit lawns seen by visitors, but the dark tangles along the walls.

My desire for friends of the opposite sex was short-lived. Boys couldn't provide what I wanted, and what boys wanted had nothing to do with me.

While I was in high school, one day our ancient spitz died. The house remained without a dog for a while, until Mother was finally prompted to replace him when my sister's marriage, soon after her graduation, left just the two of us in an unprotected home. She found someone who let her have a terrier puppy. She bought a brush and comb and began rearing the pup with the best of care, explaining that it came from a clever hunting breed. As it grew, however, it failed to display the expected intelligence and still behaved like a puppy after six months; and besides, it was timid. What it did have was energy as, yapping shrilly, it frisked about the house all day long. It may have been useless but it was a funny little fellow. Its presence made all the difference to me in my intense boredom at home. After my brother's death, my mother (a widow since I was a baby) passed her days as if at a wake. We saw each other only at mealtimes, and even then we seldom spoke. In high school a fondness for the movies was

美しい娘でもなければ、愛敬のある娘でもなかったので、一人でぎこちなく身を硬くしながら、かえってつまらない思いを味わっていた。はじめてそこに来たほかの三人のように、広い日本庭園に素直に見とれたい、と願ったが、レンガ塀越しに毎日、その木立を見ているのでは、庭園のなかに入ってはじめて見ることができる庭園の手入れの行き届いた芝生の明るさよりも、塀際の、伸びるままにまかせている雑木の暗い木立しか、思い浮かべられなくなっていた。

異性の友だちを欲しがっていたのも、その一時期で終わってしまった。私の求めていたものは持ち合わせがなく、少年たちの求めていたものは、私には無縁のものだった。

私が高校生になってから、ある日、家で長年飼っていた老スピッツ犬が死んだ。しばらくの間、そのまま家に犬のいない状態が続いたが、姉が大学を出て、すぐに結婚して家からいなくなってしまうと、いよいよ家のなかは、私と母の二人きりになり、不用心にもなったので、母もようやく犬を飼う気になって、テリア種の仔犬をどこからか貰ってきた。賢い猟犬の血筋だから、とくにやブラシも買い求め、大事に育てはじめた。しかし、この犬は成長しても期待通りには知恵がつかず、半年経っても振舞いは仔犬の時と同じで、その上、臆病な性格だった。始終、甲走った声で鳴きながら、家のまわりを跳ねまわっていた。役立たずの犬ではあっても、愛敬はあった。自分の家がつまらなくて仕方なかった私には、その犬がいるのといないのとでは大きな違いがあった。末の子の私が赤ん坊の頃、夫に死なれている母は、兄が死んでから、来る日来る日を通夜のように過ごしていた。食事の時しか顔を合わせることもなかったし、互いに口を開いて声を出すこともなかった。映画

about the worst I could have been accused of, but Mother had
no patience with such frivolity and would snap angrily at me
from time to time. "I'm leaving home as soon as I turn
eighteen," I'd retort. I meant it, too.

It was at that time that we had the very sociable dog. I
suppose I'd spoiled it as a puppy, for now it was always
wanting to be let in, and when I slid open the glass door it
would bounce like a rubber ball right into my arms and lick
my face and hands ecstatically.

Mother, however, was dissatisfied. She'd had enough of the
barking; it got on her nerves. Then came a day when the dog
went missing. I thought it must have got out of the yard. Two
or three days passed and it didn't return—it hadn't the wits to
find the way home once it had strayed. I wondered if I should
contact the pound. Concern finally drove me to break our
usual silence and ask Mother: "About the dog . . ." "Oh, the
dog?" she replied. "I threw it over the wall of Rikugien the
other day."

I was shocked—I'd never heard of disposing of a dog like
that. I wasn't able to protest, though. I didn't rush out to comb
the park, either. She could have had it destroyed, yet instead
she'd taken it to the foot of the brick wall, lifted it in her arms,
and heaved it over. It wasn't large, only about a foot long, and
thus not too much of a handful even for Mother.

Finding itself tossed into the wood, the dog wouldn't have
crept quietly into hiding. It must have raced through the area
barking furiously, only to be caught at once by the caretaker.

をよく見に行くぐらいのことしかしない高校生だったのだが、母から見れば俗世に気持を奪われている私が我慢ならず、たまに憤怒の言葉を投げつけてきたが、そうすると私は、十八になったらすぐに家を出て行くんだ、と母に言い返していた。本気で、そう思い決めていた。

そんな頃にいた、やたらに賑やかな犬だった。家のなかに入りたがる犬で、それも私が仔犬の時分に甘やかしていたからなのだろうが、ガラス戸を開けると、勢いよく、ポンとゴムまりのように、私の腕のなかに飛びこんできた。そして夢中になって、私の顔や手を舐めた。

しかし、母にはその犬が不満だった。愛想を尽かし、鳴き声に神経を苛立たせていた。そして、その犬の姿が見えなくなった日があった。外に逃げだしたのか、と思った。二、三日経っても、犬は戻ってこなかった。馬鹿な犬だから、外に出てしまったら道が分かるわけもないのだ。保健所に問い合わせた方がよいのかもしれない。私は日頃、話しかけたことがない母に、あの犬のことだが、と思い余って聞いてみた。すると母は、ああ、あの犬なら、この間、六義園の塀の中に投げ棄ててきました、と答えた。

そういう棄て方があったのか、と私はびっくりしたが、母に文句を言うことはできなかった。早速、六義園に行って、探すこともしなかった。母は犬を殺すこともできたのに、六義園のレンガ塀の下まで犬を連れて行き、抱き上げ、塀の向こう側に放り投げたのだった。体長が三十センチほどしかない小型の犬だったので、母の手でも充分に投げ棄てることができた。

森のなかに突然、放りこまれた犬は、静かに身を潜めていたはずもなく、けたたましく吠えながら、広い森のなかを駆け巡ったことだろう。それですぐに、庭園の監視員に見つかり、捕まったのに違いない。それからの

Would the next stop be the pound? But there seemed to me just a chance that it hadn't turned out that way. I could imagine the wood by daylight, more or less: there'd be a lot of birds and insects, and little else. The pond would be inhabited by a few carp, turtles, and catfish. But what transformations took place at night? As I didn't dare stay beyond closing time to see for myself, I wondered if anyone could tell of a night spent in the park till the gates opened in the morning. There might be goings-on that by day would be unimaginable. Mightn't a dog entering that world live on not as a tiny terrier but as something else?

I had to be thankful that the dog's fate left that much to the imagination.

From then on I turned my back on Rikugien more firmly than ever. I was afraid of the deep wood, so out of keeping with the city: it was the domain of the dog abandoned by my mother.

In due course I left home, a little later than I'd promised. After a good many more years I moved back to Mother's neighborhood—back to the vicinity of the park—with a little daughter and a baby. Like my own mother, I was one who couldn't give my children the experience of a father. That remained the one thing I regretted.

Living in a cramped apartment, I now appreciated the Rikugien wood for its greenery and open spaces. I began to take the children there occasionally. Several times, too, we released pet turtles or goldfish into the pond. Many nearby families who'd run out of room for aquarium creatures in their overcrowded apartments would slip them into the pond to spend the rest of their lives at liberty.

行方は、やはり保健所なのだろうか。けれども、万が一、そうではない場合だって考えられる、と私は思った。

日中の森の様子なら、せいぜい鳥や虫が多いだけだとおよその見当はつく。池のなかには鯉や亀、ナマズがいる程度だ。しかし、夜はどう変わるのだろう。自分で庭園の閉門後も居残ら、誰か、朝の開門まで、一晩中庭園に過ごしました、という人がいないものか、と思う。昼間には想像のつかないことが起きているのではないか。その世界に犬が入り込んだのだとしたら、テリア種の小型犬としてではなく別のものになって、生きながらえるのではないか。

そんな想像が許される処分を犬が受けたことを、私はありがたいと思わなければならなかった。

それから私はますます六義園に背を向けるようになった。都会に似つかわしくない深い森がこわかった。そこは母に見棄てられた犬の領分だった。

やがて、私は母の家を出た。十八歳よりは少し遅かった。それから何年も経ってから、小さな娘と赤ん坊を連れて、母の家の近くに、と言うことは、また森のそばに戻ってきた。私も母同様に、自分の子どもたちに男親というものを味わわせてやることのできない母親になっていた。それだけはいやだと思い続けていた者になっていた。

狭いアパートに住んでみると、六義園の森は貴重な緑の拡がりだった。子どもたちを連れて、時々、訪れるようになった。アパートで飼っていた亀や金魚を、何回か、池に放してやったりもした。近所の、アパート住まいの家の多くも、狭い部屋のなかでは飼いきれなくなった水槽の生きものを、この池なら寿命までのびのびと生きてくれるだろう、とそっと運んできていた。

Rocks rose from the water here and there, and each was studded with turtles sunning themselves. They couldn't have bred naturally in such numbers. They must have been the tiny turtles sold at fairground stalls and pet shops, grown up without a care in the world. More of them lined the water's edge at one's feet. No doubt there were other animals on the increase—goldfish, loaches, and the like. Multistoried apartment buildings were going up around the wood in quick succession, and more living things were brought down from their rooms each year. Cats were one animal I'd overlooked, though. If tossing out turtles was common practice, there was no reason why cats shouldn't be dumped here, and dogs, too. No type of pet could be ruled out. But to become established in any numbers they'd have to escape the caretaker's notice and hold their own against the wood's other hardy inhabitants. Thus there'd be a limit to survivors: cats and reptiles, I'd say.

Once I knew about the cat population, I remembered the dog my mother had thrown away, and I also remembered my old fear of the wood. I couldn't help wondering how the cats got by from day to day.

Perhaps they relied on food left behind by visitors—but all of the park's litter baskets were fitted with mesh covers to keep out the crows, whose numbers were also growing. For all their nimbleness, even cats would have trouble picking out the scraps. Lizards and mice were edible enough. But on the other side of the wall lay the city and its garbage. After dark, the cats would go out foraging on the streets.

Then, too, there was the row of apartment towers along one side of the wood, facing the main road. All had balconies that overlooked the park. The climb would be quick work for a cat,

池のあちこちに、岩が突き出ている。そのひとつひとつにいつでも亀が鈴なりになって甲羅干しをしている。自然に増えたにしては、多すぎる。かつては夜店や、ペット・ショップで売られていた亀たちが、なんの煩いごともなく、大きく育った姿なのだろう。池の縁を見下ろしても、亀の並んでいるのが見える。金魚やどじょうやらのほかの生きものも、亀のように増え続ける一方なのに違いないのだ。森のまわりに高層マンションが次々に建てられ、そのひとつひとつの部屋から森に運びこまれる生きものは、年を追う毎に増えていく。しかし、猫までが、とはうかつなことに思いつかずにいた。亀を捨てるのが珍しくもない行為なら、猫も、そして犬も、無造作に捨てられているはずなのだった。ペットとして飼われる生きものなら、どんなものでも考えられることで、当然、種類も限られてしまう。猫と爬虫類、といったところか。

猫も増えている、と知ってから、私は母の手で投げ棄てられた犬を思い出し、その頃の自分の森への怯えを思い出しもした。森の猫はどのようにして毎日を送っているのだろう、とあれこれ考えずにいられなくなった。人間の残していく食べものをあてにしているのかもしれないが、森のゴミ入れは、これも増え続けているカラスへの対策で、すべてに金網の蓋が付けられている。器用な猫にも、そこから食べられるものを選びだすのはむずかしいだろう。トカゲや、ネズミも食べられないことはないのだろうが、塀の向こう側は、ゴミの多い街なのだ。夜になると、猫は食べものを求めて、街に出て行く。

また、森のバス通りに面している側には、ずらりと細長いマンションが建ち並んでいる。どのマンションも、森の見える方にベランダを向けている。そのベランダに出向くことも、猫には簡単なことなのだろうから、マン

and if its favorite food was left outside a door it would soon come back regularly. Something told me there must be people who put out food: there'd be elderly tenants and women living alone. Even children. Children captivated by a secret friendship with a cat.

I don't find such a relationship odd—perhaps because it occurs so often in fairy tales. But to make it worth their while, the apartment children would have to receive something from the cat; otherwise they wouldn't keep it up. There are tales of mountain men and villagers who traded a year's haul of linden bark for a gallon and a half of rice in hard cakes. No villager could deal openly with the lone mountain men; so great was their fear of each other, in fact, that they avoided coming face-to-face. Yet when a bargain was struck, it could not have been done more skillfully. The trading was over in a flash, before either man had time to catch sight of the other or hear his voice. I think everyone wishes privately that bargains could be made like that. Though there would always be the fear of attack, or discovery by one's own side.

Supposing it was my own children: what could they be getting in return? They'd have no use for a year's stock of linden bark. Toys, then, or cakes. I'm sure they'd want all sorts of things, but not a means of support like linden bark. What, then? Something not readily available to them; something the cat has in abundance and to spare.

The children leave food on the balcony. And in return the cat provides them with a father. How's that for a bargain? Once a year, male cats procreate; in other words, they become fathers. They become fathers ad nauseam. But these fathers don't care how many children they have—they don't even

ションの住人がもし、そこに猫の好きなものを置いておけば、猫はすぐに通うようになる。そのようなことをしている住人は、現に何人かいるのではないか、という気がする。年寄りもいるだろうし、一人でいる女もいるだろう。子どもだっているだろう。誰にも言えない猫との付き合いに気持を奪われている子ども。

子どもと猫の付き合いは、少しも変わった出来事のようには思えない。童話に多い組み合わせだからなのかもしれない。しかし、続けて付き合う以上は、マンションの子どもの方も猫からなにかをもらわなければ引き合わない。山男と村の男がマダの皮一年分と三升の餅を交換していたという話もある。とても互いに認め合うわけにはいかないし、顔さえ合わすのも避けなければならない怖ろしい相手なのだが、取り引きできるのだとしたら、こんなうまい相手もいないのだ。なにかの拍子に、姿も見ず、声も聞かぬうちに、いつの間にか、取り引きが成立している。そんなことがあったらいい、と誰しもがこっそり願っている。襲われるのはこわい、自分の仲間に知られるのもこわいけれども。

マンションの子どもが、もし、私の子どもたちだったら、なにを猫からもらうのだろうか。マダの皮一年分など欲しくもない。おもちゃとか、おかしとか、欲しいものはたくさんあるのだろうが、マダの皮のような、生活そのものを支えるものではない。それならなにか。子どもたちには手に入れるのがむずかしくて、猫にはいつでも過剰なほど恵まれているもの。

子どもたちはベランダに、食べものを置いておく。すると猫はお返しに、父親を子どもたちに与える。こんな取り引きはどうだろう。一年に一度ずつ、オス猫はメス猫を孕ませる。つまり、父親になる。うんざりするほど、何度も父親になる。しかし、何匹子どもが生まれようが、この父親は頓着しない。自分が父親であるということ

notice that they are fathers. Yet the existence of offspring makes them so. Fathers who don't know their own children. Among humans, it seems there's an understanding that a man becomes a father only when he recognizes the child as his own; but that's a very narrow view. Why do we allow the male to divide children arbitrarily into two kinds, recognized and unrecognized? Wouldn't it be enough for the child to choose a father when necessary from among suitable males? If the children decide that the tom that climbs up to their balcony is their father, it shouldn't cause him any inconvenience. A father looks in on two of his children from the balcony every night. The two human children faithfully leave out food to make it so. He comes late, when they are fast asleep, and they never see him or hear his cries. It's enough that they know in the morning that he's been there. In their dreams, the children are hugged to their cat-father's breast.

We'd seen the children's human father six months earlier, and together we'd gone to a transport museum they wanted to visit. This came about only after many appeals from me. If the man who was their father was alive and well on this earth, I wanted the children to know what he looked like. To me, the man was unforgettable: I was once preoccupied with him, obsessed with the desire to be where he was; nothing had changed when I tried having a child, and I'd had the second with him cursing me. To the children, however, especially the younger one, he was a mere shadow in a photograph that never moved or spoke. As the younger child turned three, then four, I couldn't help being aware of that fact. This was the same state that I'd known myself, for my own father had died.

などに、気づきもしない。それでも仔がいる以上、父親なのだ。自分の仔を知らない父親だ。人間の場合は、生まれた子を自分のものと認めてはじめて父親になるという申し合わせがあるらしいが、ずいぶんと狭い了簡の話ではある。認められる子、認められない子、とオスが勝手に子どもを二種類に分けてしまうというのか。必要なときに、子どもが適当なオスのなかから父親を選ぶということで充分ではないか。だから、マンションのベランダに登ってくるオス猫を子どもたちが自分の父親だと思い決めても、オス猫の方では一向に差し支えはない。父親が自分の子の子どもたちのうちの二匹を、毎夜、ベランダから覗きに来る。そういうことにしておきたいので、二人の人間の子どもはベランダに猫の餌を忘れずに出しておく。オス猫の来るのは夜更けのことだから、その姿を見ることも、鳴き声を聞くことも、ぐっすり寝入っている子どもたちにはできない。ただ、ベランダに来てくれたことが翌朝、分かれば、それで満足なのだ。

夢のなかで、子どもたちは猫の父親の胸に抱かれている。

子どもたちの人間の父親の方とは、半年前に会い、連れ立って、子どもたちの行きたがっていた交通博物館に行った。私から頼みこんで、ようやく実現した機会だった。この同じ地上で父親である男が無事に生きているのならば、子どもたちに生きている姿を見せておいてやりたかった。私はその男にこだわり続け、男と同じところにいたい、という思いに取り憑かれて、一人子どもを産んでみても変化はなく、男に呪われながら二人めの子どもまで産んだのだから、忘れようもない一人の人間だったのだが、子どもたち、特に下の子どもにとっては、写真だけの、動かず、しゃべりもしない人間の影にすぎなかった。下の子どもが三歳、四歳、と大きくなるにつれて、そう気がつかずにいられなくなった。それでは父親と死別した私と同じことになってしまうではないか。

If their father had been dead, it couldn't have been helped. But as long as he was alive I wanted them to have a memory of their father as a living, breathing person whose eyes moved, whose mouth moved and spoke.

On the day, he was an hour late for our appointment. The long wait in a coffee shop had made the children tired and cross, but when they saw the man a shy silence came over them. "Thanks for coming," I said with a smile. I couldn't think what to say next. He asked, "Where to?" and stood to leave at once. He walked alone, while the children and I looked as though it was all the same to us whether he was there or not. On the train I still hadn't come up with anything to say. The children kept their distance from the man and stared nonchalantly out the window. We got off the train like that, and again he walked ahead.

The transport museum had an actual bullet-train car, steam locomotives, airplanes, and giant panoramic layouts. I remembered enjoying a class trip there while at school myself. My children, too, dashed excitedly around the exhibits without a moment's pause for breath. It was "Next I want to have a go on that train," "Now I want to work that model." They must have had a good two hours of fun. In the meantime we lost sight of the man. Wherever he'd been, he showed up again when we'd finished our tour and arrived back at the entrance. "What'll we do?" he asked, and I suggested giving the children a drink and sitting down somewhere. He nodded and went ahead to look for a place near the museum. The children were clinging to me as before. He entered a coffee shop that had a cake counter, and I followed with them. We sat down, the three of us facing the man. Neither child showed the slightest inclination to sit beside him. They had orange drinks.

I was becoming desperate for something to say. And

死んだのなら仕方がない。しかし生きているのなら、体が動き、目玉が動いて、声が出る人間の姿を、父親の記憶として残しておいてやりたかった。

その日、男は約束の時間よりも一時間ほど遅れて来た。喫茶店で待ちくたびれてしまっていた子どもたちは、それでも男を見ると、照れくさそうに黙りこんでしまった。きょうはすみませんでした、と私は笑顔で言った。言葉は続かなかった。それで、どこに行けばいいの、と男は聞き、すぐに立ち上がった。男は男で一人で歩き、私と子どもたちは男がいてもいなくても同じような顔で歩いた。電車のなかでも、言葉が思い浮かばなかった。子どもたちも男のそばに近づくまいと警戒し、窓の外を素知らぬ風に見つめている。そのまま電車を降り、また男は一人で先に歩いて行った。

交通博物館には、本物の新幹線の車輌や、蒸気機関車、飛行機、大きなパノラマ模型もある。子どもの頃に学校で行き、楽しんだ記憶があった。私の子どもたちも、喜んで館内を駆け巡りだした。次はあの電車に乗りたい、次はあっちの模型を動かしてみたい、と休む暇がない。二時間ほども楽しんだだろうか。その間、男の姿は見えなくなっていた。一巡して、また出入り口に戻ってきたところで、男もそれまでどこにいたのか、姿を現わした。どうする、と男が聞くので、ジュースでも飲んで、どこかで休みたい、と私は答えた。男は頷き、先に立って博物館を出、まわりに喫茶店を探しだした。子どもたちは相変わらず、私にしがみついている。ケーキを店頭で売っている喫茶店に男が入ったので、私も子どもたちを連れて入った。私たち三人と男と向かい合わせに坐った。子どもたちのどちらも、男の隣りにはどうしても坐りたがらなかった。ジュースを飲んだ。

なにか男に話すことはないのだろうか、と私は心を焦らせていた。男も、私に聞いておきたいことがひとつや

weren't there one or two things he'd like to ask me? Such as how the children had been lately. But to bring that up, unasked, might imply that I wanted him to watch with me as they grew. I'd been able to ask for this meeting only because I'd finally stopped feeling that way. Now it seemed we couldn't even exchange such polite remarks as "They've grown" or "I'm glad they're well" without arousing needless suspicions. It wasn't supposed to be like this, I thought in confusion, unable to say a word about the children. He was indeed their father, but not a father who watched over them. As far as he was concerned the only children he had were the two borne by his wife. Agreeing to see mine was simply a favor on his part, for which I could only be grateful.

If we couldn't discuss the children, there was literally nothing left to say. We didn't have the kind of memories we could reminisce over; I wished I could forget the things we'd done as if it had all been a dream, for it was the pain that we remembered. Inquiring after his family would be no better. His work seemed the safest subject, yet if I didn't want to stay in touch I had to think about this, too.

The man and I listened absently as the children entertained themselves.

On the way out the man bought a cake, which he handed to the older child, and then he was gone. The children appeared relieved, and with the cake to look forward to they were eager to get home. Neither had held the man's hand or spoken to him. I wanted to tell them that there was still time to run after

ふたつ、ないのだろうか。子どもたちの最近の様子。しかし、私からそれを告げるのは、男に子どもたちの成長を私と一緒に見守って欲しい、と望んでいるということを意味してしまいかねない。そうした気持をようやく捨てきることができたから、一度会って欲しい、と男に頼めたのだ。大きくなった、とか、元気でなによりだ、とか、そんな挨拶程度の言葉すら、互いに交わせば、今更、不必要な疑いを湧き起こしてしまいそうだった。そんなはずではなかった、とうろたえるのだが、子どもに関することは一言も口にすることができなかった。男は子どもたちの父親には違いないが、その子どもたちを見守り続ける父親ではないのだ。男にとって自分の子どもとは、妻の産んだ二人の子どものことだった。男が私の子どもたちに会ってくれたことさえ、男の好意にほかならないのだから、感謝するしかないことなのだった。

子どものことを話題にできないとすると、しかし、文字通り一言も、男に話せることはなにもなくなってしまった。以前、二人でしてきたことは、思い出として語り合えるようなことではなかった。できれば、夢のなかで起こったこととして忘れてしまいたいのだ。思い出すことは、互いに痛みでしかない。男の家族については、更に聞けない。いちばん、差し障りのなさそうな男の仕事の話も、これからまた二人で付き合いたいと思っているのではない限り、聞くのはやはり、ためらわれる。

子どもたちが勝手に二人でふざけ合っているのを、男と私はぼんやり聞き流していた。帰りがけに、男はケーキを買い、上の子どもに手渡して、喫茶店から立ち去って行った。子どもたちはケーキを食べるのを楽しみに、男と別れて一安心という様子で、早くアパートの部屋に戻りたがった。子どもたちのどちらも、男と手をつなぐことも、話しかけることもしないままだった。今からでも追いかけて行って、体のどこ

him and touch some part of his body, but of course they wouldn't have done it.

I don't know when there will be another opportunity for the children to see the man. They may never meet him again, or they may have a chance two or three years from now. I do know that the man and I will probably never be completely indifferent to each other. He's still on my mind in some obscure way. Yet there's no point in confirming this feeling in words. Silence is essential. As long as we maintain silence, and thus avoid trespassing, we leave open the possibility of resuming negotiations at any time.

I believe the system of bartering used by the mountain men and the villagers was called "silent trade." I am coming to understand that there was nothing extraordinary in striking such a silent bargain for survival. People trying to survive— me, my mother, and my children, for example—can take some comfort in living beside a wood. We toss various things in there and tell ourselves we haven't thrown them away, we've set them free in another world, and then we picture the unknown woodland to ourselves and shudder with fear or sigh fondly. Meanwhile the creatures multiplying there gaze stealthily at the human world outside; at least I've yet to hear of anything attacking from the wood.

Some sort of silent trade is taking place between the two sides. Perhaps my children really have begun dealings with a cat that lives in the wood.

でもいいから触っておいで、と言ってやりたかったが、無論、そんなことを言ったところで、子どもたちが従う
はずはなかった。

今度は、いつ男を子どもたちに会わせる機会が巡ってくるのか、分からない。一度も会わないままになってし
まうのかもしれないし、一二年経ったら、また、会えるのかもしれない。いつまでも、気持のどこかで気になり続ける。が、いつまでも私も男も互いのこと
に無頓着にはなりきれないのだろう、ということは分かる。いつまでも、気持のどこかで気になり続ける。しか
し、言葉にしてそうした自分の思いを確かめることもない。沈黙が必要なのだ。沈黙を続ければ、互いの領分を
犯すことなく、いつでも取り引きを再開できる状態を保っていることができる。

山男と村の男のような取り引きを黙市というのだそうだ。黙市が、生きようとしている者たちの間では少しも
珍しいものではなかったことが、私にも分かりはじめてきた。そのような者にとって、たとえば私や、母、そし
て子どもたちにも、森のそばに住んでいることは気休めになる。森にさまざまなものを捨て、でも捨てたのでは
ない、別の世界に放してやったのだと思い、自分の知らない森の姿を勝手に想像し、こわがり、なつかしがって
いる。一方、森に増えはじめている生きものたちは、森の外の人間の世界をひっそりと見つめ続けている。少く
とも、森からなにかが襲ってきた、という話は、今のところまだ聞いていない。

なんらかの形で、黙市が森のなかと外とで成り立っている。私の子どもたちも、もしかしたら本当に、森の猫
と取り引きをはじめているのかもしれないのだ。

Mogera Wogura

うごろもち[1]
鼹鼠[1]

Kawakami Hiromi

Translated by Michael Emmerich

Let me tell you about my mornings.

I'm an early riser. Most days, I wake up even earlier than my wife.

If the sun has risen, thin rays of light filter down through the cracks in the ceiling. I just lie there for a while, gazing up at all those rays of light trickling in.

No light appears on days when it's cloudy or raining, even if I wait. On the rare occasions when it snows, the room seems faintly bright even before dawn.

It's warm inside my futon, but the tip of my nose is cold. I want to rush into the bathroom right away, but I have a hard time making myself leave the futon.

After a while, my wife wakes up. She goes off to the toilet before I can manage to get up. My wife is a good riser; no sooner is she up than she's cleaning the house and setting the pot on the fire, humming all the while.

Eventually I get myself ready, and by the time I start making the rounds, checking up on the humans I picked up the previous day or the day before that or even earlier, a bright red fire is blazing in the fireplace, water is boiling away in the whistling kettle, and the whole room is fragrant with the wonderful scent of toast. My wife works fast.

The humans I've collected are in the next room.

Most of them are sprawled on the floor. There are tons of futons and blankets and pillows in there. Very few of the humans ask us if it's all right to use them. Some burrow down into the heaped-up blankets as soon as we take them into the room. Some push aside the humans who are already stretched out on the floor and snuggle up inside their nice, warm futons. Some keep wheeling around the room, stepping on the humans who are lying down. That's what these humans are like.

毎朝のことを話そう。

起きるのは、早い。たいがい、私のほうが妻よりも先に目が覚める。

夜が明けていれば、天井の隙間からは薄く日が差している。漏れてくる何条もの光を眺めながら、私はしばらく横たわっている。

曇った日や雨の日には、いつまでたっても光が差さない。ごくまれに雪が降っているときには、夜明け前なのに、うすあかるく感じる。

ふとんの中は暖かいが、鼻先は冷たい。すぐに便所に行きたいと思うのだが、なかなかふとんから出る決心がつかない。

そのうちに妻が目を覚まし、私よりも先に用を足してしまう。妻は寝起きがよくて、鼻うたなど歌いながら、起きるなり掃除をはじめたり、鍋を火にかけたりする。

ようよう私の支度ができて、昨日やおとといや、それよりもっと前に拾ってきた人間たちを見まわるころには、暖炉には真っ赤な火がおこり、やかんには湯が沸いてピーピーと音をたて、部屋じゅうにかんばしいトーストの匂いがたちこめている。妻は、手ばしこいのだ。

拾ってきた人間たちは、次の間にいる。

おおかたが寝そべっている。ふとんも毛布も枕も、ふんだんにある。使っていいかと訊ねる人間は、少ない。連れられてきたとたんに、積み上げられた毛布の中にもぐる者。すでに寝そべっている人間を押しのけて、あたたまったふとんの中に入りこむ者。部屋じゅうをぐるぐる廻り、横たわる人間たちを踏んで歩く者。そんなのば

Even so, after half a day or so everyone settles down into his or her own place or territory or what have you, and silence descends on the room.

Every morning, I go around and give each human a few soft pats on the shoulder. First, this allows me to make sure they're still alive. Second, it gives me a chance to find out if they want to leave immediately, or if they'd prefer to stay a little longer.

I drag the dead ones out of the house and drop them down a hole that has been dug outside, even deeper into the earth. The hole extends more than a hundred meters below the surface. I didn't dig the hole. Neither did my wife. It took our ancestors generations to dig it, working at their own pace.

Originally, the hole was intended to be a place where our clan could drop its dead. But as time passed, our numbers dwindled; now we have no one left in the world but our parents and our siblings, of which we each have two.

Our parents and siblings live even farther south than Kyūshū, in a place fairly deep down under the ground. They live quiet lives, free from interactions with humans. Every so often my wife's mother sends us letters, but all she says in them is that we ought to hurry up and get out of Tokyo, and come join them where they are. She seems to worry that my brother-in-law and sister-in-law might get the itch to move to Tokyo, too.

I can always tell which humans are likely to want to leave immediately because they respond when I touch their shoulders, lifting their faces to look up. The humans all have this forlorn look on their faces then. They keep their eyes locked on mine, perfectly still, and mutter things under their breath.

I give each human another soft pat on the shoulder, smiling warmly. Then I return to the main room, where my wife is, and have

かりだ。

それでも半日もたてば、居所というか縄張りというか定まり、部屋は静かになる。

毎朝、私は人間たちの肩を軽く叩いてまわる。生きているかどうかを確かめるためが、第一。じきに出ていくのか、それともまだしばらくここにいるのかを調べるためが、第二。

死んでしまった者は、そのままひきずって、地面のさらに深くに掘った穴に落とす。穴は地下百メートル以上の深さまで掘られている。掘ったのは、私ではない。妻でもない。私たちの祖先が、何代もかけてじっくりと掘ったのだ。

掘られた当初は、穴は私たちの族のなきがらを落とすためのものだった。しかし時代が下るにしたがって私たちの血縁は減りつづけ、今ではこの世界に生きているのは、私と妻の両親、そして二人ずついる弟妹たちだけになってしまった。

両親たちも弟妹たちも、九州からさらに南にくだった、地下のかなり深いところに住んでいる。人間と交わることもなく、ひっそりと暮らしている。ときどき妻の母がメールをよこすが、早く東京など離れてこちらに来いと書いてくるばかりである。義弟や義妹が東京に出たいと言いだすのを、恐れているらしい。

じきにここを出ていきそうな人間は、肩を叩いた私に反応して顔を上げるので、それとわかる。顔を上げたとき、人間はどれもよるべない表情をしている。私の目に自分の目をじっと据え、口の中で何ごとかをつぶやいたりもする。

私はもう一度人間の肩を軽く叩き、にっこりと笑いかける。それから、妻のいる居間に戻って、かりかりに焼

a few slices of crispy fried bacon and yogurt with peach jam on top.

When I finish eating, my wife and I carry into the next room the big pot of gruel that she has cooked to give to the humans. My wife ladles the gruel into bowls; I get the humans to line up. Of course, you can't expect too much from these humans: before you know it they're cutting the line, or if they find it too much of a hassle to line up, they just grab other people's bowls. They're all like that. Whenever they do something bad, I tell them to stop, and if they still don't stop I give them a swat with my claws and force them to listen. That's how I maintain order.

After all the gruel has been eaten, the room falls silent again. I start getting ready to go to work. My wife polishes the kitchen sink, then starts the washing machine, which moans as it spins. She comes to see me off; I throw open the trapdoor and go out into the street. I take my time walking to the station. I've got on my cashmere coat and my muffler. And I'm wearing my leather gloves. I get cold easily. I change trains twice on my way to work; the commute takes a little under an hour.

Arriving at work, I punch my timecard. While I'm waiting for one of the office girls to make tea I glance over the faxes that have been left on my desk. When I first came to work at this company, people sometimes threw rocks at me or pelted me with rotten vegetables and things, but over the years both my colleagues and my superiors seem to have grown accustomed to my presence.

The young humans who have joined the company in recent years don't even seem to notice how different I look. I don't think they consciously decide not to wonder about me, why my form is so unlike theirs; they simply can't be bothered. People sometimes make comments—"You're pretty hairy, aren't you?"—but no one openly stares at me anymore, or presses me for information about my background. Until a decade or so ago, people really gossiped a lot.

I sit at my computer until lunchtime, mostly dealing with statistics. Sometimes a young woman comes from general affairs and asks me to write out an address on an envelope in calligraphy,

けたベーコンや、桃のジャムをかけたヨーグルトを食べる。

食べおわると、人間たちのために妻が温めたごった煮の大鍋を、妻と一緒に次の間まで運ぶ。妻はごった煮を椀によそい、私は人間たちを並ばせる。なにしろ人間たちときたら、すぐに横入りをしたり、並ぶのを面倒がって人の椀をよこどりしたりする者ばかりなのだ。私はそういう者たちにいちいち注意を与え、注意しても聞かぬものは鉤爪でひっかいて力ずくで言うことを聞かせ、秩序を保つ。

ごった煮が食べつくされてしまうと、また部屋は静かになる。私は会社に行く用意を始める。妻は台所のシンクを磨き、洗濯機をごうごう回しはじめる。妻に見送られて、私は地上へのあげぶたをはね上げ、道に出る。それから駅までゆっくりと歩く。カシミヤのコートにマフラー。革の手袋もはめている。私は寒がりなのだ。会社までは、電車を二本乗りついで、一時間弱ほどかかる。

会社についてタイムカードに刻印し、女の子がお茶を淹れてくれるのを待つ間に、私は机の上に置かれたファックスを一通り眺める。会社に入りたてのころは、石をなげつけられたり腐ったものをぶつけられたりしたこともあったが、何年かするうちに、同僚たちも先輩社員たちも私に慣れたらしい。

近年入社してくる若い人間たちなどは、私の姿が自分たちとずいぶん違うことにも気がつかないようだ。異形のもののことを、あえて忖度しない、というよりも、気に留めようともしない、らしい。「かなり、毛深いんすね」と言われたことくらいはあるが、あからさまに凝視されたり、出自を問い詰められたり、ということもなくなった。十年ほど前までは、口さがない人間も多かったのだが。

お昼までパソコンに向かって、おもに統計処理をする。ときおり庶務の女の子がやってきて、封筒の表書きの

using a brush. I'm a good calligrapher. Everyone says I write sharper-looking characters than anyone else in the company.

I sit there quietly plowing through my assigned tasks until the time comes to open the box lunch that my wife has made me. I get cold even though the office is heated, so I put disposable heating pads on my stomach and lower back. Lunchtime rolls around right about the time the pads begin to lose their heat.

Let me tell you about my lunch break.

When I finish eating my lunch, I carefully wrap up the empty box again and go give my hands a good washing. I wash off my face while I'm at it. I eat with chopsticks, but I also make good use of my claws and the palms of my hands. My hands get sticky from the oil, and little bits of food get stuck on the fur on my cheeks and around my mouth.

I don't know if it's because no one can stand the sight of me eating or because people see no reason to spend even their lunch breaks in the office, but either way the young woman manning the phones and I are the only two left in our section. There isn't a sound in the whole office, and it gets a little chilly.

I start feeling so cold that I go out to spend what remains of the lunch break in the park in front of the station.

There are lots of humans over in the park, holed up in cardboard shacks; I make it my practice to accept the hospitality of whoever's shack looks the warmest.

"Hey, you're not human, are you?" says the drifter, who has been scrutinizing my hands and feet and face as I crawl inside. These drifters look much more closely at me than the young humans at the office do.

墨書を頼んでゆく。私は習字が得意なのだ。会社の誰よりも立派な字を書くと言われている。

妻のつくってくれた弁当を開くまで、もくもくと私はノルマをこなす。オフィスの中は暖房が効いているが、それでも私は寒がりなので、使い捨てカイロを腰と腹とに当てている。カイロがぬるくなるころに、昼食の時間となる。

昼休みのことを話そう。

妻のつくってくれた弁当を食べおえると、私はていねいに空の弁当箱を包みなおし、よく手を洗い、ついでに顔も洗う。食べるときに、私は箸も使うが、てのひらも鉤爪も活用するのである。手は油でにちゃにちゃするし、頬や口のまわりの毛も、食べ滓でくわんくわんになる。

私が食べるさまを見るのが嫌なせいか、それとも昼食の時間まで会社にいたくないせいか、同じ部署でオフィスに残っているのは、私とあとは電話当番にあたっている女の子だけだ。オフィスの中はしんとして、少し寒い。

あんまり寒いので、私は残った昼休みの時間を過ごしに、駅前の公園へ行く。

公園にはダンボールにくるまった人間たちがたくさんいて、私はそのうちの一番暖かそうなダンボールに入れてもらうことにしているのだ。

「あんた、人間じゃないだろ」

私がもぐりこんでゆくと、浮浪者は私の手や足や顔をじろじろ見ながら言う。会社の若い人間なんかよりも、よほど私のことをしっかり観察している。

"Human? I should say not!" I say, puffing out my chest.

"Don't be so hoity-toity," the drifter says, chuckling. "You're just an animal."

"What do you mean by that! Humans are animals, too, aren't they?"

"Well, yeah. You've got a point there."

Our exchange typically comes to an end around then. These drifters aren't too talkative. The humans I collect aren't too talkative, either. Generally speaking, the humans in Tokyo have all become pretty closemouthed of late.

As I sit there with my back pressed up against the drifter's, I gradually start to feel warm. It's much warmer pressing up against a human back than it is in the office, even when it's raining—even, in fact, when it's snowing. And yet humans don't seem to huddle together very often. Sometimes I wonder why humans are so distant from one another.

I never pick up drifters. The humans I collect are more unstable than they are.

I leave the drifter's cardboard shack and walk around for a while in the alleys that run behind the buildings near the station. There aren't any unstable humans there, not in the alleys. Strange though it may seem, they tend to appear in brighter, more open spaces. Around the kiosks in the station, for instance, or in well-lit coffee shops with wide glass windows, or in department stores.

There are cats in the alleys. Whenever they see me, their hair stands on end and they yowl at me. They say: *Giyaa!* Humans like cats, so they look displeased when the cats cry *Giyaa!* I try to steer clear of cats when I walk in the alleys.

Sometimes there's a hole near the end of an alley; when I scrunch up and burrow down inside, I find that the soil there is nice and soft. I dig into the soft soil with my claws, deeper and

「人間じゃないですよ、むろん」と私が胸を張って言うと、浮浪者は少し笑う。

「なにいばってんの、動物のくせに」

「なになに、人間だって動物の一種ではありませんか」

「ま、そりゃそうだな」

このくらいで、やりとりは終わる。浮浪者は、あまり喋らない。私が拾ってくる人間たちも、あまり喋らない。

総体に、東京の人間はあまり喋らなくなっている。

浮浪者と背中をくっつけあってじっとしていると、だんだんに暖かくなってくる。雨が降っているときも、雪のときでさえ、会社の中にいるよりもこうやって人間の背中にくっついているときの方が、暖かい。でも人間どうしはあまりくっつかないみたいだ。なぜ人間たちはあんなによそよそしくしあうのかと、私はときおり不思議に思う。

私が浮浪者を拾うことは、まずない。私が拾うのは、もっと安定しない人間たちだ。

浮浪者のダンボールから出て、しばらく私は駅のまわりのビル裏の路地を歩く。安定しない人間は、路地にはいない。かえってもっと白々とした、広い場所にいる。駅の売店のあたりとか、明るいガラス張りのコーヒー店の中とか、デパートの中とか。

路地には猫がいる。私を見ると必ず毛を逆立てて、ギャーと鳴く。人間は猫が好きだから、猫がギャーと鳴くと、にがにがしそうにする。猫を避けながら、私は路地を歩く。

路地の奥にはときどき穴があって、小さくなってもぐりこむと、柔らかい土に当たる。その柔らかい土を、私

deeper. Sometimes I get carried away and end up tunneling all the way home. My wife bristles when she sees my wonderful cashmere coat all covered with dirt. I give her a kiss and make my way back through the tunnel.

Aboveground, the sunlight is blinding. Even on cloudy days it takes a while after I emerge from the earth for my eyes to get used to the light; I have to wait a bit before I can even open them. I stand there for a moment, feeling the brightness through my tightly closed eyelids. The light feels cold. Even though it comes from the sun, it feels cold. My wife says this is because the sun is just too far away from the earth. Down inside the earth it's much warmer than aboveground, because there you're closer to the lowest reaches of the earth, where the magma is. Even the humans I collect look much warmer sprawled out in the second room of our house than they did when they were aboveground.

Eventually my eyes grow accustomed to the light, and I am able to open them. I brush the dirt from my coat, wrap my disheveled muffler around my neck again, and return to the office. By the time the lunch break draws to an end, the office is completely filled with humans. I switch on the monitor of my computer and call up rows and rows of figures from inside the hard drive. A young woman makes me some hot tea. I take sips of it, holding the teacup between my claws.

Sometimes my claws slip, and I drop the teacup on the floor. The young women rush right over and, without a word, begin sweeping up the fragments. The young women won't look me in the eye. None of the humans at work ever look me in the eye. They never try to talk to me, either.

I sit at my computer, tapping away on the keyboard with my claws.

Let me tell you about my afternoons.

In the afternoon, sunlight gushes into the office and it gets a little warmer. There are three potted rubber plants lined up alongside the reception desk. On the way to the toilet, I sometimes

は鉤爪でもってどんどん掘ってゆく。興が乗ると、家までトンネルを掘ってしまうこともある。せっかくのカシミヤのコートが土だらけになると、妻はぷりぷりする。妻にキスをして、私はまた穴の中を戻ってゆく。

地上に出ると、太陽がまぶしい。曇っている日でも、地中から出たとたんには目が慣れなくて、しばらくは目を開けられない。つむった瞼ごしに、しばらく私は光を感じている。光は、冷たい。太陽の光なのに、冷たい。太陽から地上までは距離がありすぎるからだと、妻は言う。地中は、地の底のマグマに近いから、地上なんかよりもよっぽど暖かいのである。拾ってきた人間たちも、地上にいたときよりも、私の家の次の間に寝そべっているときの方が、よほど暖かそうに見える。

ようやく目が慣れて開けられるようになると、私はコートの土を払い、ずれたマフラーを巻きなおし、会社に戻る。昼休みが終わりかけるころには、オフィスの中は人間でいっぱいになっている。私はパソコンの画面のスイッチを入れ、何列もの数字をハードディスクの中から呼び出してくる。女の子が熱いお茶を淹れてくれる。私は鉤爪で茶碗を持ち、お茶をすする。

ときどき鉤爪がずれて、私は茶碗を床に落としてしまう。女の子たちがさっと寄ってきて、無言で茶碗のかけらを掃き集める。女の子たちは、私の顔を見ようとしない。会社の人間は、誰も私の顔を見ようとしない。話しかけようともしない。

午後はオフィスに日が差して、少し暖かい。ゴムの樹の鉢が三つ、応接スペースの横に並べてある。便所に行

私はパソコンに向かい、キーボードをぱちぱちと鉤爪で打ちはじめる。

午後のことを話そう。

blow off a bit of the dust that has accumulated on their leaves. Dust accumulates very quickly on the leaves of rubber plants. By the time the day is half-done, they're already thinly coated with dust stirred up by passing humans.

In the toilet, I enter a stall. I'm smaller than humans are, so I can't quite reach an ordinary urinal. I'm about two-thirds as tall as a full-grown man. Once I went ahead and tried to urinate in the urinal anyway, with the predictable result: I couldn't really aim high enough, so I made a mess.

On the way to the toilet, I always talk a bit with the humans who do the cleaning in our building. In the afternoon, they can usually be found on the emergency stairs between the third and second floors. They lean against the wall, not speaking.

Sometimes the cleaning humans pass on a tip.

"There was one of *them* outside today."

They are the humans I collect.

"This guy today looked kind of dangerous."

"Oh? How did he look?"

"Like he might jump off a roof or something."

How unpleasant, the cleaning humans say to one another. I mean, once, there was this guy who actually jumped, you know, and I saw him go. The humans say things like that, and then they laugh. *Aahaha.* I don't understand why they laugh at such moments. I don't laugh. I laugh only at happy times. The humans don't really seem to be laughing because they're happy. I just don't get humans.

I take out my memo pad and note down where they saw "one of *them.*"

く途中で、ゴムの葉の上にたまったほこりを、私はふっと吹いたりする。ゴムの葉には、すぐにほこりがたまる。

半日もすると、人間たちのたてるほこりが、うっすらとたまる。

便所では、個室に入る。私は人間よりも小さいので、ふつうの朝顔には届かないのだ。私は背の高さは、成人男子の三分の二くらいである。いつか無理して朝顔に向かって放尿したら、案の定うまく入らなくて、汚してしまった。

便所に行ったついでに、わたしはいつもビル清掃の人間たちに声をかけることにしている。午後には、清掃の人間たちは、たいがい三階と二階の間の非常階段のあたりにいる。どの人間も、無言で、壁に寄りかかっている。

「今日、ビルの外にアレがいたよ」と、清掃の人間たちが、ときどき教えてくれる。

アレ、というのは、私が拾う類の人間のことである。

「今日のアレ、ちょっと危ない感じ」

「どんなですか」

「屋上とかから飛び下りそう」

いやだね、と清掃の人間たちは言いあう。いつかほんとに飛び下りた奴がいて、俺見ちゃってさ。そんなことを言いながら、人間たちは、あはあはと笑ったりする。どうしてそういうときに笑うのか、私にはわからない。私は笑わない。笑うのは、愉快なときだけだ。人間たちは愉快だから笑っているのでもなさそうだ。人間のことは、よくわからない。

私は手帳を出して、「アレ」がいたという場所を書きこむ。

When I go back to the office and sit down at my computer, a young woman brings me some tea. The tea the young women make in the afternoon is always lukewarm. Maybe humans get tired in the afternoon. If they're tired they ought to go to sleep, but instead they keep their clothes on, nice and neat, and they sit on their chairs and get up and walk around and so on and so forth, tired all the while.

When I get tired, I lie down right away, in the office or the hall or wherever I am. I spread my cashmere coat over my body like a blanket and sink for some time into a profound sleep. The humans cut a wide swath around me when they pass, being careful not to step on me. I always try to lie down near the wall, so they ought to walk straight by without worrying. But they make a big arc, heels clicking on the floor in an especially busy way, coming nowhere near my supine form.

My whole body is cold when I wake up. I've been lying directly on the floor, so it's only natural. I leap up, causing a momentary buzz among the humans. There isn't actually a buzz, just a tremor of energy that shudders through the air. I can sense it.

The humans dislike me. It's been that way for ages. Back in my ancestors' time, no one could have imagined that the day would come when I would live my life like this, among humans. In the old days, humans used to hate our clan, and if they so much as caught sight of one of us they would shoot him with guns or jab him with spades or sprinkle poison all over the place. Boy, was that terrible.

Hardly anyone tries to attack me now. Humans no longer seem so sure of what they hate and what they like. Deep down at the core of their being they feel hatred for me, yet they let me stay on at the company as if everything were just fine. They tell themselves that they let me stay on because they need me. But most of the humans have no need for me at all. Truth be told, for the vast majority of humans, we who inhabit the earth's depths cause

オフィスに帰ってまたパソコンに向かっていると、女の子がお茶を淹れてくれる。午後に淹れてくれるお茶は、いつもぬるい。人間は午後になると疲れてくるのかもしれない。疲れたら眠ればいいのに、人間はきっちりと服を着て、疲れながら椅子に座ったり歩きまわったりしている。

私は眠くなると、部屋でも廊下でもどこででも、すぐに横たわってしまう。カシミヤのコートを毛布がわりに体に掛けて、しばらくぐっすりと眠る。人間たちは、私を踏まないようにぐるりと大回りしてゆく。私はできるだけ隅の方に横たわるのだから、気にせず側を通ればいいのに、横たわる私に少しも近づかないように、かつかつと靴音をたてて、人間たちは歩きまわる。

目覚めると、体が冷えてしまっている。床に直接横たわっていたのだから、しかたがない。私がむっくり起き上がると、人間たちは一瞬どよめく。実際にどよめくわけではないが、空気が、ぴりりと立つのである。はっきりと、わかる。

人間たちは、私のことが嫌なのである。大昔から、そうだった。私の先祖たちのころは、私が今しているように、人間の中に入りこんで毎日を過ごすことなど、考えられもしなかった。私たちの族を人間は嫌い、姿を見かけようものならば、銃で撃ったり鋤でつついたり薬を撒いたり、それはもうたいへんなものだった。

今では、私を攻撃しようとする人間など、ごくわずかだ。人間たちは、自分たちが何を嫌っていて何を好いているのか、よくわからなくなってしまったらしい。気持ちの底の方では私を嫌いながら、平気で会社に置いておく。必要があって置いてやっているのだと、どの人間も自分を納得させているのだ。しかしたいがいの人間にとって、私など必要ではない。地の底に住む私たちの族など、大多数の人間にとっては害を成すものでしかない

nothing but harm.

I walk slowly through the frigid ripples of attention, return to my computer, and wait for the lukewarm tea some young woman will bring. I check my e-mail and find any number of messages from humans writing to tell me that they came across "one of *them*" in such and such a place. I note down in my pad all the places where "one of *them*" was spotted, and when I've finished I erase the e-mails.

Day after day, the number of e-mails keeps rising. The muffled voices of humans who happen to have heard someone, somewhere, talking about me keep pushing on and on in my direction, growing like the slender roots of a plant working their way through a boulder.

I drink my lukewarm tea, then drop the teacup on the floor. Every so often I drop my teacup like this, on purpose. Their bodies seething with hatred, but without letting that hatred out, sending deep black waves rippling through the air in every direction, the humans begin sweeping up the fragments of my teacup.

I gaze at the figures on my computer screen, acting as if nothing had happened. The dim red light of the setting sun streams in through the glass of the office's wide windows. The sunset has expanded until it fills the sky. A raging sunset that occupies the entire sky over Tokyo.

I begin noting down in my pad the order in which I'll go collect *them*.

Why don't I tell you about my evenings?

When I leave work, I always make a deep bow. The walls of the office building are cloaked in a dusky twilight glow that makes things look wet, and it's hard to make out their edges. The lit-up windows are like square pieces of white paper floating in the air. The humans, on their way out of the office, keep their distance

はずだ。

　私は冷たいざわめきの中をゆっくり歩き、パソコンの前に戻って、女の子の淹れてくれるぬるいお茶を待つ。

　メールをチェックすると、「アレ」をどこそこで見かけたというようなメールが、何通も来ている。「アレ」のいる場所を手帳に全部写し終わると、私はメールを消去する。

　メールは毎日増えつづけている。どこかで私のことを聞きつけた人間たちのつぶやきが、岩を割って伸びてくる植物の細い根のように、私をめがけて伸び伝わってくるのだ。

　ぬるいお茶を飲み、私は茶碗を床に落とす。ときどき、こうやってわざと茶碗を落としてみせる。人間たちは嫌悪を体いっぱいにためて、しかしその嫌悪を発散することはせずに、くろぐろとした空気をまき散らしながら茶碗のかけらを掃き集める。

　私は何ごともなかったような顔をして、パソコンの数字を眺める。オフィスの広い窓ガラス越しに、夕暮れのうすあかい光がさしこんでくる。夕焼けが、空いっぱいに広がっている。東京の空いっぱいを覆いつくす、猛々しい夕焼け。

　私はアレを拾いにゆく順序を、手帳にメモしはじめる。

　夜の始まりのことを、話そうか。

　会社を出るとき、私はいつもふかぶかとお辞儀をする。ビルの壁面は濡れたような夕闇におおわれ、輪郭が曖昧になっている。光を灯した窓は、空中に浮かんだ四角い白紙のようだ。お辞儀をする私を、退社する人間た

from me as I stand there bowing. The humans never turn to look back at the building after they've left. Even though they could die in the night, and then they wouldn't be coming back the next day. The humans just rush out and hurry on home.

Once I feel I've bowed enough, I start walking toward the part of town where all the action is.

The night is young. The darkness that fills the streets is still fairly light.

I go into a bar and order a draft beer. The young guy who comes to take my order shows a flicker of surprise at the hairiness of my body, but he takes the order without changing his expression. He doesn't take much time bringing out a snack to go along with the drink, either; he sets down a small bowl filled with slices of dried daikon.

The young guy seems startled only at first. He quickly gets used to me, and he comes out promptly with the dishes I keep ordering, one after the other. Deep-fried tofu in broth, salt-grilled gizzard, yellowtail and daikon in soup, things like that.

"Say, have you seen any of *them* around here?" I ask sometime around the second bottle of hot sake.

"Oh, no, *they* wouldn't come to a place like this!" replies the young man.

Looking around the bar, I see two or even three of *them*. One looks terribly tired, and the whites of his eyes are bleary; another is drooped over, his eyes so clear they're almost blue. The young guy hardly seems to notice when *they* order something; he just keeps bustling briskly around the room.

They slide off their chairs, wobble into walls. I stick out a claw and breezily grab hold of one of *them*, hooking him by his back. He dangles there for a while at the end of my claw, then gradually begins to shrink. It's not long before he's only half my size, and eventually he gets so small I can hold him in the palm of my hand.

Pinching him gingerly between two claws, I lower him into one of the pockets of my cashmere coat. He doesn't shout or try to

ちが大きくよけてゆく。人間たちは、会社を出てしまうと、二度とビルに来るというのに。人間たちはそそくさと出て、そそくさと帰るばかりだ。

ば、明日は同じビルに来ることはないというのに。人間たちはそそくさと出て、そそくさと帰るばかりだ。

思うさまお辞儀をしてしまうと、私は夜の街に向かって歩きはじめる。

夜はまだ浅い。街の闇も淡い。

私は一軒の居酒屋に入り、生ビールを注文する。つきだしの切り干し大根の小鉢もすぐに持ってくる。

表情は変えずに、生ビールの注文を通す。注文を開きに来た若い衆は、私の毛深いからだに一瞬驚くが、

若い衆が驚くのは、最初だけだ。すぐに慣れて、私がつぎつぎに注文する揚げ出しどうふだの、砂肝の塩焼き

だの、ぶり大根だのを、てきぱきと持ってくる。

「このへんに、アレ、いますかね」と私が聞くのは、燗酒が二本めになったあたりだ。

「うちみたいな店には、アレ、来ませんよ」と若い衆は答える。

店の中をみまわすと、アレが二人も三人も、いる。白目が濁って、ひどく疲れた様子のアレもいるし、あおく

澄んだ目の、うなだれたアレもいる。若い衆はアレがなにかを注文しても、ほとんど気がつかない様子で、やた

らにてきぱきと店の中を動いている。

アレは、椅子からすべり落ちたり、ふらふらと壁にぶつかっていったりする。私は鉤爪で、アレの背中をひょ

いとひっかける。そのまましばらく鉤爪の先にぶらさげていると、アレは次第に小さく縮んでゆく。そのうちに

私の半分くらいの大きさになり、やがては掌に載るくらいにまで小さくなる。

私はカシミヤのコートのポケットにアレをつまみ入れる。アレは、叫んだりさからったりすることもなく、静

resist; he just quietly slips down into my pocket. Almost as if he had been wanting this all along.

"Comes to thirty-five hundred yen, sir," says the young guy who works at the bar, bringing the bill.

"There were a bunch of *them* here, you know," I tell him, taking one of *them* from my pocket, holding him gingerly between two fingers.

The young guy's eyes widen as he stares at the shrunken *thing*.

"I'll be darned! So we had some here, too, huh?" he says, shrugging. He peers uneasily at the *thing*, which is flopped over with his eyes closed, and asks me, "What the hell are *they* anyway?"

"Good question. I'd say . . . I'm not really sure myself."

"But if you had to say more than that. . . ." says the young guy, urging me on. I put the *thing* back in my pocket and think for a few moments. All of a sudden, over the course of the last decade, these *things* have started increasing in number. When my parents began to feel hopeless about things, they always used to say they had "no more spirit to live." It strikes me that maybe that's what *they* are: humans who no longer have what my parents called "the spirit to live."

If they are left to their own devices, these *things* become empty, and then the places where they are, and then eventually even the areas around the places where they are. *They* make it all unreal.

You might expect them to die once they're empty, but they don't.

Evidently it takes real power even to die.

People who don't die, but who don't live, either; who just *are* wherever they are, eating away at their surroundings. Eating away at themselves, too. When you get right down to it, that's what *they* are.

When was it, I wonder, the first time one of *them* fell underground, down into the place where I live. I heard a big thump, and when I went into the next room to see what had

かにポケットにすべりこむ。まるで自分から望んだみたいに。

「お客さん、三千五百円」と店の若い衆が勘定を持ってくる。

「アレ、けっこう、いましたよ」私が言って、ポケットからアレを一人つまみ出すと、若い衆は目を丸くして縮んだアレを見つめた。

「ありゃー、うちの店にもいましたか」と言って、肩をすくめる。

「アレ、っていったい何なんすか」若い衆は、ぐったりと目を閉じているアレを気味悪そうに見ながら、聞いた。

「さあねえ、私にもよくわからないけど」

「けど？」と若い衆は促した。私はアレをふたたびポケットにしまい、しばらく考えこんだ。アレは、この十年ほどで突然増えた。生きる精がない、と私の父母などはものごとに絶望しかけたときに表現したものだったが、アレも、生きる精というもののなくなってしまった人間たちなのかもしれなかった。

アレは、ほうっておくと、虚になってしまうのだ。アレ自身も、アレのいる場所も、そのうちにはアレのいる場所の周辺をも、虚にしてしまう。実でないものにしてしまう。

虚になったならば、実の力というものが必要らしい。

死ぬのにも、死にもせず、生きもせず、ただそこにあって、周りを浸食する者。そしてまた、自身を浸食する者。それが、アレというものなのである。

アレが最初に私の住む地下に落ちてきたのは、いつのことだったろう。どさり、という音がして見にいくと、

happened, there was a human there. A human I'd never seen before. Of course, in those days my wife and I were still living quietly in our underground world, just the two of us, so we never had any interactions with humans.

"I'm scared," said the human.

"What are you scared of?" my wife and I both asked at once.

"Scared of it all," the human replied, still staring into space.

After that, we had a person a week, then one every five days, then one every three days. Little by little the frequency with which the humans came tumbling down increased, until at last one would drop into the next room every day, without fail.

At first, we just waited for the humans to fall. They would stay there in the next room for a while, then go back aboveground.

"Are you going back up?" I'd ask.

And in most cases the humans would reply: *"I'm going."*

Apparently the humans just had to stay underground for a while, and then, once they had done that, they were able to go back aboveground.

All kinds of humans dropped down into our house. We had kids with long arms and lanky legs, we had wobbly old folks, we had well-built adults. The humans all kept to themselves; their bodies gave the space around them a wild look.

Early on, my wife and I would dig a separate hole each time one of the humans who dropped into our house died, and we gave each body a careful burial. After a while we remembered the hole our ancestors had dug, and decided to throw the bodies in there. Humans grow cold and stiff when they die. We *Mogera wogura* also become cold and stiff. Humans cry when one of their number dies, but we don't. We cry when we're sad or when we feel hurt or angry. Death is simply a fact of life, so it doesn't make us sad. It doesn't make us feel hurt or angry. But when a human dies, even

次の間に人間がいたのだ。見知らぬ人間だった。もともとそのころは人間のあいだにたち交じることもなく、妻と二人で地下の世界で静かに暮らしていた。

「コワイ」とその人間は言った。

「何が、怖いのですか」私と妻が同時に聞くと、人間は空を見据えたまま、

「ゼンブがコワイ」と答えた。

以来、一週間に一人、五日に一人、三日に一人と、次第に人間の落ちてくる頻度は高くなり、そのうちに、一日に必ず一人は、次の間に落ちてくる人間を待つだけになった。人間たちは、次の間にしばらくいて、それからまた地上に帰っていった。

最初のころは、落ちてくる人間を待つだけだった。

「もう帰りますか」と聞くと、たいがいの人間が、「カエル」と答えた。人間は、しばらく地下にいて、そして、ようやく地上に出られるようになるらしかった。

落ちてくるのは、さまざまな人間たちだった。手足のひょろ長い子供もいたし、よぼよぼの老人もいたし、体格のいい大人もいた。どの人間も寡黙で、荒れた空気を体にまとわりつかせていた。

初めのころ、落ちてきた人間が死んだ際には、私と妻は別途小さな穴を掘っていちいちていねいに埋めていた。そのうちに祖先の穴を思いだしし、そちらに放りこむことにした。人間は死ぬと冷たく硬くなる。私たち鼬鼠も、死ねば冷たく硬くなる。人間たちは仲間が死ぬと泣くが、私たちは泣かない。泣くのは、悲しいときと悔しいときである。死ぬのは当然の理なのだから、悲しくない。悔しくない。しかし人間は仲間が死ぬと、あんなにいつ

though the other humans are always so hollow and reticent and uninterested, they all come together and sob and wail, so that the next room resounds with their cries. They cry in such a way that they seem to be enjoying themselves. I just don't get humans.

I started collecting humans only a few years ago. Since I started going around pocketing humans—those who no longer even have the strength to come tumbling down underground—my nights have gotten busy. Following the sequence written out in my pad, I bustle busily along, gathering humans. They just sit there perfectly motionless, so it's easy to hook them with my claws.

I go around without a moment's rest all through the night, picking up humans, collecting more and more in the pockets of my cashmere coat.

I'll tell you about the wee hours of the night.

Now that I'm done gathering up the humans, I feel exhausted.

I walk soundlessly along the long black strip of asphalt. My pockets are full of humans. From time to time I pat the outsides of my pockets to make sure none of the humans are in danger of spilling out.

When I come to the entrance to our house, I raise the trapdoor and wriggle down belowground. My wife is waiting up for me. I've told her that she doesn't have to, but she says it's harder for her to get a good night's sleep if she gets up again after she's gone to bed. So she waits for me, wearing a nice thick sweater over her pajamas, sipping a cup of hot chocolate or warm milk.

"Welcome back!" says my wife in her gentle voice. She's a gentle-voiced *Mogera wogura*. All my wife's relatives are like that. My father-in-law and my brother-in-law both have gentle voices, and my mother-in-law's and my sister-in-law's voices sound just like my wife's, though their faces don't really look all that much alike.

Helping me out of my cashmere coat, my wife asks if I'd like a little rice in some tea or something; then, with a single quick

もは空虚で寡黙で無関心なのに、そのときばかりは揃っておいおいと、次の間じゅうに泣き声を響かせる。泣くのが気持ちいいみたいな様子で、泣く。人間のことは、よくわからない。

人間を拾いはじめたのは、この数年来のことだ。落ちてくる力もなくなった人間を、ポケットに拾い集めるようになってからは、夜も忙しくなった。手帳につけた順に、てぎわよく拾ってゆく。どの人間もじっとしているので、鉤爪にひっかけやすい。

夜半まで、休む間もなく、私は人間たちをカシミヤのコートのポケットに拾い集めてゆく。

深更の話をしよう。

人間たちを集め終わり、私は疲れている。

くろぐろと延びるアスファルトの上を、靴音をたてぬように私は歩いてゆく。ポケットの中は、人間でいっぱいだ。ときどきポケットの外側を叩いて、人間たちがこぼれ落ちていないかどうか、確かめる。

家の入り口まで来て、あけぶたを開き、地下にもぐりこむ。妻は起きて待っている。待たなくていいと言ってあるのだが、一度眠った後で起きるとかえって寝つきが悪くなると言いながら、パジャマの上に厚いセーターを着こんで、ココアやホットミルクをすすりながら待っている。

「おかえりなさい」と妻は優しい声で言う。優しい声の鼬鼠なのだ。妻の血縁は、みなそうだ。義父も義弟も柔らかな声をしているし、義母と義妹は、妻にそっくりの声をしている。顔はみなあまり似ていないのだが。

お茶漬けでもどう、と聞きながら、妻は私のカシミヤのコートをうしろから脱がせ、そのまますっとハンガー

gesture, she hangs my coat on the hanger. The pockets are bulging. My wife sticks a claw down into one of the pockets and gingerly extracts a human. One, two, three . . . She counts aloud as she lines them up on the table.

At first, the humans remain perfectly still. After a while they begin to scrabble about on the table, beginning with the relatively lively ones. As their movements grow more energetic, they gradually return to their original size. My wife and I carry them into the next room before they get to be too big and let them expand to their full size in there.

The humans who are already in the other room gaze on blankly as the little humans go back to being big humans. The humans I've just collected are universally blank. No matter how unnatural and strange something may appear to humans, they never lose their blank looks. Pretty much the only time they ever cry or blow their noses or otherwise express emotion is when one of their number dies.

Once my wife and I have seen that all the humans are back to their normal size, we sit down on either side of the table and drink a hot cup of fragrant, roasted-leaf tea. Sometimes we have a few rice crackers, too. We hardly ever talk about the humans. We don't talk about my work, either. We talk about other things. About what was on sale that day at the supermarket. About how Chiro, at the pharmacy, just had puppies. About the fact that ever since she had her puppies, Chiro is always barking at my wife. My wife and I chat about this and that, sipping our fragrant tea.

In the next room, the humans climb down into the futons, under the blankets. Occasionally some of the humans will talk to one another. My wife and I press our ears to the wall that separates the next room from the living room and listen to their voices. The humans' voices are gentle. I'm talking only about the voices of the humans who drop into our house, and of the ones I collect. The humans at work don't have gentle voices at all.

"Scary, isn't it."

にかける。ポケットがふくらんでいる。ふくらみの中に妻は鉤爪をさしこみ、人間をつまみ出す。いち、に、さ

ん、と数えながら、卓の上に人間を並べてゆく。

人間たちはじっとしたままである。しばらくすると、比較的元気のいい人間から、ごそごそと動きはじめる。

動きが活発になるにしたがって、人間たちは元の大きさに戻ってゆく。妻と私は、ほどよい大きさになった人間

を次の間に運び、そこですっかり元の大きさに戻るようにしてやる。

前からいた人間たちは、小さな人間が大きな人間に戻る様子を見ながら、うすぼんやりとしている。拾われて

くる人間たちは、いったいにうすぼんやりとしている。人間にとってどんなに不自然で奇妙なことを見ても、人

間たちはうすぼんやりとした様子を崩さない。泣いたり鼻を鳴らしたりといった感情を表すのは、仲間が死んだ

ときくらいのものなのである。

妻と私は人間を戻し終わると、卓に向かいあって熱いほうじ茶を飲む。せんべいを二三枚、つまむこともある。

人間たちのことは、めったに話題にしない。会社のことも、話題にしない。今日のスーパーマーケットのお買い

得品は何だったか。薬局のチロに子供が生まれたこと。子供を生んでから、チロがやたらに妻に吠えかかるよう

になったこと。そのようなことごとを、私と妻はほうじ茶をすすりながら、喋る。

人間たちは次の間で、布団や毛布の間にがさがさともぐる。ときどき人間どうしが喋りあっていることもある。

妻と私は、次の間と居間を仕切る壁に耳を当て、人間の声を聞く。人間の声は、優しい。ここに落ちてくる人間

や、拾われてくる人間の声は、優しいのだ。会社の人間たちの声は、ちっとも優しくない。

「コワイモンダ」と人間は言っていた。

"Yeah, real scary . . . grass of remembrance . . . on the ancient eaves."

We have no idea what any of it means. Everything the humans say sounds like a broken machine. They just keep repeating *"scary," "scary,"* or bellowing *"oow," "oow."*

Scary is the word the humans say most often. I can't imagine what it is that scares them so much. Their faces blank, their voices gentle, the humans keep saying *"scary scary scary"* back and forth to one another, repeating this in a never-ending loop. What on earth do they find so frightening? And if they're so scared, why doesn't it show? I just don't get humans.

Shortly before my wife and I go to bed, we go into the next room, where the humans are.

We walk around saying things to them. Hey, that hat looks really great on you! What's your favorite food? That futon sure looks nice and warm! Little things like that. The humans reply to our questions with surprising alacrity, though among themselves they hardly ever have a conversation worthy of the name. "I like fish best, I'm particularly fond of rockfish, so I was sitting on the shore trying to catch myself some rockfish when this cat came up to me, it was a calico cat with white, black, and tea-colored stripes, and once I killed a cat and ate it but it wasn't any good." They come out with things like that, speaking very fluidly, without a pause.

My wife and I go off to bed and fall into a deep sleep.

All night long, cries and sighs come from the next room, where the humans are. At first my wife and I weren't used to those sounds, so we had trouble going to sleep; nowadays we drift off right away.

My wife snores a little. Apparently I snore a lot when I'm asleep.

「コワイモンダヨ ノキバのシノブ」

意味もなにも、わからない。拾われてくる人間たちは、壊れた機械みたいな言葉しか喋らない。ただコワイコワイと繰り返したり、オウオウ叫んだり。

人間が一番よく喋るのは、「コワイ」という言葉だ。何を人間たちは、こわがっているのだろう。うすぼんやりとした表情の、優しげな声で、人間たちは際限もなく「コワイコワイコワイ」と言いあっている。そんなにこわいものとは、いったい何なのだろう。そんなにこわがっているにしては、ちっともこわそうに見えないのは、なぜなんだろう。人間のことは、よくわからない。

眠るちょっと前に、私と妻は人間たちのいる次の間に行く。

その帽子よく似合うね、とか、好きなたべものは、とか、ふとんがあったかそうだね、などと声をかけてゆく。

人間たちは、私たちの問いには、存外はっきりと答える。お互いほどんと会話らしい会話を交わさないのに。好きなたべものは魚で、魚はめばるがとくに好きで、めばるを釣ろうと海辺に座っていたら猫がきて、猫は白と黒と茶のだんだら縞で、猫は昔殺して食っちまったことがあるけど、猫はおいしくなかった。そんなことをすらすらと喋ったりする。

私も妻も早々に寝床に入り、ぐっすりと眠る。

人間たちのいる次の間からは、叫び声やため息が一晩じゅう聞こえてくる。私も妻も、最初のうちはその音に慣れなくて寝つかれなかったが、今ではすぐさま寝入ってしまう。

妻は少し鼾をかく。私も、眠りが深くなると、かなり鼾をかくらしい。

I'll tell you about dawn.

Dawn is when we *Mogera wogura* bear our children.

My wife has had fifteen children so far. They were small, lively children, covered all over with soft hair. But they all died soon after they were born. Not a single one of our children survived. We dug a separate hole for each child, and gave each a careful burial.

The humans shed tears when they learned that our children died. Some of them cried even more vociferously than they had after one of their own number died. My wife and I don't cry, even when the death is that of a newborn child, because death is a fact of life. There are people among the humans I've collected who have strangled their own children, and yet they, even more than any of the others, howl and writhe as they cry. I just don't get humans.

It's not only *Mogera wogura*. Humans also tend to have children at dawn.

In the past decade or so, two of the humans have given birth to children. One had a boy, the other a girl. They were small, lively children, covered all over with soft hair. They were human babies, of course, and yet they looked just like baby *Mogera wogura*. None of the humans paid the slightest attention when they were born. The humans cry and generally make a tremendous fuss when one of them dies, but it seemed as if they didn't give a fart when the babies were born.

The moment the mothers laid eyes on their hairy babies, they tossed them away. Then they crawled right down into their futons and went to sleep. Both the mothers went back aboveground about two days after they had their babies, so the children were left to their own devices here underground. The humans didn't show

明け方の話をしよう。

明け方は、私たち鼴鼠が子供を生む時刻である。

妻は今までに十五匹の子供を生んだ。小さな、柔毛におおわれた、活発な子供たちだった。けれど生まれてしばらくすると、どれも死んでしまった。生き残った子供は、一匹もいない。死んだ子供は、別途穴を掘って、ていねいに埋めた。

人間たちは、私と妻の子供が死んだことを知ったときも、さめざめと泣いた。自分たちの仲間が死んだときよりも、さらに大声で泣く者もあった。死ぬのは当然の理なのだから、たとえ死んだのが生まれたての子供であっても、私も妻も泣かない。拾ってきた人間の中には、自分の子供をくびり殺してしまったような者もいるのに、そういうのに限って、ことさらに大きな声で泣いたり身をよじったりする。人間のことは、よくわからない。

鼴鼠ばかりでなく、人間も、夜明け方に子供を生むことが多い。

ここ十年ほどの間に、二人の人間が子供を生んだ。一人は男の子、もう一人は女の子を生んだ。小さな、柔毛におおわれた、活発な子供たちだった。人間の子供なのに、鼴鼠そっくりの子供だった。どちらが生まれたときにも、まわりの人間たちは無関心だった。人間が死ぬときには多いに泣き騒ぐのに、生まれてきたときには、屍の一つをひるのも惜しがるような様子だった。

子供を生んだ母親たちは、毛深い子供を見たとたんに、すぐに子供を放り出した。そのまま母親たちは布団にもぐって眠った。翌々日くらいにはどちらの母親も地上に戻ったから、子供は地下に置きっぱなしである。人間

the slightest interest when they saw them, hairy as they were.

My wife and I raised the children that the humans brought into the world. They grew claws and matured so quickly they hardly seemed human; after three years they were fully grown. We set them free aboveground, and they both scampered off somewhere. We haven't heard a word of them since.

When the sun rises, thin rays of light filter down through the cracks in the ceiling. I just lie there for a while, gazing up at all those rays of light trickling in. No light appears on days when it's cloudy or raining, even if I wait. On the rare occasions when it snows, the room seems faintly bright even before dawn.

It's warm inside my futon, but the tip of my nose is cold. I want to rush into the bathroom right away, but I have a hard time making myself leave the futon. After a while, my wife wakes up. She goes off to the toilet before I can manage to get up. My wife is a good riser; no sooner is she up than she's cleaning the house and setting the pot on the fire, humming all the while.

Eventually I get myself ready, and by the time I start making the rounds, checking up on the humans I picked up the previous day or the day before that or even earlier, a bright red fire is blazing in the fireplace, water is boiling away in the whistling kettle, and the whole room is fragrant with the wonderful scent of toast.

The next room is overflowing with humans. My wife and I drop the dead ones down the hole, separate the ones who are going to go back aboveground immediately from those who aren't, and distribute the gruel.

The humans all look very listless, as if they're dead. But they aren't dead. They keep eating away at their surroundings, eating away at themselves; they stay where they are, perfectly motionless—but they don't die. Here in our hole, unable to become *Mogera wogura* themselves, as human as ever, they wait

たちは、毛深い子供を見ても、まったく関心を示さなかった。

妻と私は、人間の生んだ子供を育てた。鉤爪も生え、三年もするとすっかり成人し、人間に似合わぬ速い成長をたどった。そのまま地上に放したら、男の子も女の子も、どこかへ駆けていってしまった。以来消息を聞かない。

夜が明けてくると、天井の隙間からは薄く日が差す。漏れてくる何条もの光を眺めながら、私はしばらく横たわっている。曇った日や雨の日には、いつまでたっても光が差さない。ごくまれに雪が降っているときには、夜明け前なのに、うすあかるく感じる。

ふとんの中は暖かいが、鼻先は冷たい。すぐに便所に行きたいと思うのだが、なかなかふとんから出る決心がつかない。そのうちに妻が目を覚まし、私よりも先に用を足してしまう。妻は寝起きがよくて、鼻うたなど歌いながら、起きるなり掃除をはじめたり、鍋を火にかけたりする。

ようよう私の支度ができて、昨日やおとといや、それよりもっと前に拾ってきた人間たちを見まわるころには、暖炉には真っ赤な火がおこり、やかんには湯が沸いてピーピーと音をたて、部屋じゅうにかんばしいトーストの匂いがたちこめている。

人間たちは、次の間にあふれている。死んだ人間を穴に落とし、じきに地上に戻る人間とそうでない人間をより分け、私と妻は人間たちにごった煮を配る。

人間たちは、どれも生気のない、死んだような顔をしている。でも死んではいない。死なずに、周囲を浸食し、自分をも浸食しながら、じっとしている。私たちの穴の中で、鼯鼠にもなれずに、人間のままで、地上へ帰れる

for the time when they will be able to go back aboveground.

Some humans die before they are able to go back; then all the others shed tears and writhe about wildly on the floor, and for just a moment their faces, otherwise dead, light up.

　時を待っている。

　地上に帰らずに死んでしまう人間もいて、そういう時には、人間たちはさめざめと泣き、激しく身をよじり、死んだような顔を、一瞬輝かせるのである。

The Maiden in the Manger

馬小屋の乙女

Abe Kazushige

Translated by Michael Emmerich

The train carrying Thomas Iguchi pulled into Jinmachi Station at nine minutes past five in the afternoon. This accorded perfectly with the East Japan Railway Company timetable, but it represented a slight departure from Thomas Iguchi's own plans. Truth be told, he had wanted to get off two stations earlier, at Tendō, but had inadvertently ridden too far. Why had Thomas stayed on the train even as it passed the station at which he had intended to disembark? The explanation was, quite simply, that shortly after the train pulled away from Urushiyama Station, two stops prior to Tendō, Thomas had gone to sleep. Thomas Iguchi had not slept well the previous night, and so, as he sat surrounded by high school students from the region, evidently on their way home from school, he had carelessly allowed himself to drift off. Thomas was not necessarily a man who suffered from insomnia on a regular basis, but the particular nature of his work, at an establishment that did business at night, meant that he was unable to get to bed until very late. He had been living this way for some time now. And perhaps for this reason, he was assuredly not what one would call a good riser. With this trip looming over him, it was only natural that he should feel anxious about the possibility that he might oversleep, and when, toward dawn, he lay down in his bed and found himself stuck there, unable to sleep, his thoughts roaming from one random topic to the next, he began to feel every bit as awake as he had feared he would. In the end, the only option left if he didn't want to miss his train was to stay up the entire night.

The Yamagata line bullet-train Tsubasa No. 115 had departed from Tokyo Station at 1:36 in the afternoon. Once Thomas Iguchi had taken his seat, 6D in the first-class Green Car, and consumed the boxed lunch of fried chicken he had bought at a kiosk on platform 22, he decided, just in case, to take five milligrams of a sedative he used when he couldn't sleep. Seeing as the train would be arriving at its final destination in just under three hours, the most he would be able to sleep was two hours or so; nonetheless, he thought he would try to make up for at least a little of the rest he had missed. In the end, though, he hadn't even managed to doze off on the bullet train. He hadn't taken a trip long enough to require a change of trains for quite a while, and this

トーマス井口の乗った列車が神町駅に着いたのは午後五時九分だった。これはJR東日本の掲げる時刻表通りの到着ではあったが、トーマス井口にとってはいささか予定外の結果となった。本当は二つ前の天童駅で降りるつもりだったというのに、トーマス井口はうっかり乗り越してしまったのだ。なぜトーマスが降車予定駅を乗り過ごすことになったのかといえば、列車が天童駅より二つ前の漆山駅を出た辺りで彼は居眠りしてしまったのだ。

昨夜まともに眠っていないせいで、下校途中らしき地元の高校生らに囲まれながらトーマス井口はつい寝入ってしまった。トーマスは必ずしも、常日頃から不眠症に悩んでいたりするわけではないが、夜間営業の商売という仕事柄どうしても就寝が遅くならざるを得ぬ暮らしをずっと続けている。それゆえ、彼は寝起きも決して良いほうではない。旅行を目前に控えて、当然ながら寝過ごすのを懸念したトーマスは、夜明け頃に入った寝床の上で寝付けぬままゴロゴロしているうちにどうでもいいような考えがあれこれ巡り、そのせいで案の定目が冴えてしまい、新幹線に乗り遅れぬための策として最終的に徹夜を選択するほかなかったのだ。

山形新幹線つばさ115号が東京駅を発ったのは午後一時三六分だった。グリーン車の6番D席に着いたトーマス井口は、22番線ホームの売店で買ったチキン弁当を食してから念のためにと5mgの催眠鎮静剤を一錠服用した。三時間弱ほどで終点に到着するわけだから、最長でもせいぜい二時間程度しか寝ることは出来まいと知りつつ、睡眠不足をちょっとでも取り戻そうとしたのだったが、新幹線の車中では彼はとうとう一睡も出来なかった。

列車を乗り継いで行くほどの遠出をするのは久方ぶりのことではあったし、山形県は初めて訪れる土地でもあるので、幾らか気分も昂り、少しばかり緊張してさえいたのかもしれない。この度の日帰り一人旅の内容自体はじつのところ観光ではなく、単に買い物が一つあるだけだった。だが、単なる買い物といってもいわゆるレア

was also his first visit to Yamagata prefecture, so he was feeling rather anxious, and might even have become a trifle tense. For the purpose of this solitary day trip was not, as it happened, sightseeing, but shopping: he was traveling all this way just to make a single purchase. Perhaps the word *shopping* is misleading, however, for the item he was on his way to buy was a so-called rarity, a product hard to come by, very difficult to acquire. Thomas was, in short, feeling no small degree of excitement, to the extent that even after taking a sedative that should have eased his tension, he still found it far from easy to get to sleep in his seat on the moving train.

Though he hadn't so much as dozed on the bullet train, shortly after he transferred at Yamagata Station to a 4:44 local train, making all stops, he found himself utterly incapable of staying awake. Perhaps it had simply taken time for him to digest his box lunch, and the medication had taken too long to kick in. Whatever the case, despite the fact that his car on the local, all-stop train to Shinjō was occupied by a crowd of exceptionally boisterous teenagers who were engaged, just then, in making all sorts of noise, clicking and tapping, Thomas Iguchi had managed to drift off and ride past not only Tendō, the station at which he had intended to disembark, but also Midaregawa Station, which came after it. Thomas was lucky, however. The way things were going it wouldn't have been at all strange if he had slept straight through to Shinjō, but one of the high school girls standing and chatting directly in front of him mashed his toe, allowing him to regain consciousness before the train eased to a stop alongside the platform at Jinmachi Station.

"A surprisingly lyrical town, this, with an Eastern ambience that makes the whole environs seem to hang heavy with the heady fragrance of Eros. Which suggests that, at the end of the day, it is none other than the perfect town for me. And yet the air enfolding me on all sides is so damn dry that . . . how might I phrase it . . . my whole face is tingling, it seems, little pinpricks of pain all over my skin. That said, I confess that I am profoundly intrigued by the culture of this town. This is nothing but a shot in the dark, what people describe, in other words, as a sort of hunch, but I'd say it is more than likely that a significant number of

物、入手の大変困難な稀少品の購入が目的なのだからやはり少なからぬ興奮も覚えており、鎮静効果や筋緊張緩和作用を持つ薬などを呑んでみたところで、移動中の列車座席上において入眠に到るのはそう容易いことではなかったわけだ。

新幹線の車内では一睡も出来なかったとはいえ、山形駅で午後四時四四分発の普通列車に移ってしばらく後には敢え無くがくんといってしまったわけだから、あるいはチキン弁当の消化に時間が掛かり、薬の効き目が現れるのが遅すぎただけなのかもしれない。何にせよトーマス井口は、普通各駅停車新庄行き列車の車中において、十代の小僧連中がピコピコパコパコと音を立てながら大層賑やかにしている最中だというのに居眠りし、降車予定駅の天童駅を過ぎてさらに次の駅の乱川駅をも乗り過ごしてしまったのだった。けれどもトーマスは運が良かった。この分では新庄駅まで寝続けてしまっていてもおかしくはなかったはずだが、彼の目の前で立ち話していた女子高生の一人に爪先を踏ん付けられたことにより、列車が神町駅のホームに滑り込むより前に目覚めることが出来たのだ。

「驚いたことに、そこいら中にエロスの芳香がむんむんと漂っているみたいな東洋的風情のある、抒情的な町並みだな。とどのつまりはこの俺に打って付けの土地というわけだ。しかし何というか、顔中の肌がピリピリとひりつくくらいに周辺の空気が乾き切っていやがる。それにしても、この町の文化にはとても興味をそそられるぜ。こいつは当てずっぽう、要するに一つの勘というやつだが、ここには恐らく相当数の善人と悪人が住み着いているに違いない。両者はうまい具合に、言わば数の面で拮抗しているんだ。あとはそう、大昔に、じつに酷たらしい事件が立て続けに起きて、大勢の人間が死に追いやられたような形跡がそこここに認められるぞ。例えばあの

good and bad people have settled here. Numerically speaking, as they say, these two groups are just about as evenly matched as one might hope. Apart from that—well, I perceive traces here and there hinting at a series of truly bloodcurdling events that took place here one after the other, years and years ago, as a consequence of which many people were driven to their deaths. Take, for instance, those absurdly gigantic stones, like those used in pickling *tsukemono,* half-buried in that stretch of land over there, five or so meters off to the side of that ancient and well-weathered shrub. They look for all the world as though they had been planted there intentionally as a trap, to trip people. I'd be surprised indeed, let me tell you, to learn that those are a token of goodwill . . ."

Thomas had not intended to go as far as Jinmachi Station, it was true, but he would have to cover the remaining distance to his destination by taxi no matter which station he got off at, so the change in plan shouldn't have caused any problem. Except that for whatever reason, not a single taxi was angling for customers in front of the station. There were, on the other hand—as if in place of the anticipated taxis—any number of bicycles lined up in the traffic circle in front of the station (there was a bicycle lot there, so that was hardly a surprise!), and as Thomas Iguchi stood taking in his surroundings, eyes darting this way and that, person after person pedaled off until finally no one was left. Thomas became particularly entranced by a yellow electric bicycle and stood stock-still, ogling it for a minute and a half, but then he quickly lost interest, opened the door of the phone booth, and lifted the receiver.

"I'd like you to send a taxi to the station," he told the taxi company dispatcher who took his call. But the response he got, something along the lines of "There won't be any need for that!" was so thoroughly dismissive and outrageously glib that Thomas Iguchi was dumbstruck and fell into such a state of shock that it took all he had just to let out a gasp and a gulp. His instincts told him immediately that the reply he'd gotten might be a sign of the region's highly insular culture, but of course if he was going to accomplish his goal on this trip he couldn't give up so easily.

"What are you saying? You don't need the business, is that it?"

No sooner had he shot the bastard this question than the man fired

辺り一帯、あそこの古惚けた生け垣の五メートルほど脇のところには、漬物の重石にでも使うみたいな馬鹿でかい石がどっしりと埋まっているじゃないか。さながら人を躓かせるための罠として仕掛けられているかのようだな。これも善意の賜物ってやつだとすれば、うむ、全く度肝を抜かれるぜ……」

神町駅に降り立つのは予定外のことではあったが、どこの駅で降りようと目的地までの道程はタクシーで移動せざるを得ぬのだから、何ら問題はないはずだった。ところがどういうわけか、神町駅前のタクシーが一台も停まっていなかった。その代わりだとでもいうのごとく、駅前広場には何台もの自転車が置かれてあって（そこは駐輪場なのだから当たり前のことなのだが！）、トーマス井口が周囲をキョロキョロと見回しているうちに人気もばったり無くなってしまった。トーマスは一台の黄色い電動アシスト車に殊の外惹かれてしまい、一分半ばかりの間それに見入りつつただ立ち尽くすほかなかったのだが、結局すぐに飽きて公衆電話ボックスのドアを開けて受話器を手にしたのだった。

「駅に一台回して欲しいのだが」
電話に出たタクシー会社の人間にそう伝えると、その必要はありませんなどという人を馬鹿にしきった、あまりにもふざけた回答が返ってきたためトーマス井口は唖然とし、息やら唾やらを飲み込むのがやっとの状態に陥ってしまった。排他的な土地柄なのかもしれぬという直感が直ちに働いたものの、旅の目的を果たすためにはこんなところでおいそれと引き下がるわけにはゆかなかった。
「お宅は商売する気が無いのかい？」
そんなふうに問い掛けてやると、尻の毛でも抜き取られたみたいな剽軽な声色で以て相手は否定してきた。ど

back a denial, his tone as amusedly surprised as if someone had plucked a hair from his ass. Well, then, considered Thomas, it seems the second party to this discussion is not entirely disinclined to do business! But in that event, what reason can he have for declining to dispatch a cab? Thomas heaved a sigh, and then, the receiver still pressed against his ear, took a moment to drip a drop of medication into each of his two eyes. The aridity of the air was enough to make his dry-eye syndrome take an immediate turn for the worse.

"Indeed, it is precisely our need to do business that renders it unnecessary for me to send a cab at this time from our location to yours. There is no need for me to go to all the bother of sending a cab from here, you see, because we always have one waiting in your vicinity. We're permanently stationed there. Which means, if you follow me, that if I were to send yet another cab to you, I would be wasting the cost of the gasoline. This would represent a major loss on our part, businesswise. At any rate, we do have a cab there, right where it should be. Trot over to the taxi stand and look for yourself, sir. I have no doubt you will realize then that what I've said is not a lie."

There was, it was true, a taxi stand out in front of Jinmachi Station. Thomas had simply overlooked it. But there was no taxi there, either. Then something occurred to Thomas Iguchi, who had already left the telephone booth. Well, well, he thought, feeling the strength drain from his body, looks as though I may have fallen right into his trap. But, nevertheless, he did trudge over to the taxi stand.

He realized that he had not, in fact, been deceived the instant he arrived at the taxi stand and raised his hand. Lifting his hand was a trick he tried only because the taxi dispatcher mentioned above had urged this course of action upon him, just as he was on the verge of hanging up. No sooner had Thomas Iguchi swung his left hand into the air than a taxi that had been standing by in a far corner of the parking lot, over by a garage some fifty meters away from the entrance, zipped toward him at a speed of thirty or so kilometers per hour and ground to a sudden halt immediately in front of him. Why the hell was this guy waiting for passengers all the way over there, mused Thomas, feeling rather suspicious. But even as this thought crossed his mind, he was

うやらあちらさんは、商売する気が全然ないわけではないらしい。だとすればなぜ車を寄越さぬのか。トーマスは溜め息を吐いてから、受話器を耳に押し当てたままひとまず両方の眼に目薬を注した。空気が乾いているため、ドライアイの症状が立ち所に悪化してしまうのだ。

「商売する気があるからこそ、こちらから今そちらへ車をやるのは無駄なのですよ。なぜならこちらから一台わざわざ回さなくとも、そちらにはずっとうちの車がおりますからね。常駐しているのです。というわけですよ、また新たに一台そちらへ回したらばガソリン代が無駄になっちまうわけです。それだと商売上、うちは大損だ。とにかく車はちゃんとおります。タクシー乗り場へ行ってごらんなさい。あたしの言ってることは嘘じゃないってきっとお判りいただけますよ」

タクシー乗り場は確かに神町駅前に存在した。トーマスが単に見落としていただけだったのだ。しかしそこにもタクシーは停まっていない。すでに公衆電話ボックスを出ていたトーマス井口は、こいつはどうやらまんまと担がれちまったのかもしれないと思い到って脱力しながらも、タクシー乗り場のほうへのそのそと歩いていった。

騙されたわけではないと判明したのは、タクシー乗り場に立って片手を上げた矢先のことだった。片手を上げたのは、電話を切る間際に例のタクシー会社の社員が試しにそうしてみろと促してきたからだ。ひょいと左手を突き上げてみると、駅構内の外れのところ、駅の出入口から五〇メートルほど離れた倉庫付近の場所で待機していた一台のタクシーが時速三〇キロほどの速度で走ってきて、トーマス井口の眼前で急停車した。何でまたあんなところで客待ちをしていたのかと大いに訝しみながらも、トーマスは大人しく後部座席に身を預けた。

「ここに行って欲しいのだが」

meekly taking his place in the backseat.

"Here's the place I'm trying to get to."

The scrap of paper Thomas passed to the driver had nothing on it but the address he was headed for, but the white-haired, sunglassed man called out an agreeable "All right!" and, giving the wheel a spin to the right, suddenly set the car into motion. Watching out of the corner of his eye as the scenery streamed past the window, Thomas Iguchi surrendered himself to a comfortably moderated sense of relief. He folded his arms, leaned way back into the seat, and then, because his eyelids were growing heavier by the second, gradually began shutting out the visual world, maintaining all the while a rhythm of intermittent nasal inhalations. The white-haired, sunglassed driver went on humming in his northern European folk-song style, occasionally pausing to snort.

Roused from his slumber by a generous whiff of a slightly cloying floral fragrance, Thomas Iguchi dabbed with his left hand at a line of spittle that had dribbled from the corner of his mouth and was starting to dry there, at the same time taking out his wallet with his right hand. The driver had turned in his seat and was staring at him. The red light of the taxi meter's digital display cast a cloudy glow across one of the lenses of the man's sunglasses. The other lens reflected, if only very faintly, the image of a small bottle of what appeared to be some variety of air freshener. Thomas's eye landed on the driver's white-gloved left hand, which was delicately swinging a white handkerchief that had been scented with the stuff this way and that, back and forth. Quite a classy way to go about doing things, I must say, thought Thomas Iguchi with admiration, and held out a two-thousand-yen note to the man, telling him to keep the change. The time then was just a few seconds past 5:40.

The address to which Thomas Iguchi had come was a shop located along Route 13 that specialized in Japanese folk art. The store, a prefab structure that had been erected in one corner of a large rest area, was so run-down and miserable it was painful to look at, and had the sort of ambience that made it pretty damn difficult for a first-time visitor to go near it. Vines had been allowed to creep up the walls of the building until they covered almost all of it, but here and there patches of foliage

手渡した紙切れには目的地の住所だけしか記されていなかったが、黒眼鏡を掛けた白髪の運転手は「オーライ」と快諾の返事を口にし、ハンドルを右に切りながら車を急発進させた。車窓の風景が後方へ流れてゆく様を横目で眺めているうちに程好い安堵感を覚え、トーマス井口は腕組みをして背凭れに深く凭れ掛かり、次第に瞼が重くなってきたので間欠的な鼻呼吸の律動を維持しつつゆっくりと視界を閉ざしていった。白髪黒眼鏡の運転手は、ときおり涎を啜りながら北欧民謡調の鼻歌を唄い続けていた。

少々きつめのフローラルの香りをたっぷりと嗅がされて目を覚ましたトーマス井口は、口端から零れ出て乾きかけた状態の涎を左手の甲で拭いながら右手で財布を取り出した。こちらに振り向いている運転手の黒眼鏡の片側レンズには、デジタル表示された運賃の赤い光がぼんやりと映っている。そしてもう片側のレンズには、芳香剤らしき液体の入った小瓶の像が非常に朧げながら映り込んでいる。白手袋を嵌めた運転手の左手が染み付きのハンカチをゆらゆら揺らしている行為が目に留まり、随分とまた粋な計らいじゃないかと感心しながら、トーマス井口は二〇〇〇円札を差し出してやった。時刻は午後五時四〇分を回ったところだった。

トーマス井口がやって来たのは、国道13号線の沿道にある一軒の民芸品店だった。大きなドライブインの敷地内の一角に設けられたプレハブ造りのその店舗は痛ましいほどに寂れており、初訪問の旅行者からすればえらく近寄り難い雰囲気を醸し出している。店舗全体を覆い尽くさんばかりに伸び放題となった蔓草は生長がある段階に達した時点で建物から養分を吸い取られてしまったみたいに斑状に茶色く枯れており、辺りの空気も一段と乾き切っている。だが不思議なことに、この敷地は主に隣のドライブインのためにこそ整備されたものと考えるのが最も自然と思えるのだが、どういうわけかそちらの店はとうの昔に閉店してしまっているらしく、悉く窓

had withered and turned brown, as if at some stage in the vines' growth the shop had sucked up all their nutrients; the air around the shop was even drier than it was elsewhere. And yet oddly enough, considering that the lot on which the shop was located had most likely been created, by and large, in order to accommodate the adjacent rest stop, the stores in that rest stop all appeared to have shut down for some reason years ago, and not only were all the windowpanes broken but also the walls were covered from top to bottom with amazingly immodest graffiti; huge quantities of trash had been tossed in through the broken windows; and here and there one could even make out charred sections of wall that had clearly been set on fire. There were two cars in the parking lot, but one was little more than scrap metal, an adorable piece of junk. All of which is to say that the rest station was nothing but a ruin, plain and simple. The folk-art shop seemed, however—despite the great dilapidation of its exterior, which had gone so far it almost inspired terror—to be managing, for the time being, at least, to go about its business unharmed. Thomas Iguchi was suddenly overcome by a desire to pee, but he decided to hold it in.

"Yes, I think I grasp what's going on here. It's precisely because the shop is in this state, no doubt, that troves of treasure are here to be found. Come to think of it, I believe the guy said as much himself."

Without so much as a speck of hesitation, Thomas Iguchi opened the door of the shop specializing in Japanese folk art.

The store, which had an area of roughly ten square meters, was occupied by two customers who had arrived before Thomas. Though they were positioned in front of one of the showcases that lined the right-hand wall, they were simply standing there in a daze, straight-backed, paying no particular attention to the items being offered for sale. One of the two was a tall, lanky man with noticeably dark skin who looked to be in his late thirties; the other was a shabby, completely shriveled old woman who kept belching, puffing out, with each and every breath, carbon dioxide or some other substance containing traces of the stench of a decomposing body—the sort of woman, in short, who looked as if she already ought to be dead. The instant Thomas Iguchi walked into the store, these two—who, judging from appearances, could

ガラスが割られているだけでなく、外壁の到るところに破廉恥極まりない落書きが記されていて内部へ大量のゴミが投げ込まれており、所々に焼け焦げた跡すら見受けられる。駐車場には車が二台停められているが、そのうちの一台はスクラップ同然の可愛らしいポンコツ車だ。要するにここは廃墟以外の何ものでもありはしない、というわけだ。にもかかわらず、民芸品店の方は外観の荒廃が凄まじいまでに進んでいるとはいえ、一応は無事に営業を続けているようなのだ。トーマス井口は忽ち尿意を催してしまったものの、我慢することに決めた。

「つまりはこういうことなのだろう。逆にこんな店だからこそ、お宝がわんさと眠っている。確かあの男もそう言っていたな」トーマスは微塵も躊躇わずに、民芸品店のドアを開けた。

およそ一〇平米ほどの広さの店内には二人連れの先客がいた。右方の壁際に設置されたショーケースの前にいながら商品に目を向けるでもなくただぼさっと突っ立っている当の二人は、一人は三〇代後半くらいの年齢に見える浅黒い肌をした長身の優男で、もう一人はすっかり乾涸び切って呼吸の度に死臭まじりの炭酸ガスか何かでも吐き出しまくっている死に損ないみたいな見窄らしい態の老婆だった。親子関係に見て取れぬでもないその二人は、トーマス井口が店の中に入ってきた途端に揃ってカッと目を剥き、新来の客の容貌をしげしげと観察し出した。極端な度合いの非礼な洞察行為と受け取りはしたものの、トーマス井口は意に介さず、真っ直ぐに店内の最奥に位置する勘定台のほうへ歩み寄っていった。近付いてくるトーマスの姿を認めて、勘定台の向こう側にいる店番の若い男が椅子から立ち上がった。

「昨日の夕方に電話を掛けた者だが」

「何ですって?」

conceivably have been mother and son—suddenly flashed their eyes and set about making a long and careful inspection of the newcomer's visage. Although Thomas Iguchi regarded this observational activity as an instance of very discourteous behavior, he paid them no heed whatsoever, proceeding instead directly to the cash register, which was located all the way in the back of the store. Noticing Thomas's approach, the young clerk behind the counter rose from his seat.

"I called yesterday evening."

"Excuse me?"

"The item I called about, I mean, the one I had you set aside for me yesterday, the Tingly Blowfish. I'd like to have a look at it, first of all. Quickly."

The clerk muttered an understanding *"Whoaoh"* and gave two or three nods, then slowly squatted down and brought out a small box from behind the counter. Without skipping a beat, he went on to remove with fumbling fingers the lid of this box, which he then held up with both hands so that its contents were visible.

"This is it, right?"

Seeing that the tip he had gotten, from a customer at work, appeared to have been correct, Thomas Iguchi let a contented smile play across his lips. He had telephoned yesterday to confirm that the information was correct, it was true, but nevertheless he had taken a chance when he decided to accept the verity of the dragging, drawn-out yarn that the unmistakably untrustworthy regular had told him, and sure enough, he had been right to take that chance. This store was indeed selling the "dead stock" of the now extremely rare, old-style Tingly Blowfish. The question remained as to whether or not it was the right model, but when he flipped the box over, there was a label on the underside that read "Made in 1989." As it dawned on him that he had found the precise item he was looking for, Thomas's heart began to leap about wildly in his chest. The 1989 Tingly Blowfish, manufactured at the pinnacle of the bubble economy, continued to figure in tales widely circulated among adult toy aficionados, who viewed it as a miraculous gem of a product; it was the ultimate masturbation sleeve, and although Thomas had only recently started out as an adult toy collector, he was committed to

「だからあれだ、昨日のうちに取り置きしてもらっておいた『しびれふぐ』をまず直に見せて欲しいのさ」

店番の男は「はあん」と理解を示す一言を口にしてから二、三度頷き、徐にしゃがみ込んで勘定台の下から一つの小箱を取り出した。そして彼は引き続き、不器用な手付きで上蓋を開けて、中身が見えるように両手で箱を持ち上げてみせた。

「こちらで?」

仕事場で客から得た情報はどうやら正しかったようだと判り、トーマス井口はほくそ笑んだ。昨日の時点でここに電話を掛けて確かめておいたとはいえ、あのいかにも胡散臭い常連客の長話を試しに信用してみたのはやはり正解だったのだ。この店は確かに、今となっては極めて貴重な旧型「しびれふぐ」のデッドストックを商品として扱っている。

問題は年式だが、箱を裏返して見ると「89年製造」の表示があり、まさにこちらが求めていたものだったと知ってトーマスは甚だ胸が躍った。バブル絶頂期に生産された「89年型しびれふぐ」は、性具通の間でも奇跡の逸品として未だに広く語り継がれている、究極のオナホールマシンなのであり、駆け出しながら性具コレクターの道を歩み続けるトーマスは差し当たってこれを手に入れることを一つの大きな目標に据えていたのだ。むろんのこと、バイブレーション技術自体は二一世紀を迎えた今日における新商品の数々のほうが遥かに発達したものとなっており、複雑かつ微妙な振動の効果さえ味わい得るはずなのだが、しかしそれでもマニアに言わせれば、「89年型は時代を超越しており、要はあれくらいの、やや雑な動作とも感じ取れる程度の中途半端な震え具合のほうが実際の使用においては高い威力を発揮し、それと手動ポンプによる圧迫感が組み合わさるともはや生きた心地がしないような驚愕の恍惚感、恐ろ

following the path, and had made the acquisition of this item one of his major short-term objectives. It goes without saying that all these new products available today, now that we have arrived in the twenty-first century, make use of considerably more advanced vibration technologies; they are also much more user-friendly, allowing one to choose different levels, and—as if that weren't enough!—even allow the user to savor the effects of complex, subtle oscillations. And yet, regardless of these advantages, true fans have their own opinions. "The '89 model transcends its age," they insist, "because—and this is the heart of the matter—in actual usage situations, the imperfect, half-baked vibrations of this device, just enough out of joint that one senses a certain crudity in its movements, conveys a greater sense of authority, and when that feeling is combined with the pressure provided by the attached hand pump, well, the most accomplished virtuoso is bound, without fail, to be led into a flight of ecstasy so astonishing he can hardly keep his wits about him, into such raptures it's almost frightening."

"Yes, this is it. Wrap it up for me, will you? Make it quick."

Not bothering to suppress the signs of his delight, Thomas Iguchi communicated to the clerk his intention to purchase the item. At almost precisely the same moment that Thomas gave voice to this request, however, he heard the squeak of the shop's door swinging open, and with that, as though the sound had been some sort of signal, the clerk transferred his gaze to the newly arrived customer and froze. Thomas gave a cough, then tapped the counter with the tips of his fingers, but the clerk didn't turn back to continue serving him. Telling him to wait just a moment, the clerk set down the Tingly Blowfish box and turned to see first to the needs of the new customer.

"You get the point, huh? Sorry, kid, but could you move? I'm gonna need you to wait a bit."

Thomas Iguchi could certainly have insisted on his rights as an earlier customer, letting the clerk know in plain terms how outraged he was. The reason he didn't do so was that, casting a glance in the interloper's direction, he instantly understood that this man was not simply another run-of-the-mill customer, but one of those who lived his

しいほどの法悦の境地へとどんな兵であっても確実に導かれるだろう」というのだった。

「そう、これだ。さあ、包んでくれ。早めにな」

歓喜の色が露となるのを抑えることもせずに、トーマス井口は購入の意を店番の男に伝えた。ところが、トーマスの注文の声とほぼ同時に店のドアが開く音が聞こえてきて、それが合図にでもなったみたいに店番の視線は新客のほうへ向いたきり、固まってしまったのだ。トーマスは咳払いをして、さらに勘定台を指先でトントン叩いてみせたのだが店番の男は元の応対に戻ってはくれなかった。店番の男は、「少々お待ちください」と述べて

「しびれふぐ」の箱を手放すと、遅れて現れた客の相手を先に済まそうとした。

「まあそういうことだ。悪いが兄ちゃん、ちょっとそこどいて、待っててくれや」

トーマス井口が、ここで先客の権利を主張せず、店番の男に対して率直に慣れをぶつけることもしなかったのは、割り込んできたのが単なる客ではなく、裏社会に生きるその筋の者だと一見して悟ったからだ。目的はよく判らぬが、所場代でも取りに来たのだとすればものの数分で片は付くだろう、とトーマスは見通しを立てたのだ。

しかしながらトーマス井口の立てた見通しは、じつのところとんでもなく甘いものだった。その筋の者と店番の男との何やら不穏な気配を漂わす交渉は、何分経っても終わりそうになかった。さっさと言われた通りにされば良いものを、店番の男はなぜだか渋面をして相手の要求を頑なに聞き入れまいとしているふうなのだ。時刻は午後六時ちょうどを回ったばかりだが、最終の新幹線が出るまでにはまだ二時間以上あるとはいえ、このまま当てもなく放置されっぱなしの状態が続くのはまことに辛い。どうしたものかと気を揉んでいると、トーマスより先に来店していた例の二人組の男のほうが脇から話し掛けてきた。

life in the shady realms of the criminal underworld. Thomas wasn't quite sure why this man had come, but assuming it was to collect the "rent" or something along those lines, the matter could probably be settled, he estimated, in a matter of minutes.

It turned out, however, that Thomas Iguchi's appraisal of the situation was wildly, outrageously naïve. The negotiations between the shady individual and the clerk, which didn't appear to be going very smoothly, gave no sign of drawing to a close, and the minutes kept ticking by. The clerk should have gone ahead and done as he was told, not wasting a moment, but instead, for whatever reason, he appeared to be responding sulkily, stubbornly refusing to acquiesce to the man's demands. It was only just past six o'clock, and Thomas still had more than two hours before the last bullet train left, but even so it was sorely trying to be left hanging for so long like this, without any idea as to when the situation might change. He was turning over in his mind the question of what he ought to do when one-half of the pair of customers who had been in the store when he came in spoke at his side.

"Seems to be some sort of trouble, huh?"

"Yeah, looks that way. Just between you and me, it's a real pain, isn't it? Does this sort of thing happen often? Around here, I mean?"

"Can't say, I'm afraid. It's our first time here, too."

"Oh, really, you, too? You wouldn't know, then, would you . . . ?"

The man's attitude was cloyingly familiar, but because Thomas was feeling slightly uneasy at that moment, having come all alone to this unknown territory, he found it heartening to have someone standing by who could offer even a tidbit of sympathy. Having someone to chat and pass the time with also helped him relax.

The man said his name was Igarashi. He explained that he and the old woman with him were traveling the country; they had simply happened across this store and stopped in to take a look. Igarashi called the woman "Ms. Sumiko." Apparently sensing Thomas's curiosity about the nature of their relationship, he clarified: "You might say, I suppose," he said, "that it's my job to look after her." They were not, he added, related by blood. The two of them were planning to spend the night at one of the inns in Tendō Onsen, an area with lots of hot springs.

「何だかややこしいことになっちまってるみたいだね」

「まあね。ここだけの話だが、参っちゃうよね」

「さあね。うちらも初めてだから」

「あ、そうなの、なるほどね……」

馴れ馴れしい態度の男ではあったが、単独で見知らぬ土地にやって来ていささか不安な心境に陥っている最中のトーマスにしてみれば、ちょっとでも同情を寄せてくれる者が傍らにいてくれるのは心強く感じられた。さらには暇つぶしの話し相手が出来たことも、気分を楽にしてくれた。

男は五十嵐と名乗った。この店には旅の途中で立ち寄っただけであり、連れの老婆と車で全国を回っているところなのだと彼は説明した。五十嵐は老婆を「スミコさん」と呼んだ。トーマスが二人の間柄に強い関心を抱いているのを察したらしく、「言ってみりゃあ、僕はスミコさんのお世話係をやらせてもらっているのさ」などと五十嵐は説き、血縁関係を否定した。二人は今夜、天童温泉のとある旅館に宿泊する予定だという。

表の駐車場に停められている二台のうち、ポンコツのほうが五十嵐とスミコさんの乗ってきた車だと知らされて、トーマスはますます興味深い二人組だと思った。五十嵐はひどく気の好い印象を齎す人物であり、赤の他人の年寄りの世話係を自ら買って出るくらいの慈善家だけに、人一倍気が利く男でもあるようだった。スミコさんは比較的、手の掛かる老人らしく、正気を保つこと自体がもはや困難なほどに精神的衰弱が著しいながらも、大層傍若無人な面も併せ持っていて、実際過去に何人もの名うての介護士が匙を投げてしまったのだと五十嵐は、自分は介護士の資格を取得しているわけではないし、正直な話えらく大変そっと小声で打ち明けた。

Learning that, of the two cars he had seen in the parking lot out front, Igarashi and Ms. Sumiko had come in the piece of junk, Thomas began to feel an even deeper interest in the couple. Igarashi seemed an awfully pleasant sort of guy, and the fact that he had the charity of spirit to take responsibility, entirely of his own accord, for an aged woman in no way related to him suggested that he was a good deal more solicitous than most people. Ms. Sumiko seemed to require more attention than the average elderly person. Igarashi confessed, in subdued tones, that her mind had now so thoroughly deteriorated that it was quite a chore just to keep her in her normal state, and on top of that her behavior could be absolutely outrageous—it was so bad, in fact, that in the past a number of celebrated nurses had thrown in the towel and left. Igarashi didn't really have the qualifications to be a nurse, he said, and frankly he often found himself regretting that he'd taken on such an enormously demanding job, but on the other hand, nothing could ever compare to the tremendous sense of achievement he enjoyed at the end of each day, so he had never felt even the slightest, teeniest smidgen of a desire to leave her. Thomas Iguchi guessed that the only reason Igarashi could open up so candidly and unreservedly to a man of unknown provenance encountered purely by chance in a store he had happened upon randomly was that there were really all sorts of discontents pent up inside him, and he was aching to tell his story to someone, no matter who. Thomas gave the man a look that said, Don't worry, I understand, I see how you've suffered.

The shady individual and the clerk were still going at it, peppering their discussion from time to time with rough language and violent gestures. By now, Thomas was becoming seriously worried; he glanced down at his watch and checked the current hour: 6:26 P.M. There was still plenty of time before he needed to start his journey home, but he was a customer, after all, and he had made his intention to purchase the item abundantly clear—how could the clerk continue acting for so long as though he didn't even exist? This was a matter about which he simply could not remain silent. At long last, then, Thomas made up his mind to let the clerk know in no uncertain terms how displeased he was, and accordingly opened his mouth; but then, suddenly, precisely as he began

な仕事を引き受けちまったと後悔することもしばしばだが、たとえそうであっても一日ごとに得られる達成感た

るや何ものにも替え難く、逃げ出したいなどとはこれっぽっちも考えたことがないという。たまたま寄った店に

居合わせただけの素性も判らぬ者に対してこうもあっさりと明け透けになれるのは、きっと本心ではそれなりに

不満が鬱積しており、自身の現状について誰でもいいから話して聞かせてみたかったのだろうとトーマス井口は

推し量り、お前の苦労はちゃんと理解したぞと胸して伝えてやった。

　その筋の者と店番の男は依然として、ときおり荒っぽい言葉遣いや激しい身振りを交えながら話し合いを続け

ていた。トーマスはいよいよ真剣に心配になり、腕時計に目をやって現在時刻を確認してみた。午後六時二六分。

帰路に就くまでの猶予はまだ充分に残されているものの、商品購入の意思をはっきりと表明した客だというのに

こういつまでも無視を決め込まれると、さすがに彼も黙ってはいられなくなった。トーマスはついに意を決し、

苦情を言い立てるつもりで口を開いたのだが、声を出し掛けたところで出し抜けにスミコさんがウーウーと呻き

出したために出端を挫かれてしまい、途端に意気込みが萎えてしまった。スミコさんはしゃがみ込んでわなわな

と震え出してさえいたが、よくあることらしく、五十嵐は慌てる素振りもなく背負っていたリュックからいくつ

ものプラスチック容器と栄養ドリンク剤の瓶を取り出した。そして五十嵐は、「さあさあ、スミコさん、お薬で

すよ」と言って多量のカプセル薬やら丸薬やらをスミコさんの口内に無理矢理詰め込み、乱暴にもそこへ栄養ド

リンク剤を流し込んだ。無茶な光景を見せ付けられて、薬の種類が気になったトーマスは、五十嵐が届いた隙に、

ショーケースの上に置かれた数々のプラスチック容器を盗み見てみた。すると意外にも、それらは薬品ではない

ことが判明した。ビタミンCやらビタミンEやらビタミンBやら鉄分やらカルシウムやら亜鉛やらの、栄養補助

to speak, Ms. Sumiko started moaning, "*Oooo oooo*," nipping his plan in the bud and instantaneously causing his enthusiasm to wilt. Ms. Sumiko was now doubled over—her whole body was starting to shake—but evidently this was a very common occurrence, for Igarashi wasn't the slightest bit upset; he just took off the backpack he was carrying and extracted a number of plastic pill bottles and one-gulp energy drinks. "Here you go, Ms. Sumiko, here's your medicine!" trilled Igarashi as he commenced to shove large quantities of pills and capsules into Ms. Sumiko's mouth, and then he roughly dumped in the energy drinks. Confronted with this outrageous spectacle, Thomas found himself wondering just what all those medicines were, so he waited until Igarashi bent down and then sneaked a glance at the crowd of plastic pill bottles arrayed on the showcase. To his shock, he discovered that they weren't medicines at all. The pills Ms. Sumiko was being force-fed were, in fact, vitamin supplements: vitamin C, vitamin E, vitamin B, iron, calcium, zinc. And then, as if that weren't enough, she was being made to wash them all down with mouthfuls of energy drink! What with this and that, her burps continued for some time.

Perhaps I shouldn't really be posing such a personal question, but I wonder if you might not have some other reason for continuing to take care of the old woman, some hidden aim? Bet you'll profit from this somehow, won't you? By inheriting a large sum of money, for instance— is that it? Thomas, who, with the passage of time, had gradually begun to lose his composure, finally slipped and gave voice to the doubts that had been gathering at the back of his mind, catapulting them at Igarashi. The questions had been prompted, it was true, by his own frustration, but he had also been driven to ask by the curiosity he felt, the intensity of which had only continued to mount. Igarashi gave a subtle smile; Ms. Sumiko, who remained slumped over, had gone limp. Thomas didn't check his watch, but he had the feeling that it was about ten minutes before seven. He began to regret that he had asked such idiotic questions. And it was at that moment that, with no warning at all, Thomas Iguchi found himself compelled to confront one element of the truth of this world.

"No, Thomas, you're wrong about that. I'm not going to get any

食品の類いをスミコさんは与えられていたのだ。しかも栄養ドリンク剤と一緒に一気に呑み込むのを強要された

ものだから、スミコさんは以後しばらくの間ゲップを出し続けていた。

あえて立ち入ったことを訊くが、あんたがその婆さんの面倒を見るのを止めないのは、本当のところは何か、

裏の狙いがあるんじゃないのか？　あんたが得するようなことがさ、あるんじゃないのかい？　例えば多額の

遺産が入るとか、どうなんだい？

時間が経つに連れて徐々に心の余裕を失い出していたトーマスは、脳裏に

浮かんだ疑問をついそのままぽろりと五十嵐に投げ掛けてしまった。苛立ちから発した問いではあったが、高ま

る一方の好奇心に仕向けられていたこともまた確かだった。五十嵐は微笑み、スミコさんはしゃがみ込んだまま

ぐったりとしていた。時計は見なかったが、あと一〇分かそこらで午後七時を回る頃だろうと判ってはいた。馬

鹿なことを訊ねちまったと自省し掛けた矢先、トーマス井口は不意にこの世界の真実の一端と直面せねばならな

くなった。

「ヘイ、トーマス、そいつは違うな。彼女の世話をし続けたところで金になんかならないのさ。彼女は資産家

じゃないし、それどころか、外の車を見ただろ、むしろとんでもない貧乏人ってわけさ。だからこれは儲け話な

んかじゃない。全然違うんだ。本当にね。しかしだよ、僕は何もいわゆるボランティア精神ってやつを働かせて

彼女に付き添ってるわけでもない。じゃあなぜか。絶対に理由があるはずだって、君は睨んでるんだろ？　も

ちろんあるよ。とても素晴らしいことがね。じゃ言葉じゃ説明しにくいことがね。ただし金とかそういうんじゃない。全く異なる性質のものを得るこ

とが出来るんだ。言葉じゃ説明しにくいから、君には直に体験して、確かめてみて欲しい。今夜、僕らが泊まる

宿に来てくれれば、それを判ってもらえると思う。確実にね。じつを言えば、君と今日ここで会うのは予定され

money from taking care of her. She's not rich or anything—quite the contrary. I mean, you saw our car outside, didn't you? She's ridiculously poor, actually. So this isn't about monetary gain. It's not that at all. Really. On the other hand, I'm not sticking with her like this because I've got some sort of 'volunteer spirit' or something, either. So why am I doing this? As you see it, I've definitely got to have some kind of reason, right? Well, of course I do! And it's a great reason! It just isn't money or anything like that. Through what I'm doing now, I'm able to acquire something of a totally different nature. It's hard to explain using words, so I want you to experience it directly for yourself, to see what it's like. I think you'll understand if you come with us tonight to the inn where we're going to be staying. There's no question, in fact. The truth is, Thomas, our meeting here, on this day, was planned from the start. We lured you here to this shop as a first step, in other words, in order to invite you to enter our world. Isn't that right, everyone?"

As the man who said his name was Igarashi came to the end of this speech, the men who had played the clerk and the shady individual–type character, who had been facing each other across the counter, turned toward Thomas and nodded, grinning broadly. Realizing from the breeze at his back that at some point the shop's door had opened, Thomas spun around; there, standing in the doorway, was the fishy regular customer who had given him the tip that this folk-art shop had some of the old-style Tingly Blowfish in stock.

"Hey, Thomas! This is our present to you!"

Hearing a voice from over by the register this time, Thomas whirled back around in that direction just in time to see a single small box being tossed lightly up into the air. He instantly stretched out both arms to try to catch it, but he couldn't. Then, blocking Thomas's hands as he reached down to try to scoop it up, Igarashi brought his foot down mercilessly on the box, crushing it, and barked, "Don't worry! There's something better waiting for you, if you'll come join us in our bedroom tonight. . . ."

ていたことだったんだ。僕らの世界へお招きするために、まずはこの店に君を誘導したというわけさ。そうだね、諸君！」

五十嵐と名乗った男がそう述べると、勘定台を挟んで相対していた店番役とその筋の者風の人物が揃ってこちらへ顔を向けてきて、二人して笑顔で頷いてみせた。背後に風を感じ取り、いつの間にか店のドアが開いているのに気づいて振り向くと、この民芸品店に旧型「しびれふぐ」の在庫品があるとトーマスに教えたあの胡散臭い常連客が立っていた。

「ヘイ、トーマス！こいつは俺たちからのプレゼントだ！」

勘定台のほうから呼び掛けられ、今度はそちらへ振り返ると、一つの小箱がポーンと宙へ放り投げられて、トーマス井口は咄嗟に両手を差し出してそれを受け取ろうとしたが叶わなかった。トーマスが拾い上げようと手を伸ばしたのを遮りつつ、五十嵐は容赦なく小箱を踏み潰してからこう言い放ってきた。「大丈夫。今夜、僕らの寝床に来れば、もっと良いものがあるから……」

Where the Bowling Pins Stand

ボウリングピンの立つ所

Ishii Shinji

Translated by Michael Emmerich

Until about twenty years ago, the fishing industry had made this a bustling, prosperous town. These days it was rare for anyone to visit, except for a few tourists in the summer. There was a paved road that stretched out, tracing graceful curves, from the train station up at the hilly end of the peninsula. Each spring, clumps of daisies and dandelions peeked out of the rich black cracks in the asphalt.

Twice every hour, a bus made the trip from the station to the port. Most of the men who used to work the boats drove their own old-model cars around the area. They could never feel comfortable, either on land or at sea, unless they were at the wheel themselves. Each morning they would head off to their respective jobs—one man was a plumber, another painted houses—and in the evenings they would drive right back down the road from the top of the hill, sending up plumes of white exhaust like signal fires.

Very rarely would these former fishermen take the steering wheels in their hands after the sun went down. Every evening they would down glass after glass in the bar across from the port, as if there were a contest on, until they fell into a drunken stupor. Their wives, back at home, would go to bed early. Exactly five minutes before midnight every night, the bartender would put in a call to the taxi company. At ten past one, the men would all be shoved headfirst into the taxis' backseats, like bonito being tossed into the hold. When the bartender had cleaned the place and finished washing up, he would smoke a lone cigarette, and then, every night at one-thirty, he would switch off the light in the sign. The sign had a picture on it of a mermaid with flowing hair and shells covering her breasts.

The taxi company was about halfway between the station and the port. In times past, the taxis used to circle the whole peninsula, carrying foreign sailors and women, slicing through the wind that came off the sea.

Dull patches began to be noticeable on the black hoods of the taxis. Tight wads of stuffing pushed their way through cracks in the leather seats. Still, the taxis' interiors were always kept

二十年ほど前まで、その街は漁業で栄えていた。いまは夏の観光客以外、訪れるものも少ない。半島の高台に位置する鉄道駅から、なだらかなカーブを描き、舗装路がのびている。毎春、アスファルトの黒々とした裂け目に、ヒナギクやタンポポの群生がのぞく。

駅から港まで、路線バスが、一時間に三本ずつ走っている。地元では、もともと船員だった男たちのほとんどが、古い型の自家用車を運転した。陸でも海でも、みずから舵を握らずにいられないのだ。朝からほうほうの職場にでかけ（配管修理や塗装）、夕刻にはのろしのように白煙をあげながら、高台からの道をまっすぐにくだってくる。

1

日が沈むと元漁師の彼らは、滅多にハンドルを握らない。夜ごと港のバーで、競い合うかのようにグラスを干し、へべれけに酔っぱらう。女たちは家で、早々と寝てしまう。バーテンダーは毎晩正確に十二時五分前、タクシー会社の事務所へ電話をかける。午前一時十分、男たちはみな、カツオが船倉に投げこまれるように、タクシーの後部座席へと頭から押しこまれた。掃除と洗い物をすませたバーテンダーは、たばこを一本だけ吸い、毎晩一時半に、看板の灯りを消した。看板には貝を胸につけた長い髪の人魚が描かれてある。

駅と港のちょうど真ん中あたりに、そのタクシー会社はあった。往時は外国からの船乗りや女たちを乗せ、海風を切り、半島じゅうを巡ったものだった。

2

黒塗りのボンネットにはくすみが目立つようになった。革シートのひび割れからみっしりと中綿がはみでている。それでも、車内はいつも清潔に保たれ、仕事を終えた運転手たちは毎晩ていねいに車体を洗った。二十年前、この地方ではじめて蝶ネクタイを結んだのは彼である。キャバいころから洒落もので知られていた。社長は若

spotlessly clean, and each night when the drivers' shifts ended they would give the exteriors a careful scrubbing. The company president had been known ever since he was a young man as a bit of a dandy. Twenty years ago, he was the very first driver in the region to sport a bow tie. At first, everyone laughed and told him he looked like the emcee at a cabaret. Now the townspeople were so accustomed to the sight of those bow ties snappily fanning out from the drivers' collars that their presence seemed like the most natural thing in the world. They were true bow ties, not clip-ons, each one knotted by hand. Even before a new driver learned the lay of the land and the preferred driving routes, he would stand by himself before the mirror, practicing, over and over, tying the perfect knot.

It was 11:00 P.M. when the phone rang. The five drivers gathered in front of the television looked at one another.

"Kind of early, isn't it?" said a man (a former cook) with a white mustache.

"Bet it's a fight, or maybe someone cut his hand on a glass."

"Nah, he'd call an ambulance for that," said a young man with close-cropped hair (a former elementary-school teacher).

But the phone call wasn't from the bar, it was from an elderly woman who lived on a farm up at the top of the hill. Once again, the five men exchanged glances.

A tall, tight-lipped man got to his feet and took his cap from the peg.

"Hey, thanks for taking this one," said another driver.

The man nodded and quickly went out. Every once in a while the bar's customers would try to show off, passing out tips nearly double the fare. The president viewed this money as each driver's personal income. This was what they got in place of a bonus.

The black car sat just inside the garage door, crouching like a dog waiting for its master, gleaming under the illumination from the streetlight outside. The man gave it a quick once-over, then

レーの司会みたいだ、と当時は皆が笑った、いまでは、運転手たちの襟元でぴんと反りかえったボウタイは、街のひとびとの目に、当たり前のようになじんでいる。ピンで留めるのでない、それぞれが自前で、鏡の前でひとり、ボウタイのほんものタイである。新入りの運転手はまず、地勢や道順をおぼえるより先に、鏡の前でひとり、ボウタイの正確な結びかたを何度も何度も練習する。

午後十一時、事務所の電話が鳴った。五人の運転手はテレビの前で顔を見合わせた。

「ばかに早いな」

と白ひげの男（元コック）。

「けんかか、それとも誰か、グラスで手でも切ったろうかな」

「なら救急車を呼ぶでしょう」

と若い短髪（元小学校教諭）。

電話はバーからではなく、高台の農家に住む老婆からのものだった。バーの客は、ときどき見栄をはって運賃の倍近いチップをはずむ。社長はそれらをすべて運転手の取り分とみなしていた。いわば賞与のかわりである。

「悪いね」

別の運転手がいうと、男はうなずき、足早にでていった。無口な長身の男が立ち上がり、帽子かけから制帽をとった。五人はまた視線を交しあった。

ガレージの入り口で黒い車体は、街灯の光を受け、飼い主を待つ犬のようにうずくまっていた。男は素早く

eased into the driver's seat. High overhead, he heard the spring
wind sighing.

This driver was a veteran with seven years of experience; he had
every street in the region in his head. Spinning the wheel deftly, he
turned onto the farm road in just under five minutes without
having to stop once for a red light. The houses that dotted the deep
darkness were all enormous, each one like a castle standing guard
over its fields through the night. The driver slowed his car. He kept
moving along at a snail's pace, checking each house number as it
came. Eventually, a figure rose up in his headlights, standing
perfectly still, all alone, in front of a one-story house that stood
somewhat apart from the others. She was a startlingly diminutive
old woman. She held a small handbag, clasping it tightly in front
of her.

When she had climbed inside, resting her hand on the backseat
and stepping in carefully, one foot at a time, the driver asked
where she wanted to go. For a second, the old woman seemed
taken aback. Then, heaving a little sigh, she said, "Just over there."

"Just over where?"

"Just over there," she repeated.

And with that, the old woman began running her tongue
around the inside of her mouth, looking well pleased. A large mole
on her cheek rocked leisurely to and fro. The tight-lipped driver
began considering the possibilities, saying nothing. There was an
old folks' home called Maria House over to the west of the port, on
a bluff overlooking the open sea. At this hour the gate would be
long since closed, of course, but maybe that was . . .

"You mean Maria House, is that it?" the man asked,
emphasizing each word.

点検をすませ、運転席に滑りこんだ、春の風がぼうぼうと上空で鳴っている。

彼は七年目のベテランで、地元の道はすべて頭にはいっている。小気味よくハンドルをたぐり、一度も赤信号を待たず、五分足らずで農道にはいった。くろぐろとした闇に点在する家々は、どれも広大で、それぞれが夜の畑を守る砦のようだった。運転手は速度をゆるめた。住居表示を確認しながら、タクシーをのろのろと走らせていく。やがて、周囲の家並みから少しはなれた平屋の前で、ぽつねんと立ちつくす人影がライトに浮かんだ。驚くほど背の低い老婆だった。腰の前にちいさなハンドバッグを握っている。

後部シートに手をつき、一歩ずつ乗りこんできた彼女に、どちらまで、と運転手はきいた。老女は一瞬、驚いたような顔をした。そして、すう、と息をすると、

「あっち」

といった。

「あっちって?」

「あっち」

老女はくりかえすと、満足げに口のなかを舌でなめはじめた。頬の上の大きなほくろがゆったりと動いている。港の西側、外海に面した岩場に、『マリア荘』なる老人ホームが建っている。この時間、もちろん戸口はとうに閉められているだろうが、

「奥さん、あそこか、マリア荘かい?」

男は一語ずつ区切ってたずねてみた。

"Yes, that's right," the old woman replied serenely.

As they approached the shore, the westerly wind grew more forceful. The electric wires hummed like bowstrings; the hemp palms lining the street all bowed together, facing inland. The taxi swept up a slope, then descended. The lights of a vending machine passed in a streak into the background.

There was only a single light burning at Maria House, in a second-floor window. When the driver suggested that he walk the woman in, she gave a faint smile and refused, shaking her head a few times. She paid the fare and got out of the car. A gust of wind, hitting her from directly behind, caught a few loose strands of hair and sent them dancing up into the air. The old woman stood there perfectly still, bent at the hip, her head bowed, as he watched her recede into the distance in the rearview mirror. Finally her figure dissolved into the darkness's deeper recesses, and disappeared completely. The driver stepped on the gas and tapped on the wheel with his fingers. It was still early enough that he might get back in time to drive customers home from the bar.

Two days later, in the late afternoon, the same driver was summoned to the president's office. The president was wearing plaid pants and a blazer with gold buttons. He heaved a sigh, then looked down at his desk and unemotionally read out a woman's name.

"Did you give this lady a ride the day before yesterday?"

The driver wasn't sure what the president was talking about, but the name's vaguely old-fashioned air made him think of the old woman.

"I took an old woman from the end of the farm road up to Maria House."

"Ah." Suddenly the president raised his eyes. He looked more exhausted than the driver had ever seen him.

「そう」

　老婆はおだやかにこたえた。

　海辺に近づくにつれ、西からの風はいっそう強まってくる。電線は弦のように鳴り、シュロ並木は陸地へむけ、いっせいにかしいでいた。坂をのぼり、さらにくだる。自動販売機の灯りが背後へ流されていく。

　マリア荘の電灯は、二階の窓にひとつだけつけられていた。ついて行こうか、という運転手の申し出を、老婆はうっすらと笑み、何度か首をふって断った。料金を支払い、車外へ出る。さかまく海風がほつれ毛を真後ろから舞いあげている。バックミラーのなかで遠ざかっていく彼女は、腰をおり、じっと頭をさげたまま動かなかった。やがて暗闇の奥へ老婆の姿は溶けて消えた。運転手はハンドルを指で叩きながら、アクセルを踏みこんだ。

　今ならまだ、バーのお客たちの帰りに、なんとか間に合うかもしれない。

　二日後の夕方、運転手は社長室に呼びだされた。社長は格子縞のズボンに、金ボタンのブレザーをつけていた。一度吐息をつくと机をみおろし、かわいた声で、女性の名前を読みあげた。

「おとつい、このひとを乗せたかね」

　運転手はとまどいつつも、どこか古風なその響きから、あの老婆に思いあたった。

「農道の奥から、マリア荘まで、ばあさんをひとり乗せました」

「そうか」

　うつむけていた目をさっとあげる。いつになく疲れているようにみえる。

"Has something happened?" the driver asked.

"She jumped," the president said. "Apparently she threw herself into the ocean from the rocks on the west. Washed up on the beach this morning, over by the summer cottages. She had her wallet and a notebook in her bag. And a receipt from us, stuck in with the rest."

The driver said nothing.

"The police have contacted me." The president sighed, looking up. "I'm sorry about this, but you'll have to go talk to them. I'll have someone take over your shift today."

At the police station, the driver explained what he had seen, just as it had happened. The senior officer in charge of filing the report was a man with doleful eyes who held out an entire pack of cigarettes and asked if the driver wanted one, and when he declined, he offered him a cough drop. They were ginger-flavored, for people trying to quit smoking.

"Her house was nice and clean and she seems to have been in good health physically. . . . There's no indication why she did it."

"Did she have any family?"

"They're on their way. Seems they had a birthday party for her grandson just last month. They said she taught the kid cat's cradle." The officer shook his head. "Sometimes these things just come over you, I guess—you can never predict how someone's life will end, huh? Can't see a single step in front of you. Hey, how

「どうかしたんですか」

と運転手はたずねた。

「身投げだよ」

と社長はいった。

「西の磯から海へはいったらしい。今朝がた別荘地の浜へ打ちあがった。かばんに手帳やら財布やらがはいっていた。うちのレシートがはさまっていたんだ」

運転手は何もいわなかった。

「警察から問い合わせがきてる」

と社長はため息をついてみせた。

「申し訳ないが、いってきてくれ。今日の連番はだれかにまわすから」

警察署で運転手は、みたとおりのことを、ありのまま話した。調書係の巡査長は悲しげな目の男で、箱ごとたばこを勧め、相手が吸わないと知るや、今度はのど飴を勧めた。禁煙用のしょうが飴だった。

「家は片づいているし、からだはじょうぶだったようだし、まったく理由がわからんのだよ」

「ご家族は?」

「いまこっちへ向かってる。先月みなで孫の誕生会をしたそうだ。ばあさんはあやとりを教えたって」

巡査長は首をふって、

「魔がさすってのか、まったく人の一生ってのは、どんなふうに終わるか、一寸先もわからんもんだよ。なあ、

about another cough drop?"

When the driver got back to the office, he noticed an
unexpected face mixed in among those of his coworkers. The man
was an old hand they called Eltrut; he had left the company three
years ago to start driving a taxi on his own. He kept lifting the
elastic suspenders that he wore over his thin sweater, then letting
them snap back against his plump stomach. It was on an
introduction from Eltrut that the tight-lipped driver had gotten
this job seven years ago. Not only was the man unusually
knowledgeable about cars, but when he drank himself senseless
and flopped down on his back, he looked, as someone noted,
exactly like a flipped-over turtle. Ever since the similarity had
been noted, people had called him Eltrut.

"What's up, man, you look like shit!" Eltrut clicked his tongue
loudly. "You've got a face like someone doused you in bed with
gasoline!"

The driver with the white mustache was in the midst of telling a
story. It was something a driver from the next town over had told
him. It seems that last month, two sisters, both in junior high,
climbed into his cab. They told him their grandmother was dying,
and gave him the name of a famous hospital in the center of the
city. The highway was totally empty. The sisters sat in the backseat
holding hands, trembling all the way. When they reached the
hospital, the sisters told him they'd have to go get money from
their father, and darted inside the main entrance. The driver
waited a whole hour, but they never came back out. Apparently
that part of town isn't known only for the hospital; it's also a busy
shopping area where youngsters like to hang out.

So the next week, the very same driver picked up this lavishly
dressed woman. I'm afraid I don't have any money on me at the
moment, she announced majestically, but I assure you that if you
are good enough to drive me, I will not be unappreciative. The
driver hesitated, but finally he did set out, without reporting it to

飴をもうひと粒いかがかね」

事務所へ戻ると、同僚たちのなかに、意外な人物がまじっていた。三年前に退社し個人業をはじめた、通称メ
カさんと呼ばれる古参の運転手である。メカさんは薄いセーターの上でズボン吊りのゴムをのばし、丸い腹の上
でぱしぱしと弾いていた。無口な運転手は七年前、彼の紹介で現在の職に就いたのだ。機械にやたらくわしいだ
けでなく、酔いつぶれて仰向けに寝そべった姿が、ひっくり返したカメそっくりだ、というので、それ以来「メ
カ」と呼ばれるようになった。

「なんだよ、ひでえ顔だなあ」

メカさんは強く舌を打ち、

「寝床にガソリンまかれたみてえな顔してやがる」

白ひげの同僚が話している最中だった。隣り街の運転手にきいた話だが、先月、中学生の姉妹を乗せた。祖母
が危篤です、といって都心の有名な病院の名をいった。高速道路はがらすきだった。後部シートで姉妹は互いに
手をまわしずっとぶるぶるふるえていた。病院につくと、いま父から財布をもらってきます、そういって正面入
り口に駆けこんでいった。一時間待ってもふたりは戻らなかった。そのあたりは病院だけでなく、若者を集める
繁華街があることでも知られている。

また同じ運転手が翌週、豪勢に着飾った奥方を乗せた。いま持ち合わせがありません、と彼女は堂々といっ
た。けれど乗せていただければきっと悪いようにいたしません。運転手は躊躇したものの、結局会社には無届け

his company, for a town three hundred kilometers to the north. Half a day later, he pulled up in front of a compound so huge it could have been a temple. A long line of men, all dressed in black, stood along the wall. The second he stopped the car in front of the main gate, the men all bowed. An imposing elderly man who had been at the head of the line handed a packet wrapped in cloth through the window. When he opened it, he found two whole bundles of bills, seals unbroken.

"It's the truth, there are all kinds of passengers in this world," the driver said, stroking his mustache. "Who knows, maybe tomorrow one of you will pick up some incredible beauty, or maybe the king of some tropical paradise. Who knows, if he's in a good mood, maybe he'll give you a little island or something!"

The other drivers burst out laughing. But then, noticing that one of them had remained silent, they quickly shut their mouths. Someone flicked off the television. Another went to turn off the burner under the kettle, which had started boiling over.

"Hey, listen up," Eltrut said, sitting up in his seat. "There's absolutely nothing you can do about things that happen to your passengers, either before they get in your cab or after they leave it." His voice was deep and as rough as a file. "We're drivers here. It's our job to deliver our passengers safely to wherever they want to go. That's all we're responsible for. And you know what? For us to get all worked up about whatever may be going on in their lives— believe it or not, it's rude. You shouldn't do that. Not concerning ourselves with things that are none of our business, and not making passengers concerned—that's part of a driver's job."

Though he spoke brusquely, there was a forlorn air to Eltrut's expression. He looked like a child left all alone in a strange place. The drivers knew he was talking to all of them.

で三百キロ離れた北の街をめざした。半日後寺院のような屋敷の前にでた。黒服の男たちが塀に沿ってずらりと整列している。正門の前で停めた途端、男たちはいっせいに黙礼をした。先頭に立つ恰幅のいい老人が運転席の窓越しに布包みを手渡す。あけてみると封を切っていない札束がふたつはいっていた。

「この世には、いろんな客がいるもんさ」

と運転手はひげをさわりながらいった。

「お前も明日は、とびきりのべっぴんか、それとも南の国の王様かなんか、乗せるかもしれない。機嫌がよけりゃ、おまえに島一個ぐらい、わけてくれるかもしれないぞ」

同僚たちは声にだして笑うが、それでも黙っている運転手に気づき、みなすっと口をつぐむ。誰かがテレビを消した。ふきこぼれるやかんの火を止めに行く。

メカさんは座りなおし、口をひらいた。

「いいか、乗せる前と乗せたあと、お客がどんな目に遭おうが、おれたちにはどうしようもねえんだぞ」

太いやすりのようにざらついた声。

「おれたちは運転手だ。お客を目的の場所へ安全に運ぶのが仕事だ。それだけは責任をもってやらなくちゃならねえ。けどな、お客の事情を心配するってのは、かえって失礼なんだよ。やっちゃいけねえんだ。相手に余計な気をまわさせねえ、まわさせねえってことも、運転手の仕事には含まれてるんだよ」

口調とは裏腹に、メカさんの表情はさみしげだった。ひとり知らない場所に取り残されたこどものようだった。運転手たちには彼が自分たち全員に対し話していることがわかった。

"I . . ." said the tight-lipped driver. "I drove an old woman to the rocks. I took her there, right to the spot where she died. The woman . . . didn't say where she wanted to go."

"She didn't say?"

"No." The driver shook his head, just a little. "'Just over there,' that was all she said, nothing else. I'm the one who decided to take her to Maria House. If I hadn't taken her, she might have walked back into her house and gone to bed, just like always. Even if I didn't refuse to take her, if I'd just headed to the police station, this wouldn't have happened."

The other drivers listened, holding their breath.

"You seriously think so?" asked Eltrut. "I wonder if you'd have had the guts to tell her to get out of your cab. Could you have gone, totally on your own discretion, and turned a poor, bewildered old lady over to the police?"

The driver stood there, unable to reply. The telephone rang, and the woman who did the office work went off to answer it, her head down.

"Listen, I know you. You're a good driver. So good that if I needed a cab, I'd want you to be the one to drive me. You keep your car clean, you take good care of the brakes. You know all kinds of stuff about everything, but you don't go around blabbing

「おれは」

と無口な運転手がいった。

「ばあさんを磯まで連れていった。わざわざ死に場所まで。あのばあさんは、行き先をいわなかったんです」

「いわなかった?」

「はい」

運転手はかすかにうなずいた。

「あっち、とだけいって、あとは何にも。おれが勝手にマリア荘まで運んだんです。もしおれが行かなきゃ、家にもどって、ふつうに休んでたかもしれない。そうでなくても、警察署に向かってりゃ、こんなことにはならなかったはずです」

同僚たちは息をのんできいている。

「ほんとうにそう思うか?」

メカさんはたずねた。

「おまえにさ、乗車拒否なんてまねができるかね。頭のぼんやりしたばあさんを、勝手に警察へ引き渡したりできたってのか?」

運転手は立ったままこたえなかった。電話が鳴り、事務員の女性が背を丸めその場をはなれた。

「いいか、おれはおまえを知ってる。おまえはいい運転手だよ。おれが客だったなら、お前に乗っけてもらおうってくらい。車はきれいにしてるし、ブレーキはていねいだしな。なんでもよく知ってるくせに、自分ではペ

your head off about it. You realize, don't you, that everyone here thinks you're the best driver there is?"

All around, there were low murmurs of agreement: "Yeah." "Sure do." "It's true."

"At the very least, right at the end, that old woman got to meet a really, truly good guy. And she had the pleasure of a nice, smooth ride. I bet you she had a nice time while she was in the car. Maybe for a moment she actually forgot the things going on around her. You didn't take her to the wrong place. Those rocks were probably just the place where she needed to be. See? I'm telling you, when she told you where she wanted to go, you heard her right."

Eltrut left off there.

The driver, too, was silent.

Everyone remained standing in a cluster, mouths shut, imagining an old woman they had never met. Each person envisioned a different face, but every face was deeply lined with wrinkles, and every face was smiling.

After that, a group of the drivers who weren't on duty went off to a bowling alley at the edge of town. They could bowl until morning, and this was one of the few diversions available in the area for the taxi drivers who worked the night shift. The president of the taxi company was also vice president of the bowling club; once, as a young man, he had come in first in a regional championship. Company drivers could bowl all night at the special low rate for club members. Without their bow ties, the older drivers' faces seemed to age even more, and the young men's faces took on a childlike look.

Rollrollrollbang!

ラペラしゃべらない。知ってるか、ここにいるみんな、おまえのことを、最高の運転手だと思ってるんだぜ」

ああ、まあな、そうだな、などと低いつぶやき声が周囲でもれる。

「少なくとも最後の最後、ばあさんはいいやつに会ったんだ。それで、きもちのいい運転でドライブを楽しんだ。車に乗ってるあいだは、楽しかったろう。少しのあいだ、身の回りのことさえ忘れたかもしれない。おまえさんはな、まちがった場所へ運んだんじゃあない。あの磯できっと正しかった。ばあさんの行き先が、おまえにはちゃんときこえたんだよ」

メカさんは口をつぐんだ。

運転手も黙っていた。

みな口をとじ、その場に集ったまま、みも知らない老婆の姿を思い浮かべた。それぞれに、思い描いた相貌はちがっていたが、誰の頭にも、微笑みをたたえた皺まみれの顔しか浮かばなかった。

それから非番の運転手たちだけで、街はずれにあるボウリング場にでかけた。深夜勤務のタクシー運転手にとって、朝までプレイできるボウリングは、このあたりでは数少ない気晴らしとなっている。社長はクラブの副会長で、若いころ、地方大会で優勝したことがあった。運転手たちはクラブメンバーの格安料金でひと晩じゅう遊ぶことができた。ボウタイをはずした運転手たちは、年寄りならふだんより老けて、若いならいっそうおさなげな表情にみえた。

がたがたぴしゃん![11]

Rollrollrollbang!

The sounds of bowling balls careening down the lanes and sending the pins flying echoed loudly through the bright white building. The tight-lipped driver wasn't a very good bowler: on a good day, he might get two strikes in a game. The new driver with the close-cropped hair sent the ball gliding evenly down the alley every time. He chalked up two turkeys in his second game, leaving his fellow drivers dumbfounded. Eltrut sat at the scoring panel with a smirk on his face, drinking from a can of beer. He couldn't bowl. In his youth, as he was getting his car ready to go out one day, he had crushed his right thumb in the tire jack.

Rollrollrollbang!

A thin former fisherman got a spare.

Rollrollrollbang!

Again the tight-lipped driver's turn came. He slid his fingers into the holes and hurled the ball with all his might from the edge of the lane. The ball swerved off course and dropped into the gutter, having done nothing more than brush up against the tenpin.

"You throw 'em too hard!" the former teacher yelled gleefully.

Then the second ball. This time, three pins were left standing on either side.

"I'm a better driver, I guess." The tight-lipped driver directed a rueful smile at Eltrut, who was beaming at him. His score went up on the digital display above the lane. The numbers on the screen were all a digit shorter than those on a taxi meter.

がたがたぴしゃん！

ボウリング球がレーンを転がり、ピンを弾きとばす音が、白々とした場内に高く響く。無口な運転手の腕は、一ゲームに二度ストライクをとれれば上出来、といったくらいだった。短髪の新入りはたえず安定して球をすべらせた。二ゲーム目に、ターキーを二度記録し、同僚たちの度肝を抜いた。メカさんは記録席にすわり、にやにや笑いながら缶ビールを飲んでいる。彼はボウリングができない。若い頃、整備中に右手の親指をジャッキにつぶされたのである。

がたがたぴしゃん！

痩せた元漁師がスペアをとった。

がたがたぴしゃん！

また、無口な運転手の番がきた。穴に指をいれ、レーン際から思いきり投げつける。球はコースを逸れ、テンピンをかすめただけでガターの先へおちた。

「力はいりすぎ！」

元教諭が嬉しげに叫んだ。

二投目。今度は両サイドに三本ずつピンが残った。

「運転ほどはうまかないな」

笑いかけるメカさんに、運転手は苦笑をかえした。デジタル表示のスコアがレーンの上に表示される。それらの数字はどれも、タクシーの料金メーターよりひと桁少ない。

He sat down on the plastic seat and watched his coworkers bowl, taking small swigs from a can of juice. The jet-black ball glides leisurely down the lane, then slams into the orderly lines of pins, knocking them over in a single blow. The pins fly, they are swept from the lane, and once again identical pins are set out, in the same orderly arrangement. And then, noiselessly, the next ball approaches the new set of pins.

Rollrollrollbang!

Rollrollrollbang!

The taciturn driver seemed to feel something cold clenched in the pit of his stomach. He had a wife and a son who had just started elementary school. They would be taking their baths about now, or maybe watching television, in their apartment among all the rest in the white public-housing complex, under the jet-black sky. The westerly wind was raging tonight, once again. He felt as though he could actually hear the gusts rattling the windows at home, deep in his ears. The driver licked his dry lips.

Rollrollrollbang!

"A spare!"

The white-mustached driver snapped his fingers. Eltrut applauded, rallying just enough to be sociable. No thumb, right to the base. That last smile the old woman had given him. The violent waves surging in toward invisibly dark rocks, one after the other, from the edge of the blackest sea. The white pins are sucked away into the darkness beyond, and then, once again, from the other side, ten new pins appear, and are set out in defenseless rows.

Rollrollrollbang!

プラスティックの席につき、缶ジュースをすすりながら、同僚たちの投球をながめた。レーンをゆったりとすべっていき、整然とならんだピンをいっせいになぎ倒す、真っ黒いボール。ピンがはじけ、レーンから取り除かれると、あとにはまた同じようなピンが、整然とならぶ。そのピンへさらに、つぎのボールが音もなく近づいていく。

がたがたぴしゃん！

がたがたぴしゃん！

無口な運転手は腹の底に、冷えたなにかがきゅっとちぢこまるような感触をおぼえた。彼には妻と小学校にはいったばかりの息子がひとりいた。真っ黒い夜の下、白い公団アパートの一室で、いまごろは風呂だろうか、テレビを見ているかもしれない。今夜も西風ははげしく吹き荒れていた。かたかたと窓を揺らす風の音が、耳の奥にありありときこえてくるような気がした。運転手はかわききったくちびるをなめた。

がたがたぴしゃん！

「ダブルだ！」

白ひげの同僚が指を鳴らす。メカさんも愛想程度に、両手を叩いて喝采を贈っている。根元から失われた親指、老婆の最後に見せた笑み。真っ暗な磯にむかって、黒々とした海のはてから、つぎからつぎへと荒波が打ち寄せてくる。暗いあちら側へと白いピンが吸いこまれ、またそのあちら側から、新しいピンが十本あらわれ、無防備に並べられる。

がたがたぴしゃん！

"You okay?" Eltrut asked the driver when he stood up. "Bathroom?"

"No," the driver said. "I've got to make a quick call."

At the pay phone by the front desk, the tight-lipped driver punched in the number of his own apartment. It rang once, a second time, and on the third ring someone picked up.

"Hello?" the driver blurted out.

"Hey!" It was the boy's voice, eager and excited. They seemed to have a bad connection, because it sounded staticky. "Hey, Dad . . . is that you?"

"It's me." The tight-lipped driver heaved a deep sigh.

"What's wrong . . . Dad?"

Rollrollrollbang! He heard bowling sounds from the lanes.

"I'll be home soon," the driver said, leaning up against the wall,

「どうした？」

席を立った運転手にメカさんがいった。

「便所か？」

「いや」

と運転手はこたえた。

「ちょっと電話をかけてきます」

受付横のカード電話で、無口な運転手は自宅の番号を押した。一度、二度、三度目の呼び出し音のあと、相手が出た。運転手は早口でいった。

「もしもし」

「あ！」

はしゃいだ少年の声。電話線の不調のためか、とぎれがちにきこえてくる。

「父……さん？」

「ああ」

無口な運転手は深々とため息をついた。

「どうしたの……ねえ？」

がたがたぴしゃん！ボウリングの音がレーンのほうからこだまする。

「もうすぐに帰る」

his voice unusually loud. "I'll be back in half an hour. Tell that to Mom for me, okay?"

His son mumbled some sort of reply; he couldn't make out exactly what it was. It was as if his son were speaking through water, or from some very distant place.

The driver replaced the receiver and glanced toward the bowling lanes. Then he spun quickly on his heel, closed his fist around the bunch of keys in his pocket, and started walking toward the parking lot outside.

運転手は壁にもたれ、ふだんにない大声でいった。

「もう半時間もすれば帰るから。そう母さんにいっといておくれ」

息子の返事は、もぐもぐとくぐもり、はっきりとはききとれなかった。彼の声は、まるで水のなか、どこか遠い場所で話しているようにひびいた。

運転手は受話器を置いて、ボウリングレーンのほうを一度見やった。そして、すばやくきびすを返すと、ポケットの鍵束を握り、屋外駐車場をめざして足早に歩きだした。

Love Suicide at Kamaara

嘉間良心中

Yoshida Sueko

Translated by Yukie Ohta

1.

Kiyo was awakened by the sound of the lighter hitting the floor. She opened her eyes and saw a faint wisp of smoke drifting toward the sunlit ceiling. Glancing over at the other bed, she saw Sammy looking at her with a cigarette between his teeth. He must have been watching her sleep for some time. Kiyo rolled over and faced the wall. She knew he'd been getting an eyeful of her hair, which was starting to turn white at the roots, and at the lusterless nape of her bony neck. She felt painfully exposed and pulled the blanket up above her ears.

Sammy wanted to leave. Kiyo knew that. She could see it in the frown on his forehead and in the frightened look in his eyes when he regarded her. They were the eyes of someone whose heart was in turmoil. Above all, she could see it clearly in the fact that he had begun to hate sex with her.

Sammy wanted to go back to his unit. He'd grown tired of his life as a deserter, tormented by the unexpected boredom and daily humdrum. This was obvious from the listlessness of his speech, the irritation in his walk, and the occasional disgusted glances he threw at Kiyo. The MPs were not going to come looking for him. The police were not going to send out a fleet of patrol cars to track him down. He realized now that being a deserter was far more ordinary and tedious than he'd imagined, and that the daily monotony had become a hell for him.

When Sammy left, he would probably head straight for that drab little shed that was the front gate of Camp Courtney, the base where he'd been stationed. There, he would be arrested by the MPs and thrown into the stir cage. Yet even with what awaited him, there was no doubt he was going to leave.

一

ライターのゆかに落ちる音におこされた。目をあけると朝日のさしこんだ天井に薄い煙が流れている。隣りのベッドに目をやると、サミーが煙草をくわえたままこちらを見ている。さきほどからずっと寝顔を見つめていたらしい。キヨは寝返りを打って壁のほうに顔をむけた。根元から白くのび始めた髪の毛とつやのなくなった細い首筋がきっと彼の目いっぱいに広がり、曝されているだろう。つらい。キヨは毛布を耳の上までひきあげる。

サミーは出て行きたがっている。キヨにはそれがわかっている。彼の苛だった眉間に、キヨを見るときのおびえたような目付きにそれが現れている。心の中に動揺のある目なのだ。なによりもキヨとのいとなみをいやがり始めたことにそのことははっきりと出ている。

彼は部隊に帰りたがっている。脱走に飽きて帰りたがっている。 脱走生活の意外に平凡で退屈な日常に彼は苦しめられている。それは彼の力のない話しぶりに、苛だたしげな歩きかたに、ときおりキヨに投げるおぞましな目の光に現われていた。MPがパトカーを並べて走りまわるわけでもない。民警がしにくるわけでもない。無聊の日々は地獄になりかかっている。

彼は脱走というものが意外に日常的でひまなものであることに気づいている。

ここを出たら彼はおそらく彼の所属するキャンプ・コートニーのあの物置小屋のようなゲートにむかってまっすぐに歩いていくだろう。そしてそこでMPにつかまり、スターケージにぶちこまれるだろう。しかしそれでも彼は出ていくにちがいない——それでも。

She didn't know if it would be today or tomorrow or ten days from now, but one day soon he was going to get up and head straight for that little shed with the tin roof, and there was nothing she could do to stop him.

Kiyo heard Sammy get up to open the window. Bright light poured across the back of her neck, and she pulled the blanket up over her head.

He thinks he's headed me off.

Now she was angry. Sammy had again moved evasively so that he wouldn't have to touch her this morning, either. He seemed to dread even the possibility of contact with her.

The ashtray clanked softly, and then there was silence. Until only recently, Sammy would stub out his cigarette and slip into bed next to Kiyo. The squeaking in the ashtray had been a precursor of Sammy's coming, but somewhere along the line, that, too, had stopped happening.

From under the blanket Kiyo watched Sammy as he stood gazing out the window. His thin, pale neck disappeared into his disheveled hair, and his enormous ears almost seemed to be the end of it—the flesh branching, bursting abruptly out from either side of his head. Looking at those ears, she felt the loneliness of morning.

"Sammy."

"Yeah." He turned back to look at her.

それが明日になるか今日になるか、あるいは十日後になるかそんなことはわからない。が、ある日突然彼はおきあがり、あのブリキ屋根の小屋にむかって歩きだしていくだろう。そして彼女にそれを阻止することは出来ないのだ。

起きあがって窓を開ける気配がした。白い光が首筋に流れこんだ。キヨは毛布をひきあげて頭からかぶった。

（先手を打ったつもりなんだ）

腹立たしくなった。そのまま今朝も触わらずにすまそうと予防線を張っている。もうさわるのもいやになったらしい。

灰皿がかすかに鳴り、静かになった。ついちかごろまで煙草をもみ消すとすぐにキヨのわきにすべりこんで来たものだが——いわばきゅっ、きゅっ、となる灰皿のきしみはサミーの前ぶれだったが、いつのまにかそれも無くなった。

毛布のすき間からサミーの様子をうかがう。サミーは窓ごしに外を見ている。細い青白い首がほさほさになった髪の中に消え、それがふたつにわかれて頭の両がわから突然にとびだしたという感じの大きな耳に朝の侘しさがとまっている。

「サミー」

「おう」

サミーがふりかえった。

"Close the window and pull down the curtains. It's too bright."

Sammy got up, closed the window, and drew the curtains.

"Come here, Sammy."

Sammy stood at the side of the bed. Kiyo reached out with one arm and put her hand on his pants.

"What time did you get back last night?" she asked.

"I think it was around twelve, or maybe one."

"You went to sleep without taking off your pants?"

"Uh-huh. I couldn't be bothered."

Kiyo knew that Sammy had not come back until dawn, around five o'clock. "Where were you?"

"At Jim's. Jim Oblender's. I told you before, about the guy from my hometown in the air force here at Kadena."

"It's okay to hang out at your friend's house, but if you wander around outside too much, the MPs will catch you," she said.

As she spoke, she thought how strange the American military was. It had been almost half a year since he ran away from his unit, but they didn't seem to be looking for him. And Sammy didn't act like a deserter, casually walking around outside day and night, pretty much wherever he liked. If she hadn't seen it in the newspapers, she probably wouldn't have believed he was a deserter.

"Undo your belt."

Sammy did as she said, rattling his buckle as he unfastened his belt, and lowered his pants a bit so that Kiyo could slip her hand in

「窓をしめて、カーテンをひいて。まぶしいから」

サミーはおきあがって窓をしめ、カーテンをひいた。

「カム、サミー」

サミーはベッドの横に立った。キヨは手をのばしてズボンに手をかけた。

「夕べは何時ごろ帰ったの」

「十二時ごろかな、一時ごろだったかな」

「ズボンもとらないでそのまま寝たの」

「ああ、めんどくさかったからね」

キヨはサミーが明け方の五時ごろ帰ってきたことを知っている。

「どこへいってたの」

「ジムの所さ、ジム・オブレンダー。ほら同郷の奴でカデナに来ているって前にはなしたろう」[1]

「友達の所で話しこむのはいいけどさ、あんまり出歩くとMPにつかまわるわよ」

しゃべりながら、アメリカの軍隊というのは不思議なものだと思う。部隊をとび出してから半年にもなるというのに捜索をしているようすもない。サミーは脱走兵らしくもなく、昼も夜も殆ど自由といってもいいくらいに気軽に歩きまわっている。新聞ででも見ていなければ、脱走兵とは信じられないくらいであった。

「ベルトをはずして」

サミーはいわれるままにバックルの音をたててベルトをはずし、キヨの手が入りやすいようにズボンをすこし

easily. Kiyo took hold of Sammy from the opening in his olive-drab GI underwear.

"Come closer," she said.

As Sammy drew closer, Kiyo slipped his underwear down and pulled him out. She sat up and buried her face between the perspiring boy's legs. She licked him, then held him in her mouth. Once inside, Sammy got hard. Kiyo put her right hand around his back. With her left hand she slowly rubbed the skin around his navel and then lowered her hand to cup him where he was soft and rounded as she gently pushed upward. Sammy groaned faintly and fell on his back. Kiyo lay on her stomach, and as she buried her face at the base of his legs, Sammy grew so hard in the back of her throat that Kiyo felt he would push right through her.

The erect Sammy, his youthful vitality aroused inside Kiyo's mouth, trembled. He thrust himself upward with awesome power as if to penetrate Kiyo. This part of him was life itself, and when Kiyo held it in her mouth, her aged cells were restored, as if she were being rejuvenated. Injected with pure youth, she felt imbued, through her lips and her cheeks, with that young vigor. The powerful force that raged inside her mouth made her want to suck in this essence of life with all its youth and joy and make it her own. Kiyo's eyes glistened in the darkness as she engulfed Sammy.

Sammy's hands, grasping Kiyo's cheeks, tightened their grip. Kiyo was lifted up; she rolled over and found herself held down under him. As his wet life came pressing impatiently into her body, Sammy convulsed violently, and then it was over.

With both of her legs still pinned between Sammy's, Kiyo groped for the head of the bed. She lit a cigarette. Sammy's body jumped at the sound of the lighter, and his legs parted. Sammy turned over. Kiyo gazed fixedly at his profile, which was shaded from the bright light. Sammy's beard, to which he had not put a razor even once in the last half year, flowed from his chin onto his chest. Kiyo thought it heightened the sharpness of his chiseled

下におろした。キヨは軍隊の草色の下着の隙間からサミーをにぎった。

「カム」

サミーがよると、キヨは下着をずらしてサミーをひき出した。上半身をおこして汗ばんだ少年の股間に顔をうめた。舌でねぶり、口に含む。口の中でサミーがふくれあがった。背中に右手を回した。左手でゆっくりとへそのあたりをさする。そのまま手のひらをずらせて柔らかい丸まったところをおしつつみ、軽く押しあげる。サミーがうっ、と小さくうめき、仰向けに倒れた。腹ばいになってサミーの両の足のつけ根に顔を埋めた。喉の奥のサミーに突き抜けるような力がこもった。

ふくれあがったサミーが、若い生命が口の中で弾み、震える。キヨをさし貫こうと恐ろしい力で突きあげてくる。それは生命そのものであり、それを含むとき、キヨは自分の中の老いた細胞が、若い生命に出会い蘇生され、再生されていくような気がする。若さそのものを注入されて口許から、両頬から、みるみる若さに染まっていくような気がする。口の中を強靭な生命があばれる。生命そのものを若さもろとも、歓びもろとも吸いとって自分のものにしたい。キヨは暗がりの中で目を光らせ、サミーを吸いこむ。

両頬を押さえていたサミーの手に力が加わりキヨは上にひきあげられ、そのまま寝返りを打つようにしてサミーの下に押さえこまれた。濡れた生命がせっかちにからだの中にとびこんで来て、激しく痙攣し、果てた。

両足をサミーの股間にあずけたままキヨは枕元をさぐった。煙草に火をつけた。ライターの音でサミーのからだがぴくりと動き、足がほぐれた。サミーは寝返りを打った。キヨは白い光にくまどられたサミーの横顔を見つめる。この半年の間一度もカミソリをあてたことのないひげが、あごから胸もとにかけて流れている。くっきり

features and made his tall face look smaller. He looked exactly like the picture she had once seen of a crucified Christ. After Kiyo lit the cigarette, she pushed it between Sammy's lips.

2.

While showering, Kiyo wondered absentmindedly what she would do all day. Her money had run out. Not one yen left. Until yesterday, she'd had about two thousand yen, but she'd spent it last night at a nearby supermarket to buy three bottles of beer for Sammy, potato chips to snack on, and bread for breakfast. Now the two thousand yen was all gone, and this morning she was broke.

Kiyo stood in front of the mirror, wiping herself dry with a small towel. Her face was discolored and bloated, perhaps from lack of sleep. It was a loathsome face. Her neck had become even scrawnier recently. Not only was it thinner, but it had also lost its color. The yellow, wrinkled skin clinging to her neck hung down, detached from the muscle, sagging lifelessly. A trace of her youthful past remained in her thin arms, but veins floated on the backs of her hands, and her yellowed palms were pitiful. Her chest, too, was bony, having lost its glow, and her flabby belly was covered with fine wrinkles. She was acutely aware that she was no longer young, which made her feel even uglier. Looking in the mirror, she carefully applied her makeup. The least she could do was to look as young as possible, for Sammy's sake. She couldn't let this Adonis of hers, who seemed to have slipped out of a Greek myth, know the hideousness of her old age.

鼻すじの通った面長の顔がのばしたひげのせいで小さくしまって見える。それは昔絵で見た十字架の上のキリストそっくりに見える。キヨは煙草に火をつけるとサミーの唇に押しこんだ。

二

シャワーに打たれながら、今日一日どうしようかとぼんやり考えた。金がなくなった。一銭もなくなった。昨日まではそれでも二千円ぐらいはあったのである。それが昨夜ちかくのスーパーでサミーのためにビールを三本買い、つまみのポテトチップと朝食のパンを買うと、二千円がきれいに消えた。今朝からはもう一銭もない。

小さなタオルでからだを拭きながら鏡の前に立った。寝不足のせいか顔が黒くむくんでいる。いやな顔だ。首がまた細くなった。細くなっただけでなく、皮膚に色艶がない。薄い小じわに覆われた黄色い皮膚は筋肉と分離して力なくたるみ、首のまわりにはりついている。細い両腕はかつての名残りをとどめているが手首の甲に静脈が浮き、手のひらの黄ばんでいるのがなさけない。胸元もうすくつやを失った。柔らかすぎる下腹部はいっぱいこじわに覆われている。もう若くはないという明確な自覚があって、それが一層自分を醜いと思わせる作用をしているようだ。

鏡にむかってキヨは念入りに化粧する。サミーにすこしでも若く見せなくては。あのギリシャ神話の中から抜け出て来たような美少年に、におい立つ老醜を感じさせてはならなかった。

She opened her dresser and changed into a two-piece outfit. Sammy was still in bed, now fast asleep.

It was drizzling when she stepped outside. She thought about going back to the apartment for an umbrella but suddenly felt anxious and changed her mind. Sammy might be awakened by the sound of the door opening, and if he woke up, he might leave and never come back. So Kiyo gave up on the umbrella and set out across the sidewalk of the neighboring vacant lot. She walked slowly at first, and as she walked, she thought of Sammy.

They had met at Pinocchio Burger, in the shadows where she always stood. As usual, she was there propositioning customers. Soldiers would float up like bubbles from beside the bottle palm trees on B.C. Street and stand in front of the small counter. After being handed their hot dog or hamburger wrapped in a napkin, they would stand there and begin chomping on it. Kiyo would watch them from the shadows. When they finished eating, they would wipe their mouths with the napkin, throw it in the trash, and begin heading back into the sea of lights.

"Hey."

It was at that moment that she'd call out. A soldier would come over, usually look at Kiyo's face and body, then start walking away in disgust. At that point, she would yell out "Ten dollars" as

洋服ダンスを開いてツーピースに着替えた。サミーはまだベッドの中でねむりこけている。

外に出ると小雨が降っていた。部屋にもどって傘をとって来ようかと思った。が、不安になってやめた。ドアを開ける音で目をさますかもしれない。目をさましたら、出て行ってそのままもどって来ないかもしれない。傘をあきらめてキヨはアスファルトの露地に出た。そのままゆっくりと歩き出す。歩きながらサミーの事を考える。

サミーと知り合ったのはいつものピノキオ・ハンバーガーの暗がりだった。そこでいつものようにキヨは客をひいていた。

兵隊たちがセンター通りのトックリやしの横からあぶくのように浮かびあがってきては小さなカウンターの前に立つ。ナプキンにくるまれたホットドッグかハンバーガーを受けとると立ったままぱくつき始める。食べ終わるとナプキンで口をふき、トレイシに投げ入れて光の海の中にもどろうとする。そこをねらって

「ヘーイ」

声をかける。兵隊が近づいてくる。たいていキヨの顔やからだつきを見て呆れたようにもどりかけるのだが、

「テン・ダーラ」

そこをねらって

cheerfully as she could. Ten dollars was less than half the market price, so a soldier short of cash would stop in his tracks. Kiyo would then rush over and grab hold of his right arm. This required considerable skill. If she was too quick, she would be brushed off, and if she was too slow, he would escape. It was all in the timing, and at first, before she had it down, she lost many customers.

It was close to midnight when Sammy appeared, around the time Kiyo was beginning to think about going home. As she emerged from the shadows and glanced up, she saw a slender soldier standing at the counter. Kiyo paused, thinking he would be the last one tonight. When the soldier had finished eating his hot dog, he began walking over to Kiyo. He looked young enough to be in high school.

"Ten dollars," Kiyo said to him.

"Five dollars," the young soldier quickly replied.

Does he really think he can have a woman for as little as a thousand yen?

Kiyo's anger was mollified somewhat by his innocent, childlike face. She had a weakness for pretty, young boys. But even so, she would not usually have been so taken by a boy's looks to have agreed to five dollars. It wasn't until they got back to her apartment that she realized what an unspoiled Adonis this boy really was.

That night Kiyo had been standing in the shadows of the hot dog stand for nearly two hours and was exhausted. All she'd wanted was to sit down somewhere. She would even have agreed to go for free just to be tucked into a warm bed with a man. It was just when she'd begun to feel this strange sense of disheartenment that Sammy appeared. He was by himself. It was

思いきり陽気に叫ぶ。十ドルは市価の半値以下だから金のない兵隊がもどりかけた足をとめる。とんでいって

キヨは右腕を押さえる。これには相当の技術が必要で早過ぎるとふり払われるし、遅過ぎると逃げられてしまう。

タイミングというもので最初のころはこれがつかめず苦労した。

サミーが現れたのは午前零時近かった。そろそろ帰ろうかと思案し始めたころだった。暗がりを離れかけて、

ひょいと目をあげるとカウンターの前に兵隊の細い姿が立っていた。キヨはこれが最後だと思って行きかけた足

をとめた。兵隊はホットドッグをたべ終わるとキヨにむかって歩いて来た。まるで高校生のような少年兵だった。

「テン・ダーラ」

キヨは声をかけた。

「ファイブ・ダーラ」

少年兵がすぐに答えた。

（たった千円ぽっちりで女が抱けると思っているのかい）

キヨは腹が立った。が、まだあどけなさの抜けきらぬ幼い顔になんとなく気持ちが和んだ。キヨは年下の美少

年に魅かれるくせがある。といってもその時も少年の美貌にひかれて五ドルでOKしたわけではなかった。少年

が初々しいばかりの美少年だということがわかったのはアパートに入ってからだ。

キヨはもう二時間ちかくもホットドッグ屋の暗がりに立ちつくして、いいかげん疲れていたのだ。どこかで腰

がおろしたかった。出来ることなら、もうただでもいいから暖かいふとんの中に男と一緒にくるまっていたかっ

た。そんなふうに妙に気持ちが萎え始めたときにサミーが現れたのだった。サミーはひとりだった。この時間に

rare for a soldier to be walking alone at that hour.

Passing the hotel on B.C. Street, Kiyo brought Sammy to the Kamaara Apartments. When they entered her apartment, she stuck out her hand and said, "Five dollars."

Sammy reached into his pants pocket, took out a frayed five-dollar bill, and placed it in Kiyo's palm.

"You sure you don't have any more?" she asked.

"Really. This is all I've got left."

"Then how are you going to afford a taxi back?"

"I'm not going back to my quarters."

"What do you mean . . . not going back?"

"I've deserted."

"Well, well."

Kiyo gazed at the boy. A fringe of chestnut-colored hair covered his forehead, below which his thin face was smiling nervously.

"Which base are you from?" she asked.

"Camp Courtney."

"A Marine."

"Uh-huh."

兵隊がひとり歩きするのは珍しい。

センター通りのホテルの前を素通りして嘉間良のアパートにつれて来た。部屋に入ると

「ファイブ・ダーラ」

と手を出した。

サミーはズボンのポケットからよれよれの五ドル紙幣を出すとキヨの手のひらにのせた。

「ほんとにもうないの」

「ほんとうだ。これが最後のお金なんだ」

「それじゃ、帰りのタクシーはどうするの」

「おれはコーター（兵舎）にはもう帰らない」

「帰らないって……どういう意味なの」

「おれは脱走兵なんだ」

「まあ」

キヨは少年の顔を見つめた。栗色の毛髪のひたいに乱れた細い顔が心もとなげに笑っていた。

「キャンプはどこなの」

「コートニー」

「マリン兵ね」

「そうだ」

"What are you planning to do now?"

"Earn some money and go up to the main island."

"To Honshū, the main island of Japan?"

"Yeah, from Honshū I'm thinking of going over to North Korea or the Soviet Union."

"You must be kidding!" Kiyo raised her voice but did not return the money.

After taking a shower, Kiyo approached the bed. The young soldier, his shoulders bared, looked out from beneath the sheets, as if watching to see what she would do. Their eyes met. He hurriedly averted his gaze. At that moment Kiyo felt a heart-wrenching sorrow. In spite of herself, she was overcome with the irresistible urge to embrace him and hold him close to her. It might also have had something to do with the way the light from the lamp struck it, but the boy's face filled Kiyo with a strange sense of pity that awakened her maternal instincts. His gray eyes, though radiating a mysterious quietude, showed fear.

Kiyo got in next to Sammy. He clung to her tightly. Kiyo felt the boy tremble as he clutched at her breasts. When she reached out her arm and put her hand between his legs, he pulled his hips away in surprise. Sammy had never been with a woman. Kiyo suddenly turned toward him and pushed the timid Sammy inside her. Sammy's face contorted, and before she knew it, he had finished and become dead weight on top of her.

That night Kiyo let Sammy, who had nowhere to go, stay in her apartment. The next morning he left with no particular destination in mind. The following day, there was a small item in the newspaper about him. Kiyo read it on the second floor of the beauty parlor.

「脱走してどうしようというの」

「お金を作ってホンシューに渡る」

「本州に?」

「ホンシューから北朝鮮かソ連にでもいこうかと思っている」

「あきれた!」

キヨは声をあげたが、お金は返さなかった。

シャワーをあびてベッドにちかづくと少年兵が肩さきをのぞかせてシーツのかげからうかがうようにこちらを見ていた。目が合った。あわてたように視線をそらした。瞬間、キヨは胸をかきむしられるような切なさを感じた。思わず抱きしめて頬ずりしたくなるような衝動にかられた。スタンドの光の具合もあったろうが、少年の顔は、キヨの母性本能をくすぐらずにはおかない不思議な可憐さを湛えていた。不思議な静けさを湛えた灰色の目がおびえていた。

キヨはサミーと並んだ。サミーがしがみついて来た。キヨは少年が自分の乳房をにぎったままふるえているのを感じた。手をのばして股間に手をやると、びくっと腰をひいた。サミーは女を知らなかった。キヨはまだ開ききらぬサミーを思いきりむいて自分の中におしこんだ。サミーは顔をゆがめ、あっというまに果ててキヨの上で重くなった。

その夜行くあてがないというサミーをキヨはアパートに泊めた。翌朝になるとどこへともなく出て行った。キヨはその記事をパーマ屋の二階で読んだ。

二日めにサミーのことが新聞に小さくのった。

MARINE AT CAMP COURTNEY STABS SERGEANT AND FLEES

Only a few lines in a small article, but Kiyo knew right away that it was Sammy.

A Camp Courtney Marine, Private First Class (age 18), got into an argument in the training area at Camp Hansen with his platoon leader, Sergeant John W. Anderson, over a minor matter, stabbed the sergeant in the abdomen with his bayonet, and fled. It is expected that Sergeant Anderson, who is seriously injured, will need one month to recover. The Marines have obtained the assistance of local police, and are investigating the boy's whereabouts.

Kiyo wasn't afraid of having slept with a person who would stab someone. She thought Sammy must have been seriously provoked to do such a thing. In the past twenty years, Kiyo had witnessed many brutal acts among the soldiers. She had even seen a man shot to death right in front of her, so a mere stabbing didn't frighten her in the least.

When Kiyo had finished getting her hair dyed and walked back to her apartment, Sammy was sitting on the front steps. He laughed weakly when he saw her, his face heavy with fatigue.

"Hi," she said.

"Hi."

Kiyo sat down next to him. His collar smelled of sweat.

"Where did you go?" she asked.

"Isabama."

"Isabama?"

「上官を刺して脱走キャンプ・コートニーの海兵隊員」

　記事は小さく地味な扱いだったがキヨにはすぐにサミーのことだとわかった。

「……キャンプ・コートニー所属の海兵隊員A一等兵（18）は七日キャンプ・ハンセンの演習場でささいなことから上官のジョン・W・アンダーソン軍曹と口論となり、もっていた銃剣で同軍曹の腹部を刺して逃走した。アンダーソン軍曹は一カ月の重傷。海兵隊では県警の協力を得て少年の行方を追っている……」

　人を刺すような人間と寝たという恐怖はまったくなかった。人を刺すというからにはよっぽど腹に据えかねたことがあったのだろうと思った。この二十年のあいだにキヨは兵隊同士の血なまぐさい傷害事件を幾度となく見て来ている。目の前で射殺されるのを目撃したことさえある。単純な刺傷事件などキヨはすこしもこわくなかった。

　ヘアーダイを終えてアパートにもどると、入口の階段にサミーが腰をおろしていた。キヨの顔を見ると弱々しく笑った。疲労のにじみ出た顔だった。

「ハーイ」

「ハーイ」

「どこに行ってたの」

「イサバマ」

「イサバマに？」

　キヨは並んで腰をおろした。襟元から汗がにおった。

"A guy from my hometown, Jim MacGuire, lives there, so I went over to his place. But I got thrown out."

"You were in the newspaper," she said.

"In the newspaper?" Sammy's lips trembled slightly.

"You stabbed your sergeant?"

"Just nicked him. He's not going to die or anything."

"They say it'll take him a month to recover."

"It was his fault, I—"

"It's okay, you don't have to tell me why. But if you stay out here, you'll get caught."

"Yeah, well . . ." Sammy's face was turning red. "Can you put me up for a while, two or three days?" Just until the money from his mother in the States arrives at MacGuire's place, he added.

Kiyo gazed at the boy's face, and Sammy blushed. Kiyo remembered his expression from that first time when she had turned toward him and pushed him inside her, and now she was getting hot. The sensation of the boy's trembling filled her entire body. The feel of his round, firm buttocks returned to the palms of her hands. That night Kiyo had held the boy down while he lay dead asleep and devoured him until there was nothing left. His response had been weak. As she had rolled around in bed realizing how wonderful intercourse between a man and a woman could be,

「あそこに同郷のジム・マクガイアという奴がいてね、そこにいたんだが、追い出されちゃった」

「新聞に出ていたわよ」

「新聞に?」

サミーの唇がすこし震えた。

「あんた、サージャンを刺したんだって?」

「かるくね、死にゃしない」

「一ヵ月の重傷だったってよ」

「奴が悪かったんだ、おれは……」

「いいわよ、理由なんかきかなくたって。それより、こんなところをうろうろしているとつかまっちゃうわよ」

「それなんだ」

サミーは顔を赤らめた。

「しばらく、いや、二、三日アパートにおいてくれないか」

スティツのオフクロからマクガイアの所に金が届くまでさ、とつけ加えた。[7]

キヨは少年の顔を見た。キヨにみつめられてサミーは顔を赤くした。キヨはサミーをむいて自分の中に押しこんだときの表情をおもいだして、からだが熱くなった。少年の震えが全身によみがえった。丸い固いお尻の感触が手のひらによみがえった。あの夜キヨは死んだように眠りこけている少年を押さえこみ、むさぼりつくした。少年の手ごたえは弱かった。キヨはベッドの中をころがりながら男と女のまぐわいというものがこうもいと

she held Sammy's head in her arms and cried. She'd never been so thankful to be in the business of selling her body. It was her line of work that had made this experience possible. Otherwise, she would never have had the chance to be held by a man like Sammy, not even in three lifetimes.

Kiyo stood up, opened the apartment door, and called out to him from behind as he sat on the steps. "It's okay, Sammy. It can't be forever, but you can stay here."

The next day Kiyo got up around eleven o'clock. As she was brushing her teeth, the doorbell rang furiously. She looked out through the peephole and saw a police officer.

Here they come.

It was the same officer from the Goya police box she'd often seen on B.C. Street. She wondered how he knew to come here. After shaking Sammy awake, she helped him escape through the window, then opened the door.

"Excuse me," said the officer as he removed his hat and looked around the room.

"What can I do for you?" Kiyo was still holding her toothbrush as she looked up at the young officer.

"Are you Yafuso Kiyo?" he asked.

"Yes. . . . What can I do for you?"

"Actually, we're searching for a marine deserter. Do you happen to know where he is?"

しいものだったかとサミーの頭を抱いて泣いた。あの時ほどからだを売るという商売に入ったことに感謝したこ

とはなかった。それもこれもからだを売る商売をしていたればこそのことである。こんな商売でもしていない限

り生涯を三度重ねたってサミーのような男に抱いて貰える機会などあるものか。

「いいわサミー、いつまでもというわけにはいかないけど、家にいなさいな」

キヨは立ちあがってアパートのドアをあけるとサミーの背中に声をかけた。

翌日十一時ごろおきだして歯を磨いていると激しくドアが鳴った。防犯用の小窓からのぞくと警官が立ってい

た。

（来たな）

と思った。センター通りでよくみかける胡屋交番の巡査であった。それにしてもどうしてここがわかったのだ

ろう。キヨはサミーをたたきおこして窓から逃がし、ドアをあけた。

「や、どうも」

と警官は帽子をとり、部屋をのぞいた。

「何かご用ですか」

キヨは歯ブラシをにぎったまま若い巡査を見上げた。

「屋富祖キヨさんですね」

「そうですが……。何かご用ですか」

「実はマリンの脱走兵を探しているんですがね、心あたりはありませんか」

The officer got right to the point.

"So why did you come all the way over to my place?"

"To tell you the truth, an employee at Pinocchio Burger said he saw someone fitting his description. As you know, that's the most popular gathering place for soldiers. The employee said he saw you heading for Kamaara with him. Do you know where he is?"

"When was this?" Kiyo asked, playing innocent.

"Three nights ago . . ."

"What does he look like?"

"He's still a boy, Caucasian. Marine private first class . . ." The officer described Sammy's features, adding that it was a particularly brutal crime for someone his age. He explained that this information came from the investigation request issued by the Marines.

"Well, I did meet a soldier in front of Pinocchio, but the description doesn't fit," Kiyo said, still playing innocent. "His hair wasn't blond, but golden, and I think he must have been at least twenty-four or twenty-five. You'd better talk to that Pinocchio employee again."

"I see. Well, that's all I needed to ask you." The officer laughed

いきなり巡査は正面からきりだした。

「どうしてわたしのところにわざわざ?」

「実はピノキオ・ハンバーガーの店員がそれらしい兵隊を見ておりましてね、ご存知の通りあそこは兵隊が一番よく集まるところでして。そこの店員が、あんたがその兵隊と一緒に嘉間良の方に行くのを見たというんです。心あたりがありますか」

「いつのことですか?」

キヨはとぼけた。

「さきおとといの晩ですが……」

「どんな兵隊です?」

「まだ子供なんですがねえ、白人の。海兵隊の一等兵で……」

巡査はサミーの特徴を説明した。年に似合わぬ凶悪犯だとつけ加えた。海兵隊からの捜査依頼にそのように書いてあるといった。

「そうねえ、ピノキオの前で兵隊と知り合ったのは事実だけど、特徴が一致しないわねえ」

キヨはまたとぼけた。

「髪の色はブロンドじゃなく、金髪だったし、年も二十四、五にはなっていたんじゃないかしら。ピノキオの店員にもう一度きいてみたら」

「そうですか、いや結構です。よくわかりました」

as he was putting his notebook in his pocket. "In any case, he'll probably show up around B.C. Street, so it's just a matter of time until we arrest him. He's got no place else to go." The officer spoke as if he'd said these same words many times before. He apologized for having bothered Kiyo as he fixed his hat and then saluted, repeating that they were sure to catch him.

Kiyo watched from the window over the sink until the officer had turned the corner at the vacant lot. She felt a thin layer of sweat on her back. That night Sammy came back after sunset.

Half a year had passed since that day. The officer didn't appear again, and the MPs never came around even once. They didn't even seem to be looking for Sammy. It surprised Kiyo that the American military could be so lax.

There was no sign that Sammy was getting any money from home. In all this time, he had not paid Kiyo a cent. Instead of receiving money, Kiyo had actually started giving Sammy spending money. Once, after the second or third month, she had demanded he pay her back, but now the circumstances were completely different. She had come to understand that this was the price an unwanted fifty-eight-year-old prostitute had to pay so she could embrace an Adonis young enough to be her grandson and handsome enough to be a movie star. And, if she thought about it, this was a bargain. Where else could a woman like her sleep with such an angelic boy for a mere ten or twenty thousand yen a month?

巡査は手帖をポケットにしまいながら笑った。

「どっちみちセンターあたりにやってくるでしょうから逮捕は時間の問題ですよ。奴らはこのあたり以外に行くあてはありませんからねえ」

慣れた口調でいった。すみませんでした、と帽子をかぶりなおして敬礼した。必ずつかまりますよ、とつけ加えた。

キヨは巡査がアスファルトの露地を曲がりきるまで流しの窓から見送っていたが、気がつくと背中にうすく汗をかいていた。その夜サミーは日が暮れてからもどって来た。

あれから今日まで半年がたつ。巡査はいっぺんやって来たきりいち度も姿を見せなかった。ＭＰも一度もまわって来なかった。まわってくるどころか探しまわっている気配すらなかった。アメリカの軍隊というのはそういうものかとキヨはあきれた。

サミーにくにから金が送られてきた気配はない。その間サミーは一銭も金を払ったことがない。お金をもらうどころかいつごろからともなくキヨがこずかいをあげるようになっている。二、三ヵ月たったころ、一度請求したことがあったが、今では事情がすっかり変わっている。五十八歳の、誰も相手にしてくれなくなった商売女が孫のように年下の、映画の中から抜け出て来たような美少年を抱く代金だと今ではわりきっている。そう思えば安いものであった。どこの世界でたかだか月一万二万の金でこんな天使のような少年が抱けようか。

3.

When Kiyo looked at her watch, it was after three o'clock.
Where should I go?
She could think of nowhere in particular.
I'll go out to the main intersection. Then I'll decide.
Kiyo walked faster. On her face fell a drizzling rain that was
sure to ruin her makeup. She took a handkerchief out of her
handbag and pressed it to her forehead.

After reaching the intersection, she turned onto a side street
and stopped at a pawnshop, where she left her ring as collateral for
a five-thousand-yen loan. It was a cheap ring, but she was able to
borrow the money because she knew the owner, Mr. Shiroma,
whose wife, like Kiyo, was from Tsuken Island. She counted the
crisp thousand-yen bills, stuffed them into her purse, and went
into a cafeteria for a bowl of Okinawan-style noodle soup with
pork.

When she left the restaurant and looked at her watch again, it
was after three-thirty. The image of Sammy kicking back on the
sofa watching television floated into Kiyo's mind. But all at once
she was overcome with the anxiety that he might already have left
the apartment for good. Kiyo stopped short in the middle of the
street and considered returning home. Then, on second thought,
she decided that he couldn't have left. After all, where could
someone go who was homeless and penniless? Kiyo began walking
again, trying to shake off her doubts.

She stood at the bus stop and thought of going to Nakagusuku
Park. From atop the stone wall of the old castle there, she'd be able
to see Tsuken Island. She wanted to look at the white crests of

三

時計を見ると三時を回っていた。

（どこへ行こう）

行くあてはなかった。

（十字路に出てみよう。どこへ行くかはそれから決めればいい）

キヨは足を早めた。

小雨が顔に落ちかかる。化粧した顔が台無しになりそうだ。ハンドバッグからハンカチをとりだしてひたいにあてた。

十字路に出ると裏通りの質屋に寄り、指輪をおいて五千円かりた。指輪は安物で五千円も貸してくれたのは主人の城間がキヨと同じ津堅島の女を妻にしていてキヨと顔見知りだったからだ。

手の切れるような千円札を数えて財布に押しこむと、キヨは食堂に入ってソーキソバをたべた。

食堂を出て時計を見ると三時半を回っている。サミーがぼんやりソファーにもたれてテレビを見ている様子が目に浮かんだ。ふいに、ひょっとしたらもう家を出て行ってしまっているかもしれない、という不安が心に来た。

キヨは道路のまん中にたちどまった。帰ろうか。いや、そんな筈はない。あの文ナシが、あのすかんぴんの宿無しがどこに行けるもんか。キヨは迷いをふりきるように歩きだした。公園の石垣の上から津堅の海が見える。遠いリーフ

バス停留所に立った。中城公園にいってみようと思った。

waves dashing against the far reef. On days when she felt down, she longed to see the outline of the island where she was born and would come to gaze at the ocean surrounding it whenever something was troubling her. Perhaps because she had fallen on hard times, Kiyo was often depressed these days. She constantly dwelled on the past, something she hated doing. Or maybe it was because she was getting old that she thought more and more about the past, especially about her husband and children, long estranged.

Since she'd left her island, Kiyo had seen her husband two or three times, but he was always so roaring drunk that she couldn't even have a conversation with him. Her two children had long ago passed their thirtieth birthdays. She heard they'd gone off to Kanagawa and Hyōgo on the Japanese mainland to get married, but they never came to see her or sent her a single letter. They must find her detestable, she thought. The realization that she must also have several grandchildren by now was almost too much to bear.

In the air-conditioned bus sat five or six passengers, all looking bored. When Kiyo sat down in an empty seat, her whole body felt heavy. She got off the bus at Ishinda, then hailed a taxi. By the time it reached the park and pulled up at the ticket booth, painted bright red just like Ryūgū Castle, the drizzling rain had stopped. There was no one in the booth, so she put two hundred-yen coins on the counter and went inside. Pale-skinned middle-aged men and women, typical tourists, came down the steep, narrow gravel slope holding on to each other to keep from falling. Kiyo stopped under a cherry blossom tree lushly covered with dark green leaves to let two of them pass, then headed up toward the castle rampart.

At the top of her climb, the gravel path opened onto a red clay courtyard framed by a grass lawn. The borders of the courtyard rose up in two or three tiers, and behind it the castle wall spread out its flowing hem in graceful waves of stone.

に打ち寄せる白い波頭を見てみたいと思った。気分がめりこむ日は故郷の島影が見たくなる。キヨは気がむしゃくしゃすると島の海を見にやってくる。生活が苦しくなっているせいかこのごろ気分がふさいでいけない。昔のことばかり考える。キヨは昔のことを考えるのが嫌いだ。けれども年のせいか近ごろ昔のこと、とりわけ別れた夫と子供たちのことを考える日が多くなった。

夫とは島を出てから二、三度会ったことがあるがいつもぐでんぐでんに酔っぱらっていて話にも何にもならなかった。二人の子供はもうとっくに三〇を過ぎていてそれぞれ神奈川と兵庫に嫁でいったらしいのだが、ただの一度も会いに来たことはない。手紙一本もらったこともない。よほど憎いのだろう。孫ももう何人も出来ている筈だが、と思うとたまらない気持になる。

冷房のよくきいたバスの中には五、六人の客が所在なげにすわっていた。空席にすわるとからだじゅうが重くなった。

石平でバスを降り、タクシーを拾った。竜宮城をかたどった真っ赤なペンキ塗りの切符売場の前にすべりこむと小雨はやんでいた。切符売場には誰もいなかった。カウンターの上に百円玉を二つのせて中に入った。観光客らしい色の白い中年の男女がいたわり合うように細い急傾斜の砂利道をおりてくる。青黒い葉を繁らせた桜の下に立ちどまってふたりをやりすごし、キヨは城壁に向かった。

砂利道をのぼりつめると芝生でふちどられた赤土の広場が広がっていた。広場の端は二段三段にきれて盛りあがり、その背後にゆるやかな本丸の石垣が波型の裾をひろげていた。

Kiyo walked around the lawn and sat down on a bench. Two high school students, who seemed to be sweethearts, yelled to each other as they played badminton. Both were barefoot, and two pairs of shoes were lined up neatly on the red clay. For some reason, Kiyo got goose bumps and averted her eyes. She stood up hurriedly and fled.

From where she stood on the rampart, Tsuken Island was hidden from view in a mist. Beneath the low clouds, a large helicopter circled overhead, flashing a red light. Below, a huge tanker was slowly heading out to sea. A damp, dark wind had begun to blow, carrying big raindrops.

When Kiyo returned to B.C. Street, the sun was starting to go down. The light from the streetlamps, which had been turned on too early, played across the tops of the bottle palms in rows along the curb. Soldiers strolled peacefully in the clear breezes at twilight. Some looked at photographs from the floor shows on signboards propped up against the entrances to bars and cabarets. Some lined up at the hot dog counter. Others leaned against the telegraph poles, casting lonely gazes at passersby. One middle-aged soldier stood next to Pinocchio Burger with his back to the street. Kiyo approached him.

"Evening," she said.

"Good evening," he replied, in a more youthful voice than she had expected.

"Wanna make love?"

広場の芝生を回ってベンチの上に腰をおろした。恋人同士らしい高校生の男女が声をかけあいながらバドミントンをしている。ふたりとも素足であった。赤土の上に二足の靴がきちんと並べておいてある。キヨはなぜか鳥肌が立って目をそらせた。

城壁に立つと津堅島はもやの中にかくれて見えなかった。たれこめた雲の下を大きなヘリコプターが赤いランプを点滅させながら旋回していた。その下を大きなタンカーがゆっくりと外海にむかっていた。黒い生温かい風が大粒の雨を運んで来た。

センター通りにもどると陽がかげり始めていた。並木のトックリやしの葉末に気の早い街灯の光が戯れていた。たそがれの透明な風の中を兵隊たちが物静かに歩いていた。

バーやキャバレーの入口に立てかけたフロアショーの写真に見入っている者。ホットドッグのカウンターの前に順番を待っている者。電柱にもたれて通行人に人恋しげな視線を投げかけている者。

いつものピノキオ・ハンバーガーの横に中年の米兵が通りに背をむけて立っていた。キヨは近づいて声をかけた。

「イブニン」

「グッド・イブニン」

予想外に若やいだ声が返ってきた。

「メークラブしない」

The soldier remained silent and shook his head.

"Suit yourself," Kiyo said, laughing awkwardly as she passed by. She regretted having spoken to him.

After she had been walking awhile, a very drunk soldier came toward her, accompanied by another soldier. Kiyo stopped, said "Hi," then made her approach. "Hey, soldier, wanna come with me?"

"Where to?" the drunk stopped to ask.

"It's up to you."

An image of Sammy watching television floated into her mind. She had noticed lately that Sammy would sometimes watch television with tears in his eyes.

"Go with you and do what?"

"Make love, of course."

"With you?" The second soldier laughed loudly, dragging his drunk buddy away. Kiyo turned her back on them. It was no use wasting her time on a drunk. She hurried away, heading back toward Pinocchio Burger.

Kiyo went up to the counter and ordered a hot dog. A man in a triangular hat silently wrapped the hot dog in a napkin and thrust it toward her. Kiyo withdrew into the shadow of the building and bit into it. Her money was fast running out. With what she had

兵隊は黙って首を振った。

「そう」

キヨはぎこちなく笑って横を通り抜けた。あんな奴に声をかけるんじゃなかったと後悔した。しばらく歩くと、ふたりづれのかなり酔った兵隊が前から近づいて来た。キヨは立ち止まり、ハーイと声をあげて近づいた。

「兵隊さん、私と一緒に行かない？」

「どこへ」

酔った一人が立ちどまって訊いた。

「どこでもあんたの行きたい所へさ」

テレビをのぞきこんでいるサミーのうしろ姿が浮かんだ。サミーは近ごろテレビを見ながら涙ぐんだりする。

「一緒に行ってどうするんだい」

「きまってるじゃないの、メークラブするのさ」

「おまえさんとかい」

もうひとりの兵隊が酔った方をひきずりながら、声をあげて笑った。キヨはくるりと背をむけた。こんな酔っぱらいと時間をつぶしたってしようがない。キヨは急ぎ足でそばを離れ、身をひるがえすとピノキオ・ハンバーガーの前にもどった。

カウンターに近づいてホットドッグをひとつ注文した。白い三角帽をかぶった男が黙ったままナプキンにくるんでつきだした。キヨは建物のかげにひっこんでホットドッグにかぶりついた。お金はあといくらもない。これ

left, she couldn't even buy Sammy a pack of American cigarettes.

Lately there were fewer soldiers on the street. Maybe her "unemployment" continued because she was old and had lost her appeal. Still, how could anyone make a living in this business with so few soldiers around? A feeling of helplessness blew up from under her feet like the cold wind.

I could go to the black soldiers' district in Miyazato.

She heard that black GIs still came around sometimes where she used to work at the top of Miyazato Hill. Maybe guys who'd been turned away at the bars around Camp Hansen were there now, looking for a good time. Kiyo wiped her mouth with a napkin and hailed a taxi.

She got off at the entrance to the Ginten shopping street. The arcade was lined on both sides with shoe stores, coffee shops, stores selling household goods, and other shops. Kiyo dragged her feet slowly along the needlessly wide street. At the end of the arcade, she entered the area of bars where she used to work. She stepped onto the asphalt sidewalk and felt a slight pain in the pit of her stomach.

Kiyo turned the corner at the fabric store. From here, if she went down the side street, she would be at the place where she used to work. The smell of damp air assaulted her nose as she turned the corner. Kiyo stopped and looked around. Dirty cinder blocks. A rotting wooden fence. Houses with low clay-tiled roofs.

She climbed the gentle asphalt slope and recognized the little stone plaque marking the end of the street. Looking up, she saw the faded T-frame eave of the familiar Pittsburgh Bar, which seemed to

ではサミーにアメリカ煙草一個買ってやれない。それにしても通りをぶらつく兵隊たちのなんとすくなくなった

ことだろう。このところずっとあぶれが続いているのは年をとって自分に魅力がなくなったせいかも知れない

が、それにしても兵隊の数がこうもすくなくなってはどうしようもない。20 キヨは足元から冷たい風の吹き抜けて

いくような心細さを感ずる。

（宮里のクロンボ町にいってみようか）

昔働いたことのある宮里の坂の上には、まだちょくちょくクロンボたちが現れるという。21 今日あたりハンセン

のバー街で相手にされないクロンボたちがあそびに来ているかも知れない。キヨはナプキンで口をふくとタク

シーに手をあげた。

銀天街の入口でタクシーを降りた。22

アーケードをくぐると靴屋、喫茶店、雑貨店、と似たような店が向かい合っている。だだっぴろい通りをキヨ

はゆっくりと足を運んだ。アーケードが切れ、昔のバー街に入った。アスファルトの歩道をのぼる。みぞおちの

奥がかすかに痛む。

生地屋の角を曲がった。ここから裏通りに出れば昔働いていた店があるはずだ。

裏通りに出ると、湿った空気が鼻をついた。立ち止まってあたりを見回す。ブロックのシミ。朽ちかけた板壁。

屋根の低い瓦家。

アスファルトのゆるやかな坂をあがる。見覚えのある石敢當が目にとまった。23 見上げると昔の「ピッツバー

be peering down at her. Kiyo dusted off the stone steps in front of the rusted screen door and sat down. She took a cigarette out of her bag and lit up. She puffed on it awhile, her eyes fixed on the far end of the alley where the veil of twilight slowly descended. Identical dirty cement buildings stood silently in a row. On the corner to her left was the bar Manhattan, on the corner to her right was the Niagara. Next to that was the Seven Star, and halfway down the hill was the New York.

She recalled the face of her friend Sumiko, who worked the Manhattan. She wondered what had happened to Sumiko, who always used to talk about how she was going to save up the money to get her front teeth replaced. Then there was dim-witted Hiromi from Iheya, who always used to talk about how she'd been sold off to pay her parents' debts, almost as if she were boasting. She got pregnant many times by black soldiers and always had an abortion. Once, she came to Kiyo to borrow money, saying she was going into the hospital. She said Anderson would give her twenty dollars on payday, and she promised to return the money as soon as she got it from him. So Kiyo lent it to her, but she never came around again.

Kiyo was reminiscing about acquaintances from the past as she peeled her nail polish when, out of the corner of her eye, she saw something small and black moving nearby. Next to some garbage bags at the end of the alley, a cat was sitting with its front paws together, staring at Kiyo. The cat was big, and Kiyo stared back for a while. It seemed interested in the plastic bag near her and was glancing back and forth between the bag and Kiyo's face. Kiyo glared at the cat, which got up, arched its back, and walked away.

After the cat had gone, Kiyo suddenly felt tired and wanted to lie down. She leaned up against the stone plaque and closed her eyes. From the top of the hill, she heard the sound of an empty can rolling. As she opened her eyes, an image of the cat flashed into her mind. She turned to look toward the garbage bags and saw an empty soda can roll slowly by, picking up speed as it tumbled

グ」のT字型の廂が灰色にくすんでキヨを見おろしている。キヨはさびついた網戸の前の石段のほこりを払って腰をおろした。バッグを開けて煙草をとり出し火をつけた。たそがれのこぼれ始めた露地の奥に目を据えたまましばらく煙草をふかす。似たようなセメントの地肌のくすんだ建物がおしだまって並んでいる。

左の角は「マンハッタン」、右の角が「ナイアガラ」。その隣が「セブンスター」、坂の途中のが「ニューヨーク」……。

「マンハッタン」のスミ子の顔を思い出す。お金をためて前歯を入れるんだと口ぐせのようにいっていたスミ子はどこに流れていったのだろう。伊平屋からでてきたうすのろのヒロミ。親の借金のかたがわりにされたと自慢するようにいっていた。ヒロミは何回も黒人たちの子を孕んでそのたびに堕ろしていた。病院にいくからといってキヨのところにお金を借りに来たことがある。ペーデーにアンダーソンが二〇ドルくれるといっていっ

たら貰ったらすぐ返すからというので貸してやったらそれっきり来なくなった。それを貫ったらすぐ返すからというので貸してやったらそれっきり来なくなった。

マニキュアを剥がしながら昔の仲間たちのことをとりとめもなく思いめぐらしていると、眼の隅で小さな黒いものが動いた。露地の十字路のゴミ袋のそばに猫が前足を揃えてすわり、キヨの顔を見つめていた。大きな猫だ。キヨはしばらく猫と見つめ合った。かたわらのポリ袋の方に気があるらしくときどき袋に視線を移してはキヨの顔をうかがう。キヨがにらみつけると、立ちあがり背を弓なりにして歩いていった。

猫がいってしまうと急にキヨは疲れを感じた。横になりたくなった。石敢當にもたれて目をとじた。

坂の上で空きカンのころがる音がした。キヨは目をあけた。さっきの猫のことが頭をかすめた。首をひねり、ゴミ袋の方に目をやると、コーラの空きカンがゆっくり転がり、次第に速度を早めながらアスファルト道路を下

down the asphalt street before falling into the gutter in front of the Niagara.

When she looked back at the garbage bags, she saw that the cat had returned. Poking its nose into a hole it had ripped in one of the bags, it glared at her from time to time out of the corner of its eye.

"Ma'am."

Kiyo heard a voice and turned around. The blurred outline of a black face floated in the semidarkness. The white eyes hurriedly looked away.

He must be disappointed.

"Excuse me?" Kiyo said.

"No, no, forget it." The soldier took two or three steps back, as if to indicate that he had mistaken her for someone else, and then turned around. Kiyo spit loudly at him as he walked away.

A pack of dogs ran right by Kiyo. The lead dog stopped, looked back at her, and stood motionless, watching her intently. Kiyo remained seated and pretended to pick up a rock. The dog turned and ran away, with the others following close behind, until they had all disappeared around a corner.

4.

When she reached the paint store on the corner, Kiyo saw a light coming from her apartment. She walked faster, entered the lot at the end of the winding asphalt street, and dashed up the

へ下へと転がり、「ナイアガラ」の前のドブに落ちた。

チリ袋に視線をもどすと、いつのまに舞いもどったのか猫が引き裂かれた穴に鼻さきをさしこみ、ときおり目尻を光らせてこちらを見ていた。

「ネエサン25」

声がしてキヨはふりむいた。うすくらがりの中に輪郭のぼやけた黒い顔が浮いていた。白い目がせわしなく動いた。（失望したな）と思った。

「ユーズ ミー?」

「ノー、ノー、スミマセン」

兵隊は人違いだったというように二、三歩あとずさりして背を向けた。キヨはその後ろ姿に音をたてて唾をはいた。

犬が群をなしてキヨのそばを走り抜ける。先頭の犬が立ち止まってキヨを振り返った。立ちどまったままじっとキヨを見つめている。キヨはすわったまま石を拾う仕草をした。犬がそっぽをむいて走り出した。仲間の犬たちがぞろぞろと続き、角を曲がって見えなくなった。

四

ペンキ屋の角を曲がるとアパートの灯が見えた。キヨの足が早くなった。曲がりくねったアスファルトの切れ

stairs. Bright fluorescent light seeped out from the small window. She turned the knob and called out Sammy's name as she bounded into the room. There was no answer.

"Hey," she called out again, but there was no sign of Sammy. Kiyo stood paralyzed in the middle of the floor. She wondered if he had gone back to his unit. Maybe he'd given up on his dream of crossing over to Honshū or Kyūshū that he talked about so often.

Where could he have gone?

After a quick stop in the bathroom, Kiyo grabbed her handbag and dashed outside. She retraced her steps to B.C. Street. Behind the Caravan bar was a house where Tom Moore, a friend of Sammy's, was renting a room. Sammy could have gone there.

Kiyo walked faster when she got to B.C. Street. Moore's room was just off the street. She went around to the side entrance of the Caravan and called out from under his window.

"Corporal Moore."

The window opened immediately. "Well, if it isn't Kiyo," he said.

"Sammy isn't there, is he?"

たところで露地に入った。　足早に階段をかけあがった。　白いあかりが小さな窓から洩れている。　ノブを回して、

「サミー」

声と一緒にとびこんだ。

返事はなかった。

「ヘーイ」

また呼んだ。　居間にサミーの姿はなかった。　キヨは部屋の中央に立ちすくんだ。　帰隊したのか。　くちぐせのようにいっていたホンシュウかキュウシュウに渡る夢はもう捨てたのか。

（どこへ行ってしまったのだろう）

キヨは急いで用を足し、ハンドバッグをつかんでまた外へとび出した。

いま来た道をセンター通りの方へひき返した。　上地の「キャラバン」の裏手に近ごろ親しくしているトム・ムーアの間借りしている家がある。　そこへ行ったかも知れない。

キヨは足を早めてセンター通りに出た。　ムーアの間借りさきは通りのすぐ裏手にある。「キャラバン」の通用門の横にまわり、　窓の下から声をかけた。

「コープル（伍長）　ムーア」

窓はすぐにあいた。

「やあ、キーヨじゃないか」

「サミーがそっちに来てない？」

"Sammy?"

"Private Samuel Copeland."

"Oh, the deserter?"

"He comes around here a lot, doesn't he?"

"Yeah, but he hasn't been here today."

"Oh . . . thanks a lot."

"Is everything okay?"

"Uh-huh. He's probably at the pachinko parlor."

Kiyo rushed out of the alley. Where could Sammy have gone? She looked in at the nearby pachinko parlor but didn't see him. She went out onto Goya Boulevard to look in at each of the two or three large pachinko parlors there but saw no sign of Sammy. Where could he have gone?

I wonder if he went back to his unit.

Kiyo's legs trembled. She had heard that if a deserter returns to his unit he is immediately placed in a holding cell at Kawasaki and sent from there back to the United States. Could Sammy have resigned himself to being sent back and returned to his company? No way. *Maybe he's already back at the apartment,* she thought. *Maybe he's just taking a short walk around the neighborhood.* Before she knew it, Kiyo was heading back toward the Kamaara Apartments. Her pace gradually quickened. At the end of the winding road, she arrived at the front of the apartment building. There was a light in the window.

「サミー?」

「サムエル・コープランド一等兵よ」

「ああ、あの脱走兵か」

「ちょくちょくまわって来たんでしょう」

「ああ、だが今日は来てないよ」

「そう、──どうも有難う」

「いいのかい」

「いいわ、きっとパチンコ屋だわ」

キヨは足早に露地を出た。サミーはどこへ行ったのだろう。キヨは近くのパチンコ屋をのぞいてみた。サミーの姿はなかった。ゴヤ大通りに出た。そこには大きなパチンコ屋が二、三軒かたまっている。キヨはその一軒一軒をのぞいて歩いた。サミーの姿はなかった。どこへ行ったのだろう。

（帰隊したのかしら）

キヨは足がふるえた。脱走兵は帰隊するとすぐに川崎の留置場に送られ、そこから本国送還になるときいている。サミーは本国送還を覚悟の上で隊に帰ったのだろうか。そんなことはない。もうアパートに帰っているかも知れない。ちょっとこの近くを散歩していたのかも知れない。キヨの足はいつのまにか嘉間良のアパートにむかっている。足が次第に早くなる。曲がりくねったアスファルトの道路が切れるとアパートの前に出た。窓に灯りがついている。

I thought I had turned it off when I left.

Kiyo's heart danced. She rushed up the stairs and pulled on the doorknob. The door opened easily. The room overflowed with bright fluorescent light. Sammy was not back.

I guess I must have left it on when I ran out.

Kiyo threw her handbag down on the table and fell onto the bed. She lay facing upward without moving for a while. Then she got up slowly and lit a cigarette.

Where is he? Did he really go back to his unit? That boy who hated the military so?

If Sammy had returned to his unit, she would never see him again. Kiyo rose, staggering to her feet as if she were losing her mind.

He didn't go back. He wouldn't . . . I know. He probably went to the yacht harbor. . . . But why would he want to go there in the middle of the night?

Suddenly the door flew open as if blown by a gust of wind, and Sammy entered. Kiyo's slender shoulders dropped. She felt as if she was going to cry.

"Where were you?" Her voice was shrill and trembling.

"I went over to Gate Street."

"If you walk around too much, the MPs will catch you."

（家を出たときには消したんじゃなかったかしら）

キヨは心がおどった。急ぎ足で階段をかけあがり、ドアのノブを引いた。ドアは何の手ごたえもなくあいた。

部屋の中には白い蛍光灯の光があふれていた。サミーは帰ってきていなかった。

（やっぱり電灯をつけっぱなしのまま部屋を飛び出したんだわ）

キヨはハンドバッグをテーブルの上に放り投げるとベッドの上に仰向けに倒れた。しばらく身動きもしなかった。それからのろのろおきあがると煙草に火をつけた。

（どこへ行ったのだろう。本当に部隊に帰ってしまったのだろうか。あんなに隊を嫌っていたあの少年が）

部隊に帰ってしまったらもう二度とサミーの姿を見ることは出来ないだろう。キヨは狂ったように立ちあがった。

（帰ってはいない。帰るものか──。そうだ、ヨットハーバーかもしれない──だが、この夜更けにヨットハーバーに行く気になるだろうか）

突然ドアが風にあおられたように開いてサミーが入って来た。キヨの痩せた肩ががくんと落ちた。涙がこぼれそうになった。

「どこへいってたの」

声がとんがり、震えていた。

「ちょっとゲート通りまで行って来たんだ[28]」

「あんまり出歩くとMPにつかまっちゃうわよ」

"Never mind that," he said with resignation. "It's all over."

Sammy clasped his hands behind his head and fell onto the bed. He lay there without saying a word. Kiyo also said nothing. The silence continued for some time.

"Is there any beer?" he asked.

"No, should I go and buy some?"

"No, it's okay."

Again there was silence.

"You know I . . ." Sammy raised his eyes to look at Kiyo. Kiyo quickly averted her gaze. She anticipated his words with her entire body. Her legs trembled.

"I made a phone call. . . ."

Kiyo said nothing.

"I told them I'd be at the front gate tomorrow morning at ten."

Kiyo felt as if she'd been hit over the head with a two-by-four. She saw stars before her eyes. "I see," she said.

「かまうもんか」
ネバー　マインド

投げやりな声が返って来た。

「もういいんだ」
イッツ　オール　オーバー

「ビールあった？」

サミーは両手のひらに後頭部をのせてベッドの中に倒れこんだ。倒れこんだまま黙っている。キヨも黙っている。しばらく沈黙が続いた。

「ないの、買ってこようか」

「いや、いいんだ」

また沈黙が続いた。

「おれな」

サミーが上眼づかいにキヨを見た。キヨは慌てて目をそらした。からだがそっくり耳になった。足が小刻みに震えた。

「電話して来たんだ……」

「……」

「明日十時にゲートに出頭することにしたよ」

角材で脳天をぶんなぐられたような気がした。目から火の玉がとび散った。

「そう」

She tried to laugh, but the skin on her cheeks only twitched. She tried to smile, but she couldn't tell if she was succeeding. As she lay next to Sammy and closed her eyes, she felt as if her body were sinking into the floor. Sammy's sweaty palm reached out for her thigh. When she opened her eyes, she saw his tense expression. Kiyo brushed his hand away and got up. Her head ached to the core. She walked away from the bed, then turned around.

"Sammy, let's run away together. Let's go to my island. No one will come looking for you there. I know lots of empty houses," she said.

"To Tsuken Island, the one you're always talking about?"

"Yeah. It's got lots of abandoned houses. They're old, but they have gardens and fields. I'll cut the grass. And you can fix the broken storm doors and floorboards."

Sammy closed his eyes and shook his head firmly from side to side.

"If they catch you, they'll send you home. You want to turn yourself in anyway?"

"I don't care. It's all over," Sammy muttered, as if to convince himself, and turned his back to Kiyo.

Kiyo stood under the shower. For some reason, she'd suddenly wanted to bathe. She washed her body carefully and then stood in front of the mirror. Wrapping her hair in a towel, she stared at her reflection. Her eyes sparkled inside the pallor of her face. She peered at herself and laughed, though it looked like she was crying. The bags under her eyes seemed to have doubled

笑おうとしたが頬の肉がピクピクと痙攣しただけだった。笑顔を作っているつもりだがうまく成功したかどうかわからない。サミーと並んで倒れこみ目を閉じた。からだが地面の底に沈んでいくような気がした。

サミーの汗ばんだ手が太ももにのびてきた。目をあけると目の前にこわばった顔があった。

キヨは手を払いのけると立ちあがった。頭の芯が痛んだ。ベッドから離れて振りかえった。

「サミー、わたしと一緒に逃げよう。私の島へいくのよ。あそこなら誰にも見つかりっこないわ。島には空き家がいくつもあるわ」

「君のいっていたツケンジマかい」

「そう。誰も住んでない家がいっぱいあるのよ。古い家だけど庭も畑もあるわ。わたし、庭の草を刈るわ。あんたは壊れた雨戸や床板をなおしてちょうだい」

サミーを目をつぶり、だがはっきりと首を横に振った。

「つかまったら本国に送られるんでしょう。それでも行くっていうの」

「いいんだ。もうすべて終わったんだよ」

サミーは自分にいいきかせるようにつぶやいてキヨに背をむけた。

キヨは頭からシャワーをかぶった。何だかよくわからないが、急にからだが洗いたくなったのだ。念入りにからだを洗って鏡の前に立った。バスタオルで髪をくるみ、鏡をのぞく。蒼ざめた顔に目がぎらぎら光っている。

キヨは自分の顔に向かって笑いかけた。泣いているように見えた。目の下の袋が二倍にふくれているように見え

in size.

Kiyo wrapped herself in a towel. As she got out of the shower, she could hear Sammy snoring. Somehow it sounded louder than usual to her. She brushed her hair carefully, then tied it back with a ribbon as she listened to Sammy snore. The kettle whistled. She threw her towel down on the makeup table and poured herself coffee. After quickly finishing two cups, she put down the empty cup and opened her dresser. She took out a gaudy pink dress but decided against it. For some reason, Kiyo suddenly felt like wearing Japanese clothes. She took out her Kumejima kimono, which she stored at the bottom of the dresser, and stared at it vacantly for a while. The snoring stopped and Sammy turned over.

Standing in front of the mirror, Kiyo finished tying her obi and then meticulously applied her makeup. Next, she got up and closed the window. As she was locking it, she heard the thunderous roar of a jet testing its engine in the distance. Checking the lock on the door, she went into the kitchen, where she opened the propane gas jets, turning on all three. Then she walked back to the bed, leaving the kitchen and living room doors open, and lay down. Perhaps her state of mind caused her to feel she was quickly losing consciousness. She thought she'd try counting to a thousand. As she began, she suddenly felt thirsty and got up to take a drink of water. When she staggered back into bed, Sammy turned over again and began to sit up. Now Kiyo picked up the lighter that was next to the bed. Lying flat on her stomach, she placed the soft pillow on top of her head. Then, gathering her resolve, she turned the flint wheel with a click.

た。

バスタオルをからだに巻いてシャワーを出ると、サミーのいびきが聞こえた。気のせいかいつもより大きく聞こえる。キヨはサミーのいびきの音を聞きながら念入りに髪をとかして束ね、リボンで結んだ。コーヒーポットが鳴った。バスタオルを化粧台の上に投げ、コーヒーを入れた。たてつづけに二杯のんだ。

空になったコップをおくと、洋服ダンスを開けた。派手なピンクのワンピースをとり出しかけてやめた。なんだか急に和服が着てみたくなった。タンスの底にしまってある久米島紬をとり出してしばらくぼんやりみつめた。

いびきがやんでサミーが寝返りを打った。

鏡の前で帯をしめおわると丹念に化粧した。立ち上がって窓を閉めた。内鍵を入れると遠くで雷のようなエンジン調整の噴射の音がした。ドアの錠前を確かめて台所に入るとプロパンガスのコックをあけた。三つあるコックを全部あけた。台所と居間のドアをあけたままベッドにもどった。横になった。気のせいかすぐに気が遠くなっていくような気がした。数を千までかぞえようと思った。ひとつ、ふたつと数え始めると急にのどが乾いた。起きあがって水をのんだ。よろけるようにベッドにもどるとサミーがまた寝返りをうち、上半身をおこしかけた。キヨは枕元のライターを手にとった。うつぶせになり、頭の上にやわらかい枕をのせた。思いきってカチリとローラーを回した。

30

Concerning the Sound of a Train Whistle in the Night *or* On the Efficacy of Fiction

(Murakami Haruki)

1. そこにはきっと何かお話があるに違いない. This sentence represents the girl's thoughts. The use of お話 suggests this most clearly, and conveys a sense of the eagerness with which she looks forward to the boy's story. Technically お話 is the honorific お + 話, but it is better to think of it as a noun in its own right meaning "tale" or "story."

2. いいかい is a familiar way of saying いいか. It is less abrupt and abrasive than いいか, but it suggests that the speaker stands in a superior position vis-à-vis the addressee, like an older sibling addressing a younger sibling.

3. 気圧のせいで . . . 張り裂けてしまいそうな──. All this is meant to clarify the nature of the feeling that the boy mentioned in the previous sentence. It is as though the word 気持ち has been omitted at the end of the clause: 張り裂けてしまいそうな気持ち。 そういう気持ちってわかるかな?

4. The 間 in 間を置く can mean "space" (either physical or emotional, as in "you've got to give him some space") or "time." In this case, it is the latter.

5. 聞こえたか聞こえないかというくらいの音だ. The boy is not sure whether he heard the sound or not. If he did hear it, the event has passed; if he didn't, he still hasn't—hence the discrepancy between 聞こえた and 聞こえない. Note that a few lines on, we get the similar but significantly different phrase 聞こえるか聞こえないか, which suggests not that the boy isn't sure he heard the sound but simply that it is almost too faint to hear.

6. The には here suggests the strength of the boy's convictions: other people might have doubted it, but he could tell.

A Little Darkness

(Yoshimoto Banana)

1. *Slam Dunk* is a manga by Inoue Masahiko, first serialized in *Weekly Shōnen Jump* from 1990 to 1996, that centers on a high school basketball team. It has been made into a TV series and a few movies, and is one of the most popular manga of all time.

2. Gジャン is a combination of two rather startling abbreviations, from an English-language perspective: "G" is short for "jeans" and "ジャン" is short for "ジャンパー" or "jumper," meaning "jacket." So it's a jean jacket. A leather jacket is a 革ジャン.

3. The narrator is referring to Alan Parker's 1996 *Evita*, starring Madonna as Eva Perón, aka Evita, the second wife of Argentinean president Juan Perón. *Colectivo* is the Argentinean word for "buses." Recoleta is one of the nicer, pricier neighborhoods of Buenos Aires.

4. In Japan, the 納骨堂 is generally a room or a series of rooms, most often within the precincts of a Buddhist temple, filled with small lockers, each holding a portion of a person's cremated remains, or perhaps a lock of hair. Here the narrator is referring to the space within each grave or mausoleum where the remains are actually stored.

5. In this context, it almost seems as if 静まり返る ought to mean "returning to silence," but it doesn't: the 返る simply amplifies the verb, emphasizing that the graves were "dead silent," so to speak. あきれ返る is another example of this usage.

6. ひとりっ子 means "an only child"; お母さんっ子 means "a mommy's girl (or boy)." All kinds of combinations like this can be formed, indicating a special relationship between the "child" (most often metaphorical) and the preceding word: an 江戸っ子, for instance, is "a true child of Edo," and a ニューヨークっ子 is "a real New Yorker."

7. In Japanese schools, students in clubs and on sports teams use the word 先輩, either on its own or prefaced by a family name, in addressing senior members of their club or team. The

humor comes from the fact that students who used to be her juniors are now in the same year, and yet they still feel the need to address her as 先輩, the way a loyal footman might keep calling the former king "king" even after the revolution.

8. The と at the end of this sentence points us back to the end of the sentence before it: this is what the narrator's mother's friends used to say.

9. つぶれる is one of a variety of ways of saying "to get dead drunk."

10. Tempura is best eaten as soon as it is prepared, of course— otherwise it can get oily and soggy. The よりによって suggests that tempura probably wasn't the best choice in light of the narrator's father's habit of missing his own parties.

11. 青山 is a fashionable area in Tokyo with lots of boutiques and design stores. Spiral Building—on Aoyama Street in Omotesandō—is a little bit like a small Guggenheim: it has an exhibition space, part of which is circled by a walkway that spirals up to a design store, Spiral Market, on the second story. People often refer to the building simply as "Spiral," as the narrator will in a few paragraphs.

Genjitsu House

(Koike Masayo)

1. もちろん、行くわ。どう、元気でやってる? These two sentences are the first of many examples in this story of what is known as "free direct discourse," in which the words or thoughts of a character seem to be reported directly, but without being tagged by quotation marks or other typographical devices. In a sense, Japanese seems especially well suited to this technique, and you will see it used over and over again in this story and in this collection.

2. Often when a sentence concludes with "のことだった" or some variant (in this case the だった has been omitted), it is setting

the scene for an anecdote or story that will follow. That is the case here. Note, by the way, that the 間 in 間もない is just like the one we saw earlier in "Concerning the Sound of a Train Whistle in the Night *or* On the Efficacy of Fiction."

3. テーオーセッカイ is written in katakana here to emphasize that the narrator is hearing the words as nearly unintelligible sound, almost as if they were in a foreign language. Written in kanji, テーオーセッカイ is 帝王切開, "imperial incision." The connection to Caesar isn't immediately clear in Japanese; hence, the narrator's puzzlement in the following paragraph about the origin of the term.

4. ゆっくり諭すように言ったのだ. Like the 間もない頃のこと in note 1, this points to the sentences that follow.

5. 切るっていったって is a colloquial way of saying 切ると言っても.

6. The そう in そう、自分につぶやいた means そのように and refers back to the phrase まだ、わたしにも、産めるかもしれないわね.

7. 思いがけない and ドスの利いた低い both modify 声. This is subtly different from 思いがけなくドスの利いた低い声, in which 思いがけなく modifies ドスの利いた低い.

8. 彼女の声を聞くのはあれ以来だ. This takes us back to the opening lines of the story, reestablishing the telephone conversation in which Yoriko invites the narrator to the dinner as the present (彼女の声を聞く), at least for the time being, and distancing the previous conversation with an あれ. Note that while あれ以来 refers to the conversation described in the previous section, it also resonates more specifically with the 思いがけない、ドスの利いた低い声 with which that earlier call ended.

9. We will soon learn that Yoriko's apartment has only two rooms, one of which is the kitchen, so it might seem rather odd for the narrator to specify that she translates in アパートの一室. The reason she does, I think, is that アパート can, and perhaps most often does, mean "apartment building" rather than "an individual apartment," and so the phrase アパートの一室 has come to be used to mark a particular apartment

within a larger building as the location where something takes place. This is why you often hear on the news in Japan that someone was found murdered in アパートの一室.

10. だったろう is a contraction of だっただろう.

11. The として in なにひとつとして力になれなかった emphasizes that the narrator has been unable to do a single thing to help out. This usage appears only in negative sentences, generally preceded by some version of the number one (ひとつ, 一人, etc.).

12. This sentence is easier to make sense of if you consider everything from しかし彼女もまた to さびしく思い返し as a parenthetical interjection in which the narrator takes a second to rethink her first reaction: first she 自分をふがいなく思い, but then she sits back and 思いかえし. The repetition of 思い . . . 思いかえし is structurally important in this sentence, in other words.

13. 永田耕衣 (1900–1997) was a haiku poet, calligrapher, painter, essayist, dance critic, and longtime worker, from age eighteen to age fifty-five, at Mitsubishi Paper's Takasago Mill.

14. The 飴 here is 水飴, which my dictionary translates as "glutinous starch syrup." It is a lot like corn syrup, though sometimes it is thicker, and it can be eaten as a candy as well as used in cooking.

15. おじさんがじっと見ている視線に気がついたのだろうか、 is the narrator's speculation as to why the florist suddenly started talking about hands. ヤワ means "soft"; often, as here, it is used as the negative opposite of the macho タフ, or "tough." にゃあ is a typically downtown Edo/Tokyo (下町) colloquial contraction of には, and the sense here is that soft hands—the hands themselves—can't do a florist's work.

16. 鶴田浩二 (1924–1987) was a movie star and singer. Google him to get an idea of what his eyebrows were like and what he could do with them, if not of the way he smiled. Note, by the way, that the subject changes in this sentence: it is the narrator who is 内心少しびっくりしている, but it is the florist who まゆげをさげて、困ったような笑顔を向けた.

17. The のである in 呼び鈴というものはないのである lends an
    emphatic note to this phrase that suggests we should read it as
    an explanation for the とんとんとん that precedes it. It is as
    though this phrase makes us ask, Why is she knocking, why
    doesn't she ring the doorbell? And then it answers this
    question for us. In the next sentence, notice how the addition
    of a single あ changes an ordinary clipped はい to a longer
    shouted はあい: "I'm coming!" instead of "Yes."

18. きへん or 木偏 is the "tree radical." 楽しいの旧字, "the old form
    of the kanji 楽" (still in common use until the language
    simplifications of the mid- to late 1940s), is 樂. If you write 樂
    alongside the tree radical, you get 櫟, "Kunugi," the baby
    girl's name.

19. しんどい was originally a word in the Kansai dialect meaning
    "exhausted," "worn out," "pooped," and so on. These days
    people everywhere seem to use it, though I have the
    impression that in Tokyo, at any rate, it generally means
    "exhausting" or "grueling" and is used to describe activities
    rather than a state of being.

20. 先 is a tricky word that can mean either "before" or "beyond."
    When people use it in a temporal sense, however, it usually
    means "beyond," as it does here, or sometimes "the future."

21. いわし have been getting more expensive lately, it seems, but
    until recently they were one of the cheapest fishes around.
    まぐろ, on the other hand, tended to be pricey.

22. どう考えても modifies こっそり入れてくれたとしか思えない, not
    わたしが妊婦.

23. A 女子学生 is a woman in college. You might imagine the word
    would be 女子大生 because a woman in high school is a 女子高生,
    but 女子大生 actually means a woman in a women's college.

24. This business with the cord sounds a bit ominous but it's not:
    it isn't just any old bit of cord, it's an おんぶ紐—a sort of baby
    backpack. The "cord" is the straps.

25. Note that this is the same 切開 that appears in the word 帝王切開.

The Silent Traders

(Tsushima Yūko)

1. あんな生きものが is an unfinished thought and implies
    something like こんなところに現れるとは思わなかった.

2. 六義園 became one of the two most celebrated gardens
    in Edo when it was built from 1695 to 1702 by 柳沢吉保
    (1658–1714), one of the senior members of the Tokugawa
    council. The garden's name, literally "Garden of the Six
    Principles," ultimately derives from the "Great Preface" to the
    Chinese Classic of Poetry, though it was built on the theme of
    Japanese poetry and alludes to famous poetic spots from
    around the country. I suppose the main point here is that it is
    the product of a bygone age: that it is, as the narrator says,
    江戸時代の名残りの、六義園.

3. こっちのこと refers specifically to "us," but it also suggests
    "things happening on our side" of the line—or rather that
    there is a line—separating the human and the animal worlds.
    It's a wonderfully, subtly eerie image.

4. これもどんなことを書きつけたのか忘れてしまったが is a
    parenthetical comment inserted between その時まで埋めておこ
    う、と and 紙きれを小さな瓶に入れて.

5. The first time I read this it looked to me as though the
    narrator's mother had bought a とくし and a ブラシ, and for a
    second I wondered what a とくし was. Then I realized that the
    と is citational, and the mother buys an ordinary くし and
    ブラシ. I may well be the only one to make this mistake, but I
    thought I'd point it out just in case.

6. 朝の開門まで、一晩中庭園に過ごしました is written in the desu/
    masu style because the narrator is imagining someone

speaking the words, perhaps even bragging of having spent the night in such a frightening, otherworldly place.

7. This story, by the folklorist 柳田国男 (やなぎたくにお) (1875–1962), appears in 『遠野物語拾遺』(とおのものがたりしゅうい) (*More Tales of Tōno*, published as part of an expanded edition of 『遠野物語』 in 1935).

Mogera Wogura

(Kawakami Hiromi)

1. Don't bother memorizing the kanji for 鼹鼠, or even the word itself, because you will almost certainly never encounter it again, and also because no ordinary speaker of Japanese knows what it means, either. Even the author, 川上弘美, confessed in an interview I once read that she had simply stumbled across it in the dictionary when she was looking up some other word beginning with う.

2. 条 is a counter (often replaced by 本 or 筋) for long, thin objects such as obi, certain kinds of fish, and ligaments. It is also used, in an elegant way, for things that extend without having a fixed shape, such as light, water, and smoke.

3. Yet another usage of 間: in this case, it means "room."

4. ノルマ is a loan word from Russian: in the USSR, *norma* referred to a "work quota" or "labor norm," which was the minimum amount of work that a worker had to do in a given period of time to be paid or given food rations. In Japan, it just means the minimum amount of work one is supposed to do.

5. 使い捨てカイロ are like huge, thick, fuzzy Band-Aids that get toasty warm when the iron powder inside them comes in contact with the air. You stick them to your lower back or feet and toss them when they cool off. The idea of the disposable heater is a fairly recent one, but the idea of a portable, personal heater is not, as the kanji suggests: in the Edo period, 懐炉 ("sleeve fireplaces") were small metal containers that

held charcoal that could be carried around in the sleeves of a kimono.

6. くわんくわん describes, for instance, the messy state a baby gets into when it has its first birthday cake—food and frosting all around its mouth. This is hardly a common word: it isn't among the 500,000 entries in the 『日本国語大辞典』, the *OED* of Japan, and seems to be specific to Tokyo, or perhaps even certain parts of Tokyo.

7. 朝顔 usually means "morning glory," but here it is slang for "urinal."

8. In Japanese bars and *izakaya,* people generally tend to start with beer before moving on to sake, as the narrator does here, and it isn't uncommon to have more than one glass of beer. 燗酒が二本めになったあたり suggests, then, that a good deal of time has passed.

9. The terms 虚 ("emptiness") and 実 ("reality," "practicality") have been used in all sorts of contexts, from neo-Confucian thought to Chinese medicine and Zen shiatsu. Read as the compound 虚実, they mean "truth and falsehood," though in the opposite order. It isn't clear what the terms mean here, which is fine: it's the resonance that matters.

The Maiden in the Manger

(Abe Kazushige)

1. 神町駅, 天童駅, and 漆山駅—as well as 山形駅, 乱川駅, and 新庄駅, which will appear shortly—are stations on the Ōu Main Line, operated by the East Japan Railway Company (JR東日本). All are in Yamagata Prefecture, which is almost directly north of Tokyo. 神町 is the setting for 阿部和重's enormous two-volume masterpiece, 『シンセミア』.

2. 夜間営業, literally "nighttime business," is as unspecific in Japanese as it is in English, but it seems likely that トーマス井口

works in some sort of club or bar. His ludicrous name may have something to do with that. Perhaps it's a name he uses on the job.

3. The bullet train つばさ runs between 東京駅 and 新庄駅. The グリーン車, which comes up in the next sentence, is the first-class car.

4. 筋緊張緩和作用. At first glance, it might be hard to know how to break up a line of kanji that is this long. The words are: 筋緊張, 緩和, and 作用.

5. ピコピコパコパコ suggests the sound of the high school kids tapping away on their cell phones, sending text messages.

6. 民芸, originally an abbreviation of 民衆的工芸 ("popular crafts"), is a term associated with a movement to appreciate the beauty of everyday household items that began in the mid-1920s. The movement eventually came to be known as the 民芸運動. In this context, however, the 民芸品店 is probably more like a souvenir store or an "antiques" shop that sells all sorts of things.

7. In this case, その筋の者 is a yakuza.

8. 天童温泉 is, as you might imagine, a hot spring in 天童市. とある means "a certain."

Where the Bowling Pins Stand

(Ishii Shinji)

1. We have just been told that this road traces graceful curves, so I suppose we should assume this まっすぐ means "directly" rather than "straight." I think the idea is really that they whiz on down the road like marbles on a track.

2. ボンネット is a loan from British English, in which "bonnet" means what "hood" does in American English.

3. おとつい is simply another way of saying おととい.

4. Judging from the context, you would think the president is

telling the driver that he will have another driver cover his shift. Except 連番 literally means "serial number," and I have never heard of it being used to mean "shift." 連番 doesn't appear in any online glossaries of taxi-driver vocabulary, either. I wrote to Ishii Shinji to ask him what he meant, and, sure enough, he meant "shift." He says he checked with a taxi driver in Matsumoto. Who knows, maybe 連番 is specific to the company that driver worked for. Or perhaps the driver misunderstood and thought Ishii was asking what word you would use when a driver who had already been driving was asked to take over for another in an emergency. In this case, the driver would be taking two shifts in a row: i.e., 連 "linked" 番 "shifts/turns." Usually, as far as I can tell, taxi drivers refer to a shift as 出番.

5. Experienced taxi drivers will sometimes buy their own taxi license and car and start out in business on their own. That's what 個人業 means here.

6. 寝床にガソリンまかれたみてえな顔してやがる looks as though it could just be the bed (or futon) that was doused with gasoline, but because this somewhat fanciful metaphor is being used to describe the taxi driver's face, I think we can assume that the implied subject is "you" and 寝床に simply tells us the place where it happened. みてえな is a tough-guy way of saying みたいな, and してやがる is a sort of tough-guy, cursing-you-out way of saying している.

7. けれど...いたしません. This is still the woman speaking.

8. A bit of quick back-of-a-napkin calculating suggests that this taxi ride would cost at least ¥108,000. Two unopened bundles of ¥1000 notes (the smallest note available) would be ¥200,000.

9. 乗っける is a slangy way of saying 乗せる.

10. おまえ is a second-person pronoun that can be either confrontational or affectionate. おまえさん can be confrontational, too, but the さん sometimes gives it a softer ring than おまえ on its own. This is how Eltrut is using it.

When おまえさん is used politely, it often takes on a sort of antiquated, fairy-tale quality, no doubt because the word originally dates back to the Edo period. There may be a hint of that here, too.

11. がたがたぴしゃん！ is, as we are told right away, ボウリング球がレーンを転がり、ピンを弾きとばす音.

12. This looks as if it could be either 力入りすぎ or 力は入りすぎ, but it's the latter.

13. タクシーの料金メーターよりひと桁少ない. When this story was published, the starting rate for taxis was generally between ¥600 and ¥660. At this point in the game, none of the players has broken a hundred.

14. 公団アパート, literally "public apartment buildings," were enormous buildings built by the semipublic Japan Housing Corporation (日本住宅公団). Here again we see that 一室 doesn't necessarily mean "one room," as one might expect: in this case it is "one apartment in the complex."

Love Suicide at Kamaara

(Yoshida Sueko)

1. 嘉手納 is the name of a town on Okinawa, more than 80 percent of which is occupied by 嘉手納基地, or Kadena Air Base. Presumably it is to this base that Sammy's friend Jim has come.

2. Until 1953, Japan's currency consisted not only of 円 but also of 銭 and 厘. One 円 was equivalent to a hundred 銭, and one hundred 銭 was equivalent to a hundred 厘. While 銭 no longer exist, the word still appears in expressions like this.

3. センター通り is short for Business Center Street, hence B.C. Street. It has since been renamed 中央パークアベニュー通り, or Central Park Avenue Street.

4. トレイシ is a katakana-ization of "trash," perhaps with a southern accent mixed in.

5. 嘉間良 is an area just outside Kadena Air Base, perhaps three-quarters of a mile east of old B.C. Street.

6. パーマ屋 is literally a "perm parlor." The term used to be much more common than it is now, because perms used to be much more common than they are now.

7. 御袋 was originally a respectful or affectionate term of address for one's own mother; now it is used to refer casually or humbly to one's mother when talking to others.

8. していたればこそ is a classical form of していればこそ.

9. Here くにから means "from home," though ordinarily it would be closer to "from the country," in the sense of "from the country to the city."

10. いつごろともなく means "at some point along the way," or, more literally, "not at any particular point along the way."

11. 津堅島 is a tiny island off Okinawa Island. It was the site of a bloody battle during the Battle of Okinawa, as American forces tried to take Nakagusuku Bay. Now it is known for its carrots, and has adopted the nickname "キャロット愛ランド."

12. ソーキ are an Okinawan specialty: spareribs stewed in soy sauce, sugar, and a strong, distilled rice liquor called *awamori,* also an Okinawan specialty.

13. 文 is another obsolete unit of currency, dispensed with in 1871 when the Japanese government switched to 円, 銭, and 厘. 文なし is short for 一文なし, i.e., "[a person] without a single mon." すかんぴん is 素寒貧, where 素 means "pure" or "unadulterated" and 寒貧 means "cold and poor." "At the end of his rope," in other words.

14. 中城公園 is a park near the center of Okinawa Island, about twenty minutes south by taxi from 嘉間良, where the narrator lives. The park is at the top of a mountain, and offers a stunning view of Nakagusuku Bay. The ruins of Nakagusuku Castle stand within the park, having survived World War II.

15. 神奈川県 and 兵庫県 are both prefectures, the first just to the southeast of Tokyo, the second just east of Kyoto.

16. 石平 is a large intersection that serves as one of the main hubs for mass transit on Okinawa.

17. 竜宮城 (or simply 竜宮) is the palace of the Sea God, or Dragon King; historically, it was also used to refer to the castle of the king of the Ryūkyū Kingdom (now known as the Okinawan archipelago).

18. 本丸 refers specifically to the main, inner citadel of a castle. Nakagusuku Castle also has a second and third citadel, called 二の丸 and 三の丸 respectively.

19. 二人連れのかなり酔った兵隊 seems at first to mean "two very drunk soldiers," and in fact it may. Later references to 酔った一人 and the 酔った方 suggest, however, that it is actually "one very drunk soldier accompanied by another."

20. あぶれ (or sometimes あふれ) can refer generally to people who can't find any work or customers, but in this case it has a more particular connotation as an abbreviation for 溢女郎, "a prostitute who can't get a customer." This story is set sometime soon after the end of the Vietnam War, after many of the American soldiers stationed on Okinawa had been repatriated.

21. 宮里 is a hilly area that lies between Kadena Air Base and Nakagusuku Bay, just over a mile from 嘉間良. The term クロンボ has a very long history and was often used in early modern times to refer to people from India, the Malay Peninsula, and Africa; now it is a derogatory term for blacks, and has been classified as inappropriate for us in broadcasts (放送禁止用語).

22. 銀天街 is a popular shopping arcade in 宮里 created in 1978. This story was published in 1984, so we can assume it was meant to feel, at the time, as though it were set in the present or very recent past.

23. 石敢當 (いしがんとう or せきかんとう) can be large stones or small plaques with the three characters 石敢當 (literally "no enemy before you rock") carved into them. You find them at

intersections and dead ends in Okinawa, and even sometimes in Kyūshū, where they serve to keep corner-loving bad spirits away.

24. 伊平屋 (read いへや not いへいや) is the northernmost of all the populated islands in Okinawa. It is also the name of a town spread over this and one other island. The bars that appear in the previous paragraph—the New York, the Niagara, etc.—all appear to have been as real as 伊平屋, by the way.

25. ネエサン is 姉さん (or 姐さん), a word used when casually addressing or speaking about a young woman, or when calling to a waitress or maid in a restaurant or inn.

26. ゴヤ大通り is a large street that traces the outside of the Kadena Air Base.

27. 川崎 is best known as the name of a large city in Kanagawa Prefecture, but in this case it refers to the area on Okinawa Island where Camp Courtney is located. It is about a twenty-minute drive from 嘉間良.

28. ゲート通り is a street a little under a mile to the southwest of 嘉間良.

29. からだがそっくり耳になった isn't any sort of fixed phrase. It almost seems as though it could be a reworking into Japanese of "she was all ears."

30. 久米島紬 is a kind of 紬—pongee, a type of material woven from threads hand-spun from the floss of silkworm cocoons—typical of Kumejima, a large island to the west of Okinawa Island.

ACKNOWLEDGMENTS

"Concerning the Sound of a Train Whistle in the Night *or* On the Efficacy of Fiction" ("*Yoru no kiteki ni tsuite, aruiwa monogatari no koyo ni tsuite*") by Haruki Murakami, translated by Michael Emmerich. © 1995 by Haruki Murakami. First published by Heibonsha. Published by arrangement with International Creative Management, Inc.

"A Little Darkness" ("*Chiisana Yami*") by Banana Yoshimoto, translated by Michael Emmerich. Copyright © 2000 by Banana Yoshimoto. All rights reserved. Originally published in Japanese in *Furin to Nanbei* by Banana Yoshimoto, published by Gentosha Inc., Tokyo. English translation rights arranged with Zipango S.L. on behalf of the author.

"Genjitsu House" ("*Genjitsuso*") by Masayo Koike, translated by Michael Emmerich. Copyright © 2004 Masayo Koike. Originally published by Chikumashobo Ltd. Published by arrangement with The Sakai Agency on behalf of the author.

"The Silent Traders" ("*Danmariichi*") by Yuko Tsushima, translated by Geraldine Harcourt. Copyright © 1982 Yuko Tsushima. Translation appeared in *The Shooting Gallery* by Yuko Tsushima (Pantheon Books). Translation copyright © 1988 by Geraldine Harcourt. Published by arrangement with the author and the translator.

"*Mogera Wogura*" ("*Ugoromochi*") by Hiromi Kawakami, translated by Michael Emmerich. Copyright © 2002 Hiromi Kawakami. Published by arrangement with the author. Translation first appeared in *The Paris Review*, Spring 2005.

"The Maiden in the Manger" ("*Umagoya no otome*") by Kazushige Abe, translated by Michael Emmerich. © 2004 by Kazushige Abe. First published in the Japanese literary magazine *Shincho* in 2004. Published by arrangement with International Creative Management, Inc. English translation first published in *A Public Place*, Spring 2006.

"Where the Bowling Pins Stand" ("*Boringu pin no tatsu tokoro*") by Shinji Ishii, translated by Michael Emmerich. Published by arrangement with the author.

"Love Suicide at Kamaara" ("*Kamaara Shinju*") by Sueko Yoshida, translated by Yukie Ohta. English translation published in *Southern Exposure: Modern Japanese Literature from Okinawa*, edited by Michael Molasky and Steve Rabson. © 2000 University of Hawaii Press. Published by arrangement with the author and the University of Hawaii Press.

The Tale of Genji
Murasaki Shikibu

ISBN 978-0-14-243714-8

Written in the eleventh century, this exquisite portrait of courtly life in medieval Japan is widely celebrated as the world's first novel. Genji, the Shining Prince, is the son of an emperor. He is a passionate character whose tempestuous nature, family circumstances, love affairs, alliances, and shifting political fortunes form the core of this magnificent epic, published here in Royall Tyler's masterly translation.

Also available:
The Tale of the Genji (Abridged)
ISBN 978-0-14-303949-5

PENGUIN
CLASSICS

Rashōmon

Ryūnosuke Akutagawa

Introduction by Haruki Murakami

ISBN 978-0-14-313984-6

Akutagawa (1892–1927) was one of Japan's foremost stylists—a modernist master whose stories are marked by original imagery, cynicism, beauty, and wild humor. Here are eighteen of his best stories—half of them published in English for the first time.

"Rashōmon" and "In a Bamboo Grove" inspired Kurosawa's magnificent film and depict a past in which morality is inverted, while such tales as "The Nose" and "Loyalty" paint a richly imaginative picture of a medieval Japan peopled by Shoguns and priests, vagrants and peasants.

PENGUIN
CLASSICS

AVAILABLE FROM PENGUIN CLASSICS

Kokoro
Natsume Sōseki

No collection of Japanese literature is complete without *Kokoro*, the story of a poignant friendship between two unnamed characters, a young man and an enigmatic elder. It is published here in the first new English translation in over half a century.

ISBN 978-0-14-310603-6

Sanshirō
Natsume Sōseki

Sōseki's only coming-of-age novel, *Sanshirō* depicts the eponymous twenty-three-year-old protagonist as he leaves the sleepy countryside to attend a university in the constantly moving "real world" of Tokyo.

ISBN 978-0-14-045562-5

Kusamakura
Natsume Sōseki

Sōseki wrote *Kusamakura* intent on creating a "haiku style novel . . . that lives through beauty." This translation—the first in more than forty years—marvelously captures the elegance of the original.

ISBN 978-0-14-310519-0

PENGUIN
CLASSICS